Smoke & Mirrors

Love in Flames 3

Elouise East

Contents

List of characters (alphabetical order)

Alejandro/Alejo, Matías's brother

Ave, George's wife, foster parent, friends with everyone

Casey, paramedic

Dean, Red Watch firefighter, Oliver's boyfriend (Out of the Frying Pan)

Diego, Matías's father

Elena, Matías's aunt

Eli, wedding planner

George, Ave's husband, foster parent

Harry, photographer, Jason's boyfriend (Smokescreen)

Hayden, Eli's father

Isabella, Matías's sister

Jasmine, Eli's assistant and friend

Jason, Red Watch firefighter, Harry's boyfriend (Smokescreen)

Kade, Detective

Karen, Eli's mother

Layton, Green Watch firefighter
Lukas, Eli's brother
Maddox, Green Watch firefighter
Mariana, Matías's aunt
Matías, Blue Watch firefighter
Nash, Blue Watch firefighter
Oliver, Owner and Chef of Nourris Moi, Dean's boyfriend (Out of the Frying Pan)
Opal, Eli's sister
Paul, Cam Fire & Rescue Station Commander, Quinn's husband
Quinn, manager at Shelter Kitchen, Paul's husband
Rafe, Matías's best friend
Robbie, Eli's brother
Sarah, another wedding planner
Sofía, Matías's mother

Chapter 1

Matías

"Mum, please. I don't need you to introduce me to anyone." Matías Lopez barely restrained a sigh, knowing exactly how it would go over with his mother. Sofía Lopez was a force to be reckoned with.

"I just want to introduce you to Dominic. You'll have someone to talk to." She patted him on the cheek.

"I know eighty per cent of the people here. I think I'll be able to find someone to talk to." He briefly closed his eyes; he had no chance of her stopping this train wreck.

She held her hands out in front of her. "But what about dancing later? You need a partner. Dominic will be happy to meet you." She smiled, and he resigned himself to getting to know yet another man his mother believed he *needed* to meet.

"No, I don't need a partner."

"It won't take but a minute, hijo. Come."

She turned away, knowing Matías would follow because he would do anything for his family, even if it meant he had to spend the next few hours interacting with someone he might not like. If Dominic felt as uncomfortable as Matías did, it would be an interesting evening.

His attendance at his sister's wedding was mandatory, for obvious reasons, but mainly because he loved his family with everything in him. They had already had the wedding service and were finishing up the reception. He'd given his speech and gained a few laughs, but Matías wanted to spend time with his cousins instead of fending off the potential advances of a stranger.

Matías and Sofía weaved through the guests, stopping for greetings and hugs along the way. Their family was extensive, but not everyone had been able to make it, mainly those who still lived in Spain. Isabella had arranged to have the wedding service streamed for their grandparents, which he thought was a stroke of genius. He had no idea how the wedding planner had pulled it off, but from what he'd seen of Eli and from what Jasmine had told him, the man was a magician.

"I'm taking him to meet Dominic. They're perfect for each other." His mother smiled over her shoulder at him.

"I'd much prefer a beer," he mumbled, shoving his hands deep into his pockets.

He dropped his gaze to the floor when Sofía glared at him. He needed to work on his mumbling ability.

"You need to broaden your horizons, Matías," his aunt Elena said. "There are many people out there who would kill to spend time with you. You just need to give them the opportunity."

"I do, tia Elena. I meet people when I go out, but I want to relax tonight."

Elena waved her hand. "You can relax and chat. Two birds, one stone."

"You're thirty-eight, Matías. You're not getting any younger. I want some grandchildren from you because I'm not getting any younger. I want to see you settled. Maybe it will be with Dominic."

He doubted it. His family's idea of the perfect man for him differed widely from his own, but fate had another idea, it seemed. If he didn't at least meet the guy, he would never hear the end of it.

As expected, an hour later, he and Dominic had run out of things to discuss, and both sat nursing their drinks, watching the guests on the dance floor. The man was nice enough, but there was no spark. They'd found they had nothing in common and had ended up talking about their respective jobs—Matías as a firefighter and Dominic as a supermarket manager.

"Would you like another drink?" Matías asked, needing to get away even for a few minutes.

Dominic looked at the bottle in his hand. "Do you know what? I'm going to find Keegan. I think it's time I went home. Thank you for keeping me company." Dominic stood, resting his bottle on the table.

"I'm sorry," Matías said.

"Hey, it's no problem. Just don't let your family come after me." Dominic chuckled, and Matías returned it, feeling his body ease.

"I won't. Promise."

Dominic nodded. "Have a good evening."

"You, too."

Matías watched the man wander off, noticing more than one person following his progress across the room. There was nothing wrong with Dominic at all, but there was no interest between them.

"Matías! Why is Dominic leaving?"

Matías sighed and faced his mother. "We didn't hit it off, Mum. Sorry. I tried."

Sofía threw her hands up in the air. "I'm never going to get grandchildren. You need to try harder, hijo. Dominic was a good man. You could've learnt to love him."

And wasn't that the crux of the matter? Matías didn't want to settle. He wanted something real.

"Where's Dominic?" Elena asked, and Matías dropped his head, focusing on his drink.

"Matías ran him off."

Matías's head shot up. "I didn't run him off. We didn't click, that's all."

"All I ask is that you..." Sofía paused.

A hand slid across his shoulder blades, sending a shiver down his spine.

"Hey. Sorry, I got busy."

Eli, the wedding planner, sat beside him and kissed Matías's cheek. Matías stared at him, eyes wide. What the hell was the guy doing? Eli's hand rested on Matías's forearm and squeezed.

"Hi," he croaked.

"I didn't mean to leave you alone for so long, although I bet your family kept you company."

Eli glanced up at his mother and aunt and smiled. Matías looked at his family out of the corner of his eye, the same stupefied expressions on their faces as on Matías's, he was sure. He studied Eli, trying to figure out what his plan was.

"I wondered if I could borrow you for a few minutes?" Eli flicked a gaze to Sofía. "I'll only take him away for a moment."

"Okay," was all he could manage. He hoped he would get some answers. He stood, and Eli threaded his arm through Matías's as they weaved through the crowd. "What—?"

"Wait a few more minutes," Eli whispered, smiling at a guest.

The man steered them down a hallway and into a room before closing the door and leaning back against it. They stared at each other, then the corners of Eli's mouth dropped, and he pushed away from the door.

"I apologise. I hadn't planned on that happening."

He strode for a small ornate table against one wall where a kettle, cups and drink necessities sat. He flicked the kettle on and placed two cups in front of him, putting teabags in both. Neither said a word as Eli prepared the drinks and when he brought Matías's cup over, he brushed past him to sit on an elegant sofa.

Matías shook his head, trying to collect his thoughts. He drank his tea and sat adjacent to Eli.

"Does it not burn your mouth?" Eli asked, raising his eyebrow.

Matías snorted. "I don't feel it anymore. It's a hazard of the job. I've learnt to drink the hot drinks the instant I get it because I never know when I'm going to get called out."

"Called out?" Eli frowned for a second before his expression cleared. "Oh, yes. You're a firefighter."

"I am."

Eli cleared his throat and crossed his legs, resting his cup on his knee. "I'm sorry if I've made things difficult for you. Out there." He inclined his head towards the door.

Matías exhaled. "What exactly was that?"

Eli stared at his cup so long, Matías didn't think he would answer. His chin-length, dyed-blond hair fell forward, and Eli tucked it behind his ear again, showing his defined cheekbones and jaw. The man was slender, and if not for his eyes, which showed more expression than anything else, he would look strict and unbending with his thin nose and lips. Matías acknowledged Eli was good-looking.

"I've heard your family talk down to you many times today." Eli's voice made Matías flinch as he'd been too engrossed in his perusal of the man. "I hate it when the people you love do that to you, and I wanted to help. I didn't think it through, though. I reacted."

"It won't make it any worse than usual, but they will have questions about the scene. What am I supposed to tell them?"

Eli cupped his hands around his mug and held it near his face, closing his eyes and inhaling, if Matías wasn't mistaken. Eli's shoulder relaxed, and he caught Matías's gaze.

"You can tell them whatever you need to. I'll back you up. I just wanted them to stop harassing you."

Matías chuckled. "It's nothing I'm not used to. Every unmarried couple gets roasted until they get married, and every member who is single gets lectured until they're in a relationship. It's the family's way of making sure everyone is taken care of."

Eli's eyes narrowed. "You don't need a partner to be taken care of."

Matías held out his free hand. "Hey, I know it, but most of them are old-school. They want everyone to be as happy as they are. I know I do."

"Do what?"

"Want to be happy like them. I would love to have what my parents have. I haven't found the right guy yet, though."

Eli frowned. "How often do they bug you like that?"

"Every damn day." Matías chuckled again. "They mean well."

"They might mean well, but their execution leaves a lot to be desired." Eli stood, returning to the table and almost slamming the mug down.

Matías tilted his head. It didn't sound like Eli had an issue with Matías's family but rather something else, and Matías's family was getting the brunt of Eli's anger towards whoever it was. Matías didn't like Eli worked up like he was, so he rose and wandered over to him. He raised his hand to rest it on the man's back but paused, wondering why he needed to help him. Shaking his head, he continued until he touched the fabric, feeling Eli straighten and tense.

"Not everyone is bad, Eli. They don't know how else to help, other than to find us our true loves." Matías snorted. "They love us unconditionally. They do," he repeated when Eli scoffed. "If they didn't, I would've been put out to pasture by now."

Eli chuckled, and Matías grinned, happy to have lifted some of the melancholy. Eli turned to face him, leaning his hip against the table. Matías's hand dropped away from the heat of his body. Eli crossed his arms.

"Be honest, now. Have I made things worse for you?"

Matías studied the room, sighing. "Honestly? Probably. They will want to know what happened between us and will dissect every meeting we've ever had to see what went wrong, and they'll complain I didn't tell them anything about you."

Eli closed his eyes and dropped his head. "I'm sorry."

"Don't be."

Eli's forehead creased. "Why?"

Matías shrugged. "It is what it is. I'll deal with it."

"But—"

The door opened, and in trailed Jasmine, Eli's wedding assistant and one of Matías's colleague's friends. Jason, from Red Watch, had introduced them a couple of months back when Matías bemoaned having to go to this wedding alone. Jasmine had promised to give him a place to hide should he need it, but he hadn't. He'd been managing fine until Eli came along.

"Eli, there's a problem with the flowers, the bridesmaid wouldn't listen to me when I asked her to stop smoking in the bathroom, and one groomsman needs to be given a ride home. If I have to deal with his advan—" She stopped, both her words and her steps, when she saw them. "Sorry." She did an about-turn and retraced her path.

"Wait, Jasmine," Eli called, moving away from Matías.

It was only when he moved that Matías realised how close they'd been standing because a rush of cool air pebbled his skin.

"What's the problem with the flowers?"

Jasmine glanced at Matías, then focused on Eli. "The five pots on the head table? Guests are arguing over who should have them."

Eli picked up a folder and flicked through it. "I don't have the information here. Speak to Isabella. She might have a preference as to who she wants to give them to. Which bridesmaid?"

"Chloe."

"I will speak with her shortly. She needs to understand I will ban her from the celebration *and* the hotel if she continues. And as for the groomsmen, I have a feeling I know what you were going to say. Speak to Mrs Mitchell, the groom's mother. She said if any of the groomsmen became problematic, she would see to them." He held out the folder to Jasmine.

"Perfect, thank you." Jasmine grinned and whirled around, leaving as quickly as she came.

"Wow," Matías said, amazed by how Eli had calmly and confidently dealt with the issues.

Eli raised his eyebrows. "What?"

"Nothing. You're good at your job."

Matías watched Eli's cheeks turn pink as he averted his gaze. "Thank you." He cleared his throat. "Now, onto your dilemma. I have a proposition." Eli came to stand in front of him. "If I pretended to be your boyfriend, would it give you some leniency with them?"

Matías's mouth dropped open. "What? Why would you do that?"

Eli waved his hand. "I have no plans of ever having a relationship or getting married, so I'm as free as a bird. I'm happy to pretend to be your boyfriend if it will give you a break from their pushing. We won't do anything. It can be in name only."

Matías frowned, ignoring the first part of Eli's words for the moment. "It wouldn't work. My family would expect you to visit for dinner and any family events we have."

Eli tilted his head, tapping his finger on his chin. "Providing it didn't coincide with my bookings, I can make a dinner or two. You could tell them I have a busy schedule, which isn't a lie."

Matías rubbed at his neck, staring at the floor. "It would be nice not to have them going on at me at every turn, but I can't ask you to do that."

"You didn't ask. I did. It's neither here nor there for me, as I said." Eli shrugged a shoulder and rested against the table again, flipping open another folder.

Matías studied him, trying to understand why the man would offer something like this. They hardly knew each other, but...meeting up with a stranger in a bar or coffee shop was no different. At least this way, they knew a few things like Eli was a workaholic.

"What would you get out of this?"

Eli stared at him. "Why do I need to get anything out of it?"

"Surely there's something you want in return?"

Eli narrowed his eyes. "I'm not doing this for any sort of gain, Matías. I honestly thought it would help you, but if you don't want it, that's fine. All you had to do was say no."

He stepped past Matías, heading for the door. Matías caught his arm.

"I'm sorry. That's not what I meant. I wanted to be on the same page, that's all." He inhaled. "I don't understand why you would want to do this."

"You seem like a nice guy, Matías. I'm trying to help. You don't have to agree to it because I know in the end, you will have to 'break up' with me, and it will upset your family. Only you can decide, but the offer is there if you want it."

"Are you sure?"

Eli nodded. "Tell you what. Let's pretend tonight; otherwise, it might cause more problems for you, but come and visit me this week sometime, and we can sort out the details."

"Can I have your number?"

Eli reached into his pocket, pulling out a small rectangular card. "It's easier to reach me on my business number. I tend to ignore my personal phone because my family bugs me."

Matías chuckled. "Are you sure I can't help you with them?"

Eli waved his hand in front of him, a look of horror on his face. "No, no, no. There's no way I'm bringing a man home to my family. I would never hear the end."

"Understood. Thank you, Eli."

"You're welcome. Stay in here as long as you need to."

Matías grinned. "I better get back because otherwise, the family will come looking, and you don't want that."

"If they ask me about us, I'll tell them I'm busy working and can't discuss my personal life until I'm off the clock," Eli said, smiling.

Matías threw his head back and laughed. "Good luck with getting them off your back."

"I have my ways." Eli winked and exited, closing the door behind him.

Matías shook his head and huffed a laugh. He hadn't been expecting that turn of events. He wouldn't be able to visit Eli until Wednesday afternoon at the earliest because he started his night shift in two days. At least it would give them both time to think things through before they got together to discuss things.

His family would be having a conniption by now, so he inhaled deeply and left the room in search of his sister. Maybe she would help divert some of the attention away from him. It was her wedding, after all.

Chapter 2

Eli

Eli paused after closing the door, needing to find his equilibrium again. Although Matías was not much more than a stranger, he felt a pull towards him like he'd never had with anyone else. He didn't know what possessed him to offer a pretend relationship apart from that he hated the look on Matías's face when his family kept on at him about his lack of boyfriend. It wasn't fair to the guy. Not everyone was lucky enough to find the person they wanted to spend their life with. Eli hadn't even tried because, as he'd told Matías, he was happy being alone and didn't want the problems that came with a relationship, mainly the lack of control.

He wasn't a controlling person at all, but he didn't enjoy having to discuss things with someone else. He preferred to decide and do it. Having someone in his life would only complicate matters, and after what happened with his father, there was no way he could trust anyone in those circumstances.

He pushed off the door and stalked down the hallway, his emotions and personal thoughts pushed aside in favour of his work persona—the aloof, slightly scary wedding planner. His mouth curled at the thought. It hadn't been his intention to appear like that, but he found it worked. Bridezillas, few and far between as they were, found him condescending and controlling, so they told him, but most brides were happy for someone to take charge. He worked with what he had.

The tablet in his hand gave him information about the bridesmaid he would be talking to. Chloe was Isabella's cousin and came across as strong-willed, but Eli knew exactly how to deal with her.

The first place he checked was the ladies' bathroom, but surprisingly, she wasn't there. He stepped into the ballroom, where the reception was wrapping up and his employees were converting the room into the evening dinner dance. Scanning the area, he found Chloe at the bar, surrounded by three women, all laughing and slightly inebriated, if Eli was to guess.

"Miss Lopez, could I please have a word?" Eli asked, his voice holding a note of warning.

Chloe rolled her eyes at him. "Whatever you have to say, you can say around my friends."

Eli smiled, though he knew it wasn't a friendly smile. It was the smile he gave when someone was being a bitch and he knew he had to knock them off their pedestal. "Of course. It has been brought to my attention you have been smoking in the ladies' bathroom. Unfortunately, this is prohibited by the hotel due to fire issues, and you will need to go to the outside area allocated for smoking."

"It's too damn cold to go outside. I'm not hurting anyone by smoking in there. It has loads of water around me. What issue could it be?"

"Regardless, Miss Lopez, you are not permitted to smoke in the bathrooms. It's the hotel policy. I will point out, if you continue to do it, I will remove you from the party *and* the hotel premises."

"It's fucking unfair!" Her voice rose, and she stepped closer. "I'm not hurting anyone. What right do you have to tell me what to do?"

Eli smiled again. "I have the authority from the hotel and Isabella and Justin to take whatever action I see fit. As I said, there is a smoking area outside. Please use it."

He pivoted and strode away, hearing her protests following him. He didn't care if she listened to him or not because it would only be her who suffered in the end. He would throw her out of the party and anyone else who tried to ruin what he'd created for the bride and groom. No one messes with him and his business.

He found Jasmine. "Did you speak with Mrs Mitchell about the groomsman?"

She nodded. "She has arranged for his brother to take him home."

"How are you?" He touched her elbow, wanting to check in with her, especially if she was on the receiving end of a lecherous asshole.

She waved her hand. "I'm fine. I'm getting used to it."

"You shouldn't have to. If anyone, and I mean anyone, does even the slightest thing, I want you to let me know. And make sure everyone else knows, too. I will call a meeting on Monday to discuss it with everyone."

"You worry too much." Jasmine grinned at him.

"I pay you to do a job, not get harassed by people. If that happens, I could lose employees, so it's selfish, really."

"Uh-huh." Jasmine raised her eyebrows, the disbelief visible on her face.

Eli wandered off, a small smile on his lips. He needed to give her a pay rise.

"Ah, just the man I would like to talk to. How do you know my son?"

Matías's mother stopped him short with her words.

"Through the wedding, Mrs Lopez, but I won't discuss my relationships during working hours. I'm sorry." He wasn't, but he wanted to soften his words.

"That will not do at all, Eli. I should've known my son was in a relationship. I introduced him to another man tonight, and Matías didn't breathe a word about you. He sat there talking to this man as if you didn't exist. It breaks my heart. It makes me think Matías is not serious about you, and I'm hurt he would do such a thing." She sniffed.

The strength of Eli's decision not to say a word about them waned, and he found himself consoling her. "You have nothing to worry about. Matías and I have only just begun. I told him I didn't want anyone to know about us until after the wedding. I didn't want to take any of the attention away from Isabella. Matías did what I wanted him to by talking to the man. I trust him. Implicitly. You don't need to worry."

"But he said he tried to find a spark with Dominic. He shouldn't have been trying when he had you. I didn't bring him up that way."

He knew she was manipulating him into speaking about their relationship, but he couldn't stop himself. She was like his own mother. "You have nothing to worry about," he repeated. "I promise."

"Well, it won't do. You're working while we're enjoying ourselves. I insist you take a break and sit with us."

Eli's heart raced. Nope. No way in hell. "I'm sorry, Mrs Lopez. I can't. I'm managing this wedding, and I will continue to do so. I would be happy to discuss it at a later date."

Sofía narrowed her eyes on him, and he felt the sweat bead on his forehead. "I'm not happy about it, Eli, but I suppose I have no choice."

She shuffled off quicker than Eli could take back his words. Shaking his head, he turned to his tablet, checking the list of tasks to be done. Jasmine and the rest of his employees had done a good job of completing most of what needed to be done. The last thing was to ensure the buffet was stocked and replenished as needed through the evening; therefore, he headed to the kitchen to speak with the manager.

As the evening wore down, more and more guests left until only the hard partiers remained. Eli couldn't leave until everyone had gone, and he was flagging. Matías had come and said goodnight an hour ago, but it was Eli's job to get the last guests on their way. Unfortunately, Chloe was one of them.

"You can't tell me what to do," she slurred, stumbling against her friend, who wasn't in much better condition than her.

"I know, but maybe I could suggest a taxi home?"

There was no suggestion in his tone, and he steered them towards the entrance after ensuring they had their belongings and helped them into the taxi. Eli had made sure to have everyone's addresses so guests didn't have to remember it. It had saved many problems in the past, and tonight was no different.

"I can't remember my address," Chloe whined.

"4 Maple Drive, please," Eli said through the taxi window while closing the door on the two women.

"No problem."

The hotel used this taxi firm regularly, and they came highly recommended. Eli had used them religiously since his first few weddings because they were professional in both appearance and execution. He wandered back into the hotel, finding his employees tidying up the ballroom. The DJ had long gone, and the hotel staff was also helping to clean up and put the room back to the way it should be. Eli clicked on his tablet a few times until soft jazz music filtered through the speaker. He didn't turn it up too loud—it would defeat the object of winding things down so everyone could sleep when they got home—and set to work helping.

By the time he'd dropped two employees and Jasmine home, Eli was exhausted. He let himself into his house and left everything in the hallway to deal with in the morning. Luckily, he didn't have to be up until noon because the wedding he was organising didn't start until four o'clock.

Forgoing a shower because it would only wake him up, then he wouldn't be able to sleep, he strip-washed and fell into bed.

The February sky looked like snow was ready to fall, although the forecast hadn't predicted any. Eli had learnt to take the forecast with a pinch of salt when it came to weddings and be ready for any kind of weather. Many times, it had predicted sunshine, but they had ended up with downpours. From the first time it happened, Eli had changed his process to ensure they accounted for all weather possibilities, even at the height of summer.

The four o'clock wedding had gone off without a hitch, which left Eli in his office at seven-thirty on a Sunday night, trying to decide what to do. He wasn't one for sitting and reading. He didn't play video games. He didn't have any hobbies unrelated to his work. He had no idea how to spend an evening if it wasn't work-based, except to watch films, but he wasn't in the mood, so he opened his laptop and brought up his schedule.

The phone rang, and Eli frowned at the clock. It was nearing nine o'clock at night.

"Devoted Weddings. How can I help?"

"Oh, thank you! I'm sorry for calling this late, but I have a problem, and I need someone to help me."

"Okay. What's your name?"

"Amalia."

"Nice to speak to you, Amalia. My name is Eli. What can I do for you?"

"I'm getting married in two days, but my wedding planner has been in an accident. She's in a coma!"

Eli could hear the hysterics crowding into the woman's voice. "All right, Amalia. Calm down and breathe for me." He waited a few seconds. "What's your wedding planner's name?"

"Sarah from I Do Weddings."

Eli had heard of her and knew, unfortunately, she was the sole planner on her books like he was. He had spoken to her several times, but they had never worked together.

"I'm sorry to hear about Sarah. Do you know what was in place for your wedding?" Eli pulled a pad of paper towards him and clicked his pen.

"No! I left all the details to her." Eli raised his eyebrows. That was unusual. "I'm a lawyer and work long hours. I gave her my preferences and let her do what she thought was best. She sent me a choice of things along the way, but I have no idea what the plan is, just dates and times."

"Okay, give me what information you have first, and we'll work on the rest."

Eli spent the next several minutes tweaking information out of the woman. "Okay, Amalia. This is what we're going to do. You need to get some sleep because I'm sure you have work tomorrow. You're going to forget all about the problems and leave them to me. Everything will be in place for Tuesday, without fail. I promise. Tomorrow, I will start my investigations. I will give you an update tomorrow evening. Is that okay with you?"

Amalia sighed into the phone. "I'm a little unsure about leaving all this in your hands now. What if something happens to you?"

Eli smiled. "I can understand. Okay, I will work on it on my end and email you with all the details I have each time I get something new. That way, if something happens, you'll know who to contact, who to check in with, and what's happening when. How does that sound?"

"Thank you, Eli."

Eli slouched back in his chair, rubbing his forehead. "Be careful what you wish for, Eli," he murmured with a shake of his head. He checked his watch. Visiting hours at the hospital would be over now, but he might catch some of Sarah's family in the waiting room or somewhere. They would be the best place to start because he needed someone to give him access to her business records, and he doubted anyone would do it without serious questions.

As he drove to the hospital, his thoughts veered to Matías. He'd received a text message from the man earlier that day, thanking him for what he'd done the previous evening and saying he'd be in touch on Wednesday because that was when his shifts finished. In a way, it was nice to have a breather between meetings, then Eli could get his head on straight before they spoke again.

By the time he reached the hospital, his energy levels were depleting rapidly. He grabbed his folder, pulled on a coat and headed for the entrance. They gave him directions to where Sarah was, and when he asked at the reception there, the nurse pointed out Sarah's family.

Inhaling, because this wouldn't be a straightforward conversation, he strode over to them.

"Mr and Mrs Carter. I'm a colleague of Sarah's. I'm sorry to hear what happened."

Mrs Carter stood, gripping his hand in a shaky handshake. "Bea, please."

"Bea." Eli shook hands with Mr Carter, too. "I know this isn't the best time, but I've been told Sarah had several weddings booked in this week. I would like to help."

"How dare you!" Mr Carter said, towering over him. "She's not dead, and you're trying to steal her business!"

Eli bristled but stood his ground. "I am trying to save your daughter's business. I have enough of my own. Wouldn't you like to ensure she had a business to come home to?" He inwardly winced at his tone but stayed strong.

Mr Carter glared at him for several seconds, then sank back into the uncomfortable wooden chairs, dropping his head into his hands.

"I'm sorry. We're devastated about this. Of course, we want to make sure she has a business left. I also don't want those couples to have their wedding days ruined. How can we help?"

"I'm going to need access to her records. I don't know anything about her weddings apart from one, and the bride doesn't know who Sarah was using for the event. Would you be willing to give access to my assistant and me?"

Mrs Carter closed her eyes and nodded. "Of course. Let me call James. I'll get him to let you in."

"I'll do it, Bea." Mr Carter stood and moved away to make the call.

"I will put my assistant in charge of everything while Sarah is...unwell. My assistant is very capable, but I will still monitor everything. The moment Sarah is up to it, we'll hand everything back over again."

"Thank you. You don't know what it means to us."

Mr Carter gave Eli an address to meet James at, and Eli said goodbye before heading out. It was lucky he hadn't any weddings booked in for Monday or Tuesday because he had a feeling he would be working all the hours of the day and night to get Sarah's weddings up to speed. He refused to call Jasmine until the morning because at least one of them needed to be working at full energy.

James, who was Sarah's brother, let him into her house and office, giving him the keys to the filing cabinet as well. He also gave Eli access to Sarah's password-encrypted laptop. As soon as he had that, Eli had everything he needed.

"Thank you, James. Is it okay if I stay here for a while?"

"Sure. Dad said to give you the keys so you can come and go as you need to. He said they will call you with news about Sarah."

"Thank you. I appreciate it."

It surprised him when James left the bunch of keys on the desk and left the house. It had been far too easy for him to gain access to Sarah's house, and if he hadn't been as honest and upstanding as he was, he could've taken advantage of the fact. After everything went back to normal, he would mention it to them and make sure they weren't so accommodating if something like this happened again.

He focused on the laptop, searching for Sarah's schedule, and groaned when he saw she had five weddings booked for the week. Jasmine was going to have her work cut out for her, but Eli knew she was ready. He was the person holding her back. He wasn't capable of sharing his business yet. This situation, however sad, would give Jasmine the opportunity to be what she was training for, and Eli would support her. Maybe once it was over, he would feel better about bringing Jasmine into his business as a full-time wedding planner.

Shaking off the thoughts, he dived into the folders.

It was going to be a long night.

Chapter 3

Matías

"Lorry fire. Westbound on the A14, before the Milton Interchange," Matías said after he'd climbed into the front of the fire engine.

Nash nodded and tore out of the station, the sirens blaring. The rest of the Blue Watch crew scrambled to get their equipment on before they arrived on the scene.

"Any casualties?" Iris asked.

Matías shook his head. "I don't know."

As far as Matías was concerned, this was one of the worst parts of the job. Not knowing what they were facing until they were there. Unaware whether anyone had lost their lives, unaware if anyone *would* lose their lives. *That* was the worst part of all. Fire was unpredictable at the best of times, but losing someone in one was devastating.

Heading towards the plume of black smoke billowing into the sky, Nash used the hard shoulder to whip down beside the stopped cars, creating a line of traffic over a mile long. There would be no diversions unless the police could figure out a way to get them to turn around and head back down the carriageway.

They pulled up a short distance from the lorry, the heat already climbing, and they hadn't even climbed out yet.

"Kai and Willow, get the hoses rolled out and on the engine. We're going to need water and foam as usual. Iris and Nash, take the second hose and be ready."

Matías jumped from the engine and headed towards the police officer in charge. The crackling and sizzling of the fire was loud, overtaking most other sounds in the vicinity. The occasional whoosh of another blast of fire muted the shouts of his team members. He barely registered the smoke filling his nose anymore.

He held out his hand to the officer. "Frank. What's the situation?"

"Unknown cause of the fire. The driver had no idea it was even on fire until he saw the flames in his mirrors. Some occupants of the cars," he pointed over his shoulder at the waiting audience, "told us the lorry had been visibly on fire for several miles. The driver was bloody lucky."

Matías glanced at the raging fire. "He was. What's inside?"

"Pallets full of stationery items."

Matías sighed. "It could burn for a while. We need to cool that cab down to stop it from exploding."

"Timeframe?"

He blew out a breath. "Two or three hours, maybe."

Frank huffed. "All right. I'll get this lot working on turning the cars around and sending them back to the previous junction."

Matías nodded once and returned to his crew. They needed to keep the flames from spreading onto other sources, like the grass and trees next to it while keeping the cab cool. They were far enough away from houses, but close enough to office buildings to be problematic.

"Matías!"

He turned to his watch commander, Pearce, after he'd finished getting an update from his crew and, in turn, relayed it to him.

"We have another engine pulling up the other side," Pearce said.

"Understood."

He wandered back to the crew, making sure they were okay. Despite how it looked from the outside, holding a hose when water blasted from it was not easy. It took strength and tension to keep it from taking them with it, hence why he tried to put two people on the hoses instead of one when he could.

"Pearce! Have they contacted those businesses?" He pointed across the carriageway to the half a dozen buildings in the path of the black smoke. If the smoke got into the building, it would take weeks to get the smell out. Matías should know.

"I'll check with Frank!"

A crash had him whirling around, and he watched as the side of the lorry fell to the ground in a plume of fire. There would be more where that came from before it was under control. He watched, mesmerised by the yellow and orange flames licking through the back of the lorry and mixing with the black clouds as they rose to the sky. The crew focused the water on the cab and the area around the lorry, hopefully, to stop the chance of it catching fire, but there was no stopping the contents from burning. Sometimes, it was better to let the fire extinguish whatever flammable items were in its path than it was to contain it, except when it came to fuel and engines.

Another blast shot a fireball from the underside of the lorry, barely missing Iris and Nash, who immediately turned the hose to put out the small fire now behind them.

"Pull back!" he shouted. They didn't need to stop, just move a few steps back.

"We're going to lose the cab!" Nash shouted.

Matías moved forward, seeing the fire spreading close to the cab. "Get the water on it. We can't let it burn." He jogged over to Pearce. "They're focusing on the cab."

"All right. Keep watch. Let's see how long this takes."

Matías stepped back to the crew, and they watched the fire increase in temperature and height of the flames. No one could ever doubt a fire wasn't beautiful, but it had a mind of its own. In all his years of firefighting, the one thing he had learnt quickly was the fire was in control, not him. They had to let the fire do what it needed to, and they could deal with the repercussions of it.

The yellow and orange flames consumed the back of the lorry, leaving a barely standing shell, and probably wouldn't be for much longer. The heat was unimaginable without having experienced it, and sweat coated his skin.

The crew from another station parked the engine on the other side of the fire, out of the path of the flames and smoke. He watched as the men and women exited the cab and headed over to them.

He nodded at the crew commander, Robin.

"Anything we need to know?" Robin asked.

"The cab is fire free at the moment. We need to monitor the surrounding area."

"Okay. I'll station the crew on the opposite side. Two bird's-eye views are better than one."

"Thanks."

Pearce came up as the other crew left. "I have another engine on standby in case we need more."

"So far, it's following the usual course. Let's hope it continues." Matías stared at the fire, watching the usual places for signs of the fire not behaving as their trainers had taught them.

"It shouldn't. Hopefully, it will burn itself out." Pearce snorted. "Frank is turning the cars around, along with plenty of huffing and moaning."

Matías grinned. "Doesn't he always?"

He kept an eye on the time, and it was around half an hour before the fire had consumed the whole lorry. The flames were still going strong, but it was on the downslide now, and they had escaped an explosion. Though it wasn't impossible that they could still get one.

He set the crew on hosing down the fire. It took a couple of hours before they were completely done, including the clean-up. The lorry was a shell of its former self, barely anything left of it bar the metal parts, and even those were bent and twisted from the heat.

As the crew packed away the equipment, he checked in with Pearce, Frank and Robin, then they were on their way back to the station. It had been a long night, and he was ready for a shower and some food, which was lucky because the scent of bolognese wafted through the station when they pulled in.

"I'm starving," Willow groaned, climbing down from her seat.

"That's good because dinner is served," Paul called from above them.

Matías glanced up at him and grinned. "I didn't realise you were coming in tonight."

Paul shrugged. "I hadn't planned to, but I saw the fire on the news and knew no one would be in the mood to cook after dealing with it."

Matías pointed at him. "You. Are. A. Lifesaver."

"I try." He grinned. "Go get cleaned up. You're off rotation for an hour."

Everyone cheered and headed for the changing rooms. Sometimes, when the crew had dealt with a big fire, they were taken out of the rotation for being called out for a short period, so they could shower, change and eat, and basically recuperate from the physically exhausting job. They would only call them in if there was no one else available.

He jumped straight into the shower, scrubbing to dilute the scent of the smoke—he never got completely free of it. It was as if it lived in his pores. Once he felt clean, he dressed in his uniform and headed for the dining room.

The bolognese he'd smelled earlier turned out to be lasagne, and it had never tasted so good. The tomatoes, meat, cheese, pasta all melted in his mouth, and he didn't say a word to anyone until his plate was clear.

"Perfect, Chief. Thanks."

"Thank Quinn when you see him." Paul chuckled. "No way would he let me feed you when he was around to do it. You know what he's like."

"Either way. It filled the hole in my stomach."

Iris gasped, and he whipped his head around to her. "You're full?"

Matías rolled his eyes. "I'm never full, Bobcat. I said it filled a hole, not that there weren't more holes I could fill."

"TMI, Matías. I don't want to know about the holes you fill or need filling, thank you very much," Kai said, pulling face even as he shovelled food into his mouth.

"Fuck you. You know full well that wasn't what I meant."

Kai grinned, ducking so the napkin Matías threw missed him.

"I keep meaning to ask, Matías. Have you added to your tattoo yet? I know you said you were going to," Willow asked.

His phone beeped, and he pulled it out of his pocket as he answered Willow, "Not yet. I can't decide what to have done. The tribal design needs something that fits in with it, and I've not decided what does. I might have to ask the tattoo artist for advice. Anyway, I'm hoping I will do it in a couple of weeks."

"Are you going for a full sleeve?"

"Yeah, eventually. The idea is to have both sleeves done and join them up around my collarbones and shoulder blades. Or something like that anyway."

He pressed on the message from his mother.

MUM: *Don't forget to ask your young man to dinner. I won't have you forgetting again like you said you did yesterday. I hope everything's okay. Send me a message back so I know you're safe. Love you x*

He sighed. His family had let up about Eli a little, but they still wanted him to visit for dinner. He wasn't sure if Eli would be happy about it, though.

MATÍAS: *I'm safe. Just finished eating. I'll ask Eli this afternoon. Love you, too x*
MUM: *Bring Nash along, too. Maybe even the rest of your crew. They can have one of my home-cooked specials.*
MATÍAS: *I'll see what they say. Get some sleep.*

He chuckled. She would never give up like he'd told Eli. He hoped they weren't bugging him now the wedding was over. His sister might be in Spain on her honeymoon, but it didn't mean his mother wouldn't use her as an excuse to contact Eli. He might need to warn the guy about the possibility. A tingle ran through him at the thought of seeing him that afternoon. While he liked Eli from what he'd seen of him, Eli didn't seem the type to want to be part of a big family, though why he got that idea, he didn't know.

He shook off the thought and relaxed with his crew, finishing his shift with a few smaller callouts. The second his head hit the pillow at home, he was out.

His phone ringing woke him, and he fumbled for it, turning his head to the side so he could answer but keeping his eyes closed.

"'Lo?"

"Your mother keeps calling me about a party?"

"What?" He blinked, trying to get his mind working, and squinted at the clock.

"Your mother. She keeps ringing and asking me to come to a party on Thursday. When I asked them why, they told me you would explain and gave me your number as I didn't have it. What's going on?"

Matías rubbed at his face and shuffled to a sitting position, stifling a yawn. He hadn't checked the display. "Who is this?"

"It's Eli." The voice sounded exasperated.

"Eli." It took a minute for his mind to catch up. "Eli?"

Eli sighed. "Yes, it's Eli. Now, answer the question."

"You're going to have to repeat it. I'm still half asleep."

"It's midday. How long do you sleep?"

Matías snorted. "Usually until two, when I'm coming off a night shift."

There was silence, then Eli said, "Oh shit. I'm so sorry. I completely forgot. This week has messed with my brain. I'll go. Just...call me when you can, or it can wait until I see you later."

"No! It's fine. I'm awake now. Give me a second, okay?"

"Sure...?"

Matías dropped the phone to the bed and dashed to the bathroom, splashing water on his face, and hoped it would be enough for him to understand what Eli was talking about.

"Okay, I'm back. Now, explain again from the start."

"Your mother called me and invited me to a party she's having on Thursday. I was confused because we haven't even spoken about our...agreement yet, and I thought I annoyed her at the wedding. When I asked what the celebration was, she told me I needed to ask *you*. So, here I am. Asking."

Matías dropped his head back against the headboard as he grinned at the show of unease he could tell Eli rarely felt. "I have no idea what the party is about. It's the first I've heard about it. I can only assume she's excited about meeting you when you're not distracted by work."

"Okay."

"Are you free on Thursday? If so, come. It should be fun if you exclude the unending questions about our upcoming nuptials."

"What? We're not getting married."

"I know, and you know, but they don't care." Matías felt bad for putting Eli through that and quickly added, "Do you know what? It's probably better if you decline. You shouldn't have to go through all this."

Eli didn't respond straight away, and if Matías couldn't hear him breathing on the other end, he would've thought he'd hung up. He waited him out.

"I suppose...I could...attend. I don't have a wedding on Thursday."

The reluctance in Eli's voice muted the thrill of being able to see him again. "No, it's okay. Mum means well, but she doesn't know when to stop. I'll speak with her and tell her to end it. We can forget the agreement, and you won't have to hear from us again."

The silence, once again, was complete, not even breathing this time. Matías ignored the urge to check the phone, not wanting to miss Eli's words.

"I haven't been out for a while. Socially, I mean," he mumbled. "I suppose I could." Eli sighed and spoke more firmly, "Yes, all right. I'll come. I'm not going back on the agreement, but we need to discuss a few things. Are you still coming over this afternoon?"

"Yes, if that's okay?"

"Sure."

Matías stopped himself from jumping for joy, knowing he'd only disappoint himself from getting up hope when there was nothing to hope about.

"You're welcome to invite Jasmine or another friend for moral support."

"Thanks." He cleared his throat. "I'm sorry I woke you."

"It's okay. I can go back to sleep easily."

"I suppose I'll see you this afternoon."

Matías grinned. "Yep."

"Bye."

Matías didn't have time to respond because the call ended, but the smile on his face didn't. Despite all the warnings in his head, he wanted to get to know Eli better. They would end up as nothing but friends because he had plenty of experience to know Eli didn't want a relationship. It didn't stop Matías from enjoying being with him, though.

He never said he wasn't a glutton for punishment.

It was unlikely he would fall back to sleep as easy as he told Eli he would, so he did the next best thing. He dialled a number, rolling his eyes when it went to voicemail.

"Mother!"

Chapter 4

Eli

After hanging up the phone with Matías, Eli dropped his head onto his desk. How could he have forgotten Matías had been working last night?

Trying to coordinate his own bookings and helping Jasmine get her head around Sarah's was taking its toll. Jasmine had been over the moon when he'd spoken to her earlier in the week. She was excited to get started, which had been good because she had to jump in the deep end without any floats. Eli, luckily, hadn't had any weddings on Monday, so he had helped her find her feet with the Tuesday weddings and had taken over the organising and planning for the Wednesday and Friday weddings.

He had been concerned about whether she'd manage, to begin with, but the instant the first wedding was under her belt, his mind had eased. He knew she could do it, and he supposed he was already mourning the loss of his assistant. The moment their situation was back to normal, he would discuss things with her and see if she wanted to take on some new bookings independently from Eli—still within the business, but on her own, without Eli looking over her shoulder. She deserved every opportunity, and Eli felt like crap for keeping her as his assistant when she was more than capable of planning a wedding from beginning to end.

A few potential brides had called Sarah's business for bookings, and once Sarah's parents had given Eli the go-ahead to continue in Sarah's name, he'd begun booking weddings for the future. He hoped Sarah agreed with the decision once she was feeling better. From what her brother had told him, she was still in a coma but showed signs of waking up, which was great news. He had no idea what her recovery period would be, but he made sure to keep her family included with the business details so when Sarah was coherent enough, they could discuss it with her.

His phone rang, and he sighed. "Devoted Weddings. How can I help?"

Hours passed as he worked through two businesses' bookings and made sure everything was in place for each of them. Jasmine had called to say the wedding had gone off without a hitch, and she was going home for a break. She deserved it.

The doorbell chimed, and Eli frowned, checking his watch, and raised his eyebrows when he realised it was time for him to meet with Matías. How did the time go so fast?

He rose, hustling to the door and flinging it open. "Hey. Come on in."

Eli led the way, trying to ignore how Matías looked in his dark wash jeans. It was only when he entered his kitchen that Eli realised he'd taken Matías to his kitchen instead of his office, as planned. Sustenance was good, though.

"Coffee? Tea?"

"Tea, please. I've not had my quota today." Matías grinned.

"How do you take it?"

"No sugar and a splash of milk, please."

Eli flicked the kettle on, making drinks for them both. Chamomile tea should help calm his nerves, though why he was nervous, he didn't know. It wasn't like they were doing anything wrong. He tilted his head as he stared at his cup. That was incorrect. They were doing something wrong. They were lying to the people Matías loved.

"What's the matter?"

Eli blinked at Matías. "Huh?"

"You look sad, maybe. Upset?"

Eli sighed and shook his head. "It occurred to me we'll be lying to your family."

Matías stared at the tabletop and ran a finger along a groove in the wood. "We will. Hopefully, they won't find out about it and will assume when we break up it is a normal break-up. That way, no one gets upset."

"But you'll go back to having them bug you about a relationship again."

Matías nodded. "Yes, but you will have given me a breather." He studied Eli, and Eli barely stopped from fidgeting. The gaze seemed to strip him down to the bone. "We don't have to do this. It's not a problem at all. We can be friends, which I wouldn't say no to."

Eli would be happy with friends, but he knew Matías needed the break from his family's interference more. "I'm fine with it." He sat opposite Matías and cupped his mug. "So, how do you want to play this?"

Matías shrugged and chuckled, the sound sending a tingle through Eli. "I don't know. I suppose we need to figure out where we got together."

"Well, they know we didn't know each other before the wedding, unless we were pretending then, too, but I'd probably choose a time during the wedding preparation. Maybe one of the suit fittings?"

Matías sat straighter. "Yes! Remember the one where we argued over what colour to go with?" Eli nodded with a smile. "That one."

"Probably a good one. They will remember the incident, I'm sure. The way you pouted when I got my way."

Matías held up his finger. "Nah, you didn't. Isabella did. She's always known how to get me to bow down to her wishes."

"You love your family. It's plain to see. Plus, it was her wedding. You had to agree with her, and therefore, me." Eli smirked, lifting his mug to hide it.

"I still don't agree grey is a good colour for me."

"You'd be surprised."

Matías shook his head. "It reminds me too much of smoke for some reason, especially when it had a shimmer to it."

"I never thought about that. You're right. About the smoke thing, not that it doesn't suit you. Grey looks good on you." *Although white looked even better.* Eli tried not to let his mind wander too far off track, but when Matías had taken his coat off, it had left him with a tight white T-shirt, showing every muscle he had. Coupled with those jeans, which fit him like a glove, Eli wouldn't turf him out of bed.

The thought had him setting the mug down harder on the table than he'd planned to, and tea sloshed over the edge, covering his hand. He stood and rinsed his hand under the tap.

"Are you okay?" Matías asked, peering over his shoulder.

"Yeah, I'm good. The tea had cooled plenty."

He reached for a towel and dried his hands, the heat from Matías competing with the tea.

"There is another thing we need to discuss," Matías whispered, his breath caressing Eli's cheek, and he tensed to stop himself from leaning into him. Matías's hand rested on Eli's lower back.

"What's that?" His voice was barely a whisper.

"PDAs."

Eli turned his head to meet Matías's gaze and felt his heart rate increase with how close they were. They didn't need to be this close when there was no one to see them, but Eli couldn't pull himself away from Matías's embrace. His breath stuttered when Matías lifted a hand and skimmed his fingers across his cheek, leaving a stream of electricity in their wake. He swallowed hard.

"What about them?"

Matías's gaze dropped to Eli's lips, and Eli licked them unconsciously. Bringing their eyes back together, he said, "What is acceptable and what is not."

Eli tried to get his mouth to work. "Um, holding hands is fine by me."

"What about me touching your back or putting my arms around you?"

He inhaled. "That's fine."

Matías's index finger dragged along Eli's bottom lip. "What about kissing?"

Eli's eyelids fluttered, and he scraped his teeth along his lip to get rid of the tingle. "In certain circumstances."

"Like what?"

Eli tried to collect his thoughts. "A peck on the cheek or head is fine."

Matías cupped his chin. "And what about on your lips?"

"If the situation warrants it."

"Hmm. You might have to be the one to instigate those. I won't know what situation is good." The corner of Matías's mouth curled upwards.

Eli's stomach fluttered. "Okay."

"Do we need to practise?" Matías whispered.

Eli said nothing. Instead, he lifted his head and pressed their lips together, his eyelids closing of their own accord. Eli planned to pull back after one taste, but he couldn't. He felt surrounded with Matías's arm around his waist, his hand on his chin and their lips fused. He never wanted it to end. Eli slid his arm up and around Matías's neck. The kiss broke, and they paused with their lips millimetres apart, sharing the same air. He knew Matías was waiting for him, and Eli wasn't sure what the right course of action was. They didn't need to practise any more than they had already, but he shut his head down and let his body take over.

He joined them together again and twisted in Matías's grip until he plastered the whole of his body against the man. Matías teased his lips with his tongue, and Eli gasped, giving Matías entry. It had been so long since anyone had kissed him like this. Such strength. Such passion. Such need. It coursed through him with no care for the repercussions.

Matías turned them until Eli had the counter pressed into his back and Matías's hands tangled in Eli's hair. Eli didn't care about anything but the next taste of the smoke-scented, addictive man in front of him. Matías's tongue explored Eli's mouth and encouraged Eli to do the same to Matías's.

When Eli's lungs burned, he pulled his mouth away and dropped his head back, gasping to fill his lungs. Matías pressed kisses against his jaw and neck before resting his head on Eli's shoulder.

"Holy crap, Eli," Matías said.

Eli chuckled and smiled before lifting his head. "I don't think we need to practise."

Matías laughed, long and hard. "I think you're right." He stared at Eli. "I was being truthful, though. You will need to initiate any lip kissing. It's only fair."

Eli nodded. "Okay."

Matías dropped a kiss on his cheek and stepped back. Eli fisted his hands to stop him from pulling the man back into his arms.

"Anything else we need to discuss?" he asked instead.

"We need to sort out going to visit my family. Tomorrow is a party of undetermined reason. Do you have time to join me there?"

Eli nodded. "I've already written it in my diary." A question formed. "How long do you want to keep this up for?"

Matías collapsed into the chair at the table and rubbed his face. "Well, it depends on you. Would April be too long?"

"It's what? Two months?"

"Yeah. It's my birthday, and I know they'll be having a party for me. It would be nice not to have to be badgered on my birthday."

"What date?"

"Fifteenth."

"It's fine. I don't do relationships, anyway, so I don't have any other plans, except when I visit my family."

Matías tilted his head. "Are you sure you don't want me to help you with them?"

"No! No, definitely not. I will not hear the end of it if I bring you home." He shivered. There was no way he was subjecting himself to the third degree.

Matías lifted his mug, sipping the brew, which Eli had to assume was cold now. Eli withheld a shudder at the idea of drinking lukewarm tea of any kind.

"Why?"

"Why what?"

"Why would it be so bad? Surely, they want to see you with someone?"

Eli snorted. "Of course, they want to see me with someone. All families do. The problem is they don't believe I know what I want. And I don't want any kind of relationship other than friendship. One night is fine. A couple of one-off nights. Fine. But nothing permanent."

He turned to the kettle, flicking the switch again. He wouldn't explain his reasons. They were his reasons, and nobody needed to know how important it was that he had the strength and ability to be independent. Just because his father had been a liar and a thief didn't mean Eli was. In fact, Eli had been working hard since his father left them when Eli was fifteen to ensure he made enough to take care of his family financially. No one could take that away from him. No one would get close enough to him to have a joint bank account they could drain at any moment. He was not his father.

"I'm sorry."

Matías's words made him jump. He hadn't heard the man move.

Eli waved him away. "It's fine." He changed the subject. "What time do I have to be there tomorrow?"

"Are you free from six o'clock?"

"I can be."

"Can I pick you up?"

Eli chewed on his lip. "No. I'd like to drive myself in case I need to leave."

Matías frowned but nodded. His gaze dropped to Eli's lips, but he didn't move any closer. Eli realised Matías was waiting for Eli to initiate a kiss. And Eli realised he *wanted* a kiss, although he shouldn't. He lifted his chin and pecked Matías on the mouth. He couldn't do more because he didn't feel as in control as he should be.

"Have a good evening."

Matías winked, then pivoted and wandered out of the kitchen. Eli stayed where he was until he heard the front door close. Resting his hands on the counter, he dropped his head forward.

"What the hell are you doing, Eli?"

Eli smoothed a hand down his shirt front and smiled at a woman he passed. He'd been let into the house and pointed towards the back of it when he said he was here to see Matías. As he weaved his way through the crowds, he reconsidered his idea of what a family party was because it wasn't like this.

"Eli!"

He studied the people, trying to figure out where the voice came from when Matías appeared in front of him.

"Hey. I'm glad you came," Matías said.

"Hi. How are you?"

Matías smiled. "I'm good. Would you like a drink?"

"Sure."

Eli followed Matías, and they entered a spacious kitchen area with a centre island, around which several older people sat.

"Mum, Eli's here."

Mrs Jackson stood, coming towards him with open arms. "I'm so glad you could make it."

"Sorry, I'm late."

"It's fine." She looked between him and Matías. "You two look good together."

"Mum..." Matías said.

"What? It's true."

"Mrs Jackson—"

"Sofía, please."

Eli inhaled. "Sofía, thank you for inviting me."

Sofía clapped her hands. "They're here!"

The older men and women smiled, though they didn't rise from their positions. Eli wondered if it was a ritual for all people to work their way through a crowd before being granted permission to see the elders. The idea made him chuckle, causing Matías to glance at him in question. Eli shook his head but couldn't hide his smile.

"Angelica, Yuri. I'm so pleased for you," Sofía said, cupping a young woman's face and pressing a kiss on each cheek.

"Gracias, tia Sofía."

"Do we have a due date yet?" another woman asked.

"July 3," Angelica answered with a smile. Yuri slid an arm around her waist.

At least Eli understood the reason for the party now.

"Let's get you that drink?" Matías asked.

"Sure."

Matías disappeared, and Eli people-watched. It was something he always loved doing, especially at weddings, because he could always tell which people were happy and which were not. There was something in their behaviour or demeanour that gave it away. The same as his mother's demeanour did. She'd never been completely happy since his father had left, though she put on a brave face. Eli could tell, and he wished he could help, but all he'd been able to do was help with the financial side of things and with looking after his siblings.

A glass appeared in front of him, and he sent a smile to Matías. "Thank you."

"I realised when I got there, I hadn't asked what you liked, so I took a guess. It's lemon San Pellegrino."

Eli raised his eyebrows at the good guess. "Perfect." Matías sipped his drink, and Eli watched him studying the room of people. "Do you have events like this often?"

Matías glanced at him. "Sometimes. It depends on the celebration. As you can see, we're a big family, and sometimes, it's too much to do this. Mum did it at short notice because everyone was around for the wedding. From tomorrow onwards, people are heading back home."

"Home?"

"Most of the family lives in different parts of the country. Mum and her siblings seem to have spread far and wide when they left home." Matías grinned. "Couldn't imagine why."

Eli chuckled. "That good, eh?"

"Abuela is...fierce. I can see where tia Elena gets it from."

"Abuela?"

"Ah, it's the Spanish word for grandmother. It's what we call her." Matías points to the elderly woman sitting in an armchair in the corner of the kitchen.

Eli nodded. "And tia must be auntie?"

"Yes. We speak mainly English, but some words slip in sometimes or are a staple in our life. I forget some people don't know the meanings."

"Matías! Eli! I'm so glad you are here together."

Speaking of Elena.

The woman pulled Matías in for a hug, then set on Eli, who didn't know what to do but accept the greeting.

"Nice to see you, tia."

"I'm so glad I no longer have to worry about you. You've spent too long alone, Matías. You're an amazing man, and I'm so thrilled you've found someone you can spend time with." Elena smiled, patting both their cheeks.

Eli smiled back, expecting a slither of annoyance to show, but there was nothing but acceptance, which he supposed was a good thing in this situation. If he was pretending, he couldn't do it while trying to hide his aversion to being in a relationship.

"Have you eaten?" Elena asked.

The second she finished talking, Eli's stomach growled. Not loud enough for everyone to hear, but enough, he felt it and placed a hand over it. Matías laughed.

"I would take it as a yes, tia."

"Good, good. Come with me. There's plenty to eat, but also plenty of mouths to eat it. You need to get something in that stomach of yours before everything is gone."

Elena headed out of the kitchen, and everyone gave way when they saw her coming. Matías grabbed Eli's hand and followed her. Eli ignored the tingles emanating from his palm where their skin touched, pretending it wasn't the reason for the goosebumps flowing up his arm. Matías squeezed his hand once, and Eli looked up from where he'd been staring at their hands.

"You okay?" Matías asked. "Or rather, is this okay?"

Eli nodded. "Fine."

Matías smiled and stopped them beside a large table filled to the edges with different tapas. Eli had eaten at Spanish tapas bars before, so he recognised some of them, but others were a mystery.

"Don't worry. I'll tell you what's in each of them," Matías said with a grin.

"I'll have you know, I know what some of them are," Eli said, lifting his chin and pointing his nose to the ceiling, then ruined it by laughing. "But, yes, some of them I'll need help with."

"Not a problem."

They filled a plate and stood to the side of the room, eating and talking while people came up and said hello before heading off again.

"Oh, so who's this lucky fella?"

Chapter 5

Matías

Matías closed his eyes and inwardly groaned. Rafe was the very last person he wanted to see at the moment. He loved his cousin, but he was so...

"He's going to chew you up and spit you out, Matti."

He was also Matías's best friend despite his flaws.

Matías chuckled and grabbed Rafe for a hug. "I didn't expect to see you today. I thought you were working tonight."

Rafe grinned and winked in Eli's direction. "I couldn't miss the big announcement, so I took the night off."

Matías clutched at his chest. "Oh, my god! The great and mighty Rafael Garcia put his business in someone else's hands! I think I'm having a heart attack."

"Ignore him," Rafe said to Eli. "He's jealous because I get all the guys."

"Yeah, including the ones you don't want." Matías loved teasing his cousin as much as his cousin loved teasing him.

Rafe was Sofía's brother's son, and they had grown up together because they had been born within two months of each other—Matías being the oldest—and they had lived on the same street for the whole of their childhood. They went to school together and everything in between that point and now. They knew each other inside and out, which meant Rafe would be the hardest to sell his relationship to.

"Aren't you going to introduce us?" Rafe asked, glaring at Matías.

"I apologise." Matías inclined his head and placed a hand on Eli's back. "Eli, this is my cousin and occasional best friend, Rafael Garcia, also known as Rafe."

Rafe held out his hand. Immediately after Eli slid his hand into it, Rafe enclosed it with his other hand. "My dear boy, you have your work cut out for you with this one." Rafe tilted his head towards Matías, who slid his arm around Eli's waist, the move not going unnoticed by Rafe. "When he gets too tedious for you, come find me."

Matías pushed his hand against the side of Rafe's face, shoving him away from them with a laugh. "Get your own boyfriend."

Rafe held his hands over his heart. "I'm trying, Matti. I'm trying."

"How are you, anyway? How's business?" Matías glanced at Eli, who appeared amused by their antics, which was good. He often forgot how to behave when his wild cousin was around. "Rafe owns the nightclub Zoo."

"I'm doing good, and so is the club. I've left Rox in charge tonight. Should be interesting to see if the place is still standing when I go back to lock up." He chuckled.

"Rox? Are you sure it was a good idea? Wasn't he the one who left the back door open and let those stray dogs inside?"

"The one and only." Rafe held up his hands. "What can I say? I struggle to find good employees. Anyway, he did his time." Eli made a noise, and Rafe chuckled again. "I mean, he had to clean up the mess those dogs made. I could hear him gagging from two floors away."

Eli laughed. "I can imagine. Not the best job in the world."

Rafe waggled his finger in the air. "Ah, but he hasn't forgotten to shut the door since."

"Mistakes pay off," Eli said.

Rafe tilted his head and narrowed his eyes. "You sound like you have experience with it."

"Definitely. I've been in this business for twenty-five years. I've made more mistakes than I care to admit, but I've made it work in my favour. Business decisions don't always make sense to others, but when you've made a mistake, it helps build your brand because you know from experience."

Rafe pointed at him. "Exactly!" He studied Matías. "You've got a good one here. I might have to steal him."

Matías groaned. "Never going to happen." He pressed a kiss to Eli's temple, tugging him closer, sighing when Eli curled into him a bit.

Rafe grinned. "No need to get possessive. You know I'm kidding."

"Rafael Santiago Angel Garcia!"

Rafe froze. "That doesn't bode well." He pivoted. "Yes, Mother?"

"Don't you 'Yes, Mother' me. Since when do you visit with your cousin before you say hello to your mother, eh?"

"Lo siento, Mamá." He lifted his arms and wrapped them around his mother. They were the same height and build, and Rafe was the spitting image of the woman.

Matías could hear them talking, and they pulled back with smiles on their faces. Aunt Mariana cupped Rafe's cheeks and tapped him gently.

"The love between you all is visible every time you get together. It's amazing," Eli said, his gaze on Rafe and Mariana.

"I suppose we are over the top with our displays of affection. It's part of us. Do you not have something similar with your family?"

Eli shifted on his feet, and Matías dropped his arm away, though he didn't want to. "Not really. We hug hello and goodbye and always say 'I love you' at the end of a phone call, but nothing so..." He trailed off.

"Awkward? Unnecessary? Crazy?" Matías listed off.

Eli chuckled, which was what Matías had wanted. The man stared at him and slid his arms around Matías's waist. Matías returned the embrace. He wished he could understand what was going through Eli's head because it looked like he was trying to work out a difficult equation with how creased his forehead was.

"None of the above. Nothing so visibly loving, I suppose."

Matías dropped a kiss on his forehead. "You'll find we are always like this, and you might get fed up with it soon."

Eli smiled. "I'm sure I can put up with it."

They stared at each other, and Matías wanted nothing more than to drop his lips to Eli's, but he'd told Eli he needed to make the first move, and he would abide by that. It didn't stop him from wanting it, though.

Instead, he said, "There's more food if you're still hungry. Or if not, there's dessert. I'll even make sure there's something without fruit on it."

Eli raised his eyebrows. "How did you know I didn't like fruit?"

"I saw you eating everything but the fruit at the wedding. I assumed. Was I wrong?"

"No. Dessert sounds good."

Matías didn't mistake the huskiness of Eli's voice, but it took extreme effort to ignore it. He grasped Eli's hand and guided him towards the table again.

"Wow. Your family goes all out. They should consider being caterers," Eli said.

"Actually, some of them are. I have two cousins and an aunt who went into business together a few years ago. It's doing well."

"You'll have to introduce me. I'm always on the lookout for more local businesses to support. And now I'm running two businesses at the minute. I need all the help I can get."

Eli chose a slice of toffee cheesecake, and Matías grabbed some chocolate gateau. "What do you mean, two businesses?"

Eli sighed. "I received a call from a distressed bride late on Sunday night because her wedding planner had an accident and was in a coma. I visited her family and offered to keep her business afloat until they decided what was going to happen. Sarah, the wedding planner, woke up properly today, so hopefully, she'll make a full recovery."

Matías's mouth fell open. "How are you managing to work all the weddings?"

"That's where Jasmine comes in. She's been training for this. So, with Sarah's parents' permission, Jasmine took over the running of them, and I oversee and help her when she needs it. She's done three so far with another two tomorrow." Eli sighed. "It goes to show I didn't give her enough credit."

"Why do you say that?"

"Because I've been holding her back. I don't like...letting go of control of the business. It's something I'm working on." He gave a rueful smile. "It means she's been my assistant for probably longer than she needed to be. I'm surprised she hasn't left already."

"I think she knows she has a good boss, Eli. You look after your employees well. They would be foolish to leave."

Eli smiled. "Thanks." He inhaled. "I've decided when we've sorted everything with Sarah's business, I'm going to ask Jasmine if she wants to be a full-time wedding planner without me looking over her shoulder. She deserves it."

"I think it's a fantastic idea."

They spent another hour talking with Matías's family and friends before Eli said he needed to get home. Matías guided him through the throng with a hand on his lower back and collected their coats. It was too cold to be outside with next to nothing on. They wandered down the driveway and across the road to where Eli had parked.

"Thank you for a great evening. I loved meeting your family," Eli said, flicking his keys around his finger.

Matías shoved his hands into his pockets. "Thank you for coming. I know you don't enjoy lying to them. The minute you're unhappy with the situation, you need to tell me. Okay?"

Matías dipped his head down to catch Eli's averted gaze. The man nodded. "Okay."

"Drive carefully."

Eli unlocked his car but paused with one hand on the handle, glancing over at him. "Matías?" Matías raised his eyebrows at him. "Kiss me goodbye? They might be watching."

Matías tried to withhold his smile but couldn't. "Anytime."

He stepped closer, crowding Eli against his car. He rested his hands on the car, either side of Eli's shoulders, and lowered his head. "You sure?"

Eli lifted his chin, their mouths meeting. He could feel the chill of the air had already lowered Eli's temperature because the end of his nose was cold, and so was his chin. Matías didn't go slow into this kiss. He opened his mouth straight away and licked at Eli's plump mounds, encouraging him to open. Eli groaned and did so, and Matías swooped inside, tasting cheesecake and tea on his tongue. His arms closed around Eli's shoulders, and Eli's arms tightened around his waist.

He knew they couldn't go too far, but it took a lot of effort to stop. When he pulled away, streams of steamy air escaped them both as they panted to regain their breath. He waited until Eli had found his footing again and stepped back.

"Goodnight, Eli," he said, slipping his hands into his pockets again to stop the need to drag Eli back into his arms.

"Goodnight, Matti," Eli said with a wink. "The name suits you."

Matías grinned and watched Eli drive away.

"You are truly whipped, you know that?"

He whirled around to Rafe, who stood shivering in his shirt. "Bloody hell, Rafe. It's freezing out here. Get back inside." He stormed over to him and herded him back towards the house.

"It's tia Sofía's fault. She asked me to find you."

"I was saying goodbye to Eli."

"So, I saw." Rafe snorted. "Far too much heat between you to notice little old freezing me standing there waiting for you to finish."

Matías cuffed the back of his head as they entered the house. "Shut up."

Rafe pulled on his arm. "I'm serious, Matti. You look good together."

Matías fought the urge to spill everything to his best friend. He could. Rafe wouldn't mind, but there were too many chances this could go wrong. He didn't want Rafe to bear any repercussions to Matías's secrets. It would be bad enough if his immediate family found out what he'd done.

"Thanks," was all he could manage.

The thoughts plagued him for days after the party. Several times, he had convinced himself to come clean, then minutes later, told himself he was doing the right thing.

He hadn't spoken to Eli except through text messages, but he wanted to thank him in some way. When he'd come up with the idea of taking him for dinner, Matías had second-guessed himself again. Annoyed, he'd slapped himself on the cheek and asked Eli out on a date.

Eli had agreed, but only after Matías had explained his family would expect him to take Eli out for dinner and to be seen with him. He'd confirmed they would meet outside Romano's at seven o'clock. Matías had wanted to pick Eli up, but Eli had declined. Eli probably wanted some way to escape if things turned bad, which Matías could understand.

Parking wasn't great, and he chose a side road a few streets away and jogged to the restaurant so he wouldn't be late. He didn't push himself too hard, though, because sweat stains on a shirt were not a good look—for anyone.

As he came closer, he saw Eli standing by the door on his phone. Matías studied him as he drew closer, his heart racing for an entirely different reason this time. His chin-length hair was tucked behind his ears, with not a strand out of place. His skin shone in the lamplight, not a blemish to be seen. He leaned against the wall with his foot resting against the wall, bent at the knee as if he didn't have a care in the world. He wore dark-coloured trousers and a thigh-length coat, which stopped Matías from seeing what shirt he wore. Several people looked at him twice as they passed by.

Matías stopped in front of him and waited.

Eli glanced up, then down, then up again and straightened from his lean. "Hi. Sorry, I was miles away."

"Business?" Matías pointed to the phone.

Eli rolled his eyes. "Family."

Matías nodded in camaraderie. "Are you ready? I booked us a table."

Eli smiled, small though it was. "Yes."

Matías opened the door and waved for Eli to go first—his mother had taught him well. Eli's cheeks flushed.

"Good evening, Matías," the maitre d' said.

"Good evening, Rosalia. I have a table for two booked at seven o'clock."

"Perfect. Come this way."

Rosalia was the manager of Romano's and also the co-owner with her brother, Raffaele. Their father, who everyone called Old Joe, had founded the restaurant many years ago but died the previous year, leaving his children in charge. Old Joe had been an integral part of the community, and it was a sad day when Matías had found out about his death. Matías had spent many an evening at the place and socialising with both sides of the families—their families often got confused when they were all together; Rafe and Raf were called to the right and wrong person over the course of an evening. His experience with the restaurant was the reason Matías had chosen the place—he knew it would be perfect.

Rosalia showed them to a table near the back of the restaurant next to the wall, giving them a little more privacy for the conversation Eli and he needed to have.

"Can I get you any drinks to start?" Rosalia asked.

Matías glanced at Eli. "Do you drink wine?" Eli nodded. "Any preferences?"

"No. I like different types, so you choose."

"Could we have a couple of glasses of the house red, please?"

"Perfect. I'll be back with those in a few minutes."

Rosalia disappeared, and the two men opened their menus, Matías getting lost in the delicious-sounding food.

"There are too many to choose from," Eli muttered.

Matías chuckled. "I know. I try to have something different each time I come, but I'm a sucker for the spaghetti bolognese."

"I think I'll try the spigola alla griglia. Please choose something with garlic in it, so I'm not stinking the whole place out." Eli's cheeks pinked, and he shifted in his seat.

Matías laughed, though his entire brain sparked with the thought of a potential kiss at the end of the night. "Will do. I'll get the penne arrabbiata. Plenty of garlic in that."

They folded the menus away, and Matías leaned his crossed arms on the edge of the table, gazing at Eli.

"What?" Eli stroked a hand down his shirt, which Matías could now see was a deep red colour, almost like red wine.

"I'm trying to decide if this is a date or not?"

"Well, we said we were going to go out and be seen together, so technically, yes, I suppose." Eli cleared his throat. "Are there many people here, you know?"

Matías had his back to the room, so he glanced over his shoulder, taking in the guests and returning his gaze to Eli with a wince. "A few. There is one couple I wished weren't here, but only because I know them really well."

"Who's that?"

"Ave and George Oxford. Do you know them?"

Eli smiled and scanned the room. He paused when he must've found them and waved. "Yes, I do. Ave is wonderful. She sometimes helps with making the stationery for the weddings."

"She helps a lot of people around here."

Rosalia arrived with their drinks, and they placed their food order. Matías sipped the wine, rolling it around in his mouth before swallowing. He opened his eyes, having not realised he'd closed them, and found Eli staring at him, frozen.

"What's wrong?"

Eli shook his head. "Nothing. Sorry." He took a sip. "This is lovely."

"Gentlemen. What do we have here?"

Matías sighed and stared at Eli, whose smile lit up his entire face. Eli rose, hugging Ave and George, and Matías did the same thing.

"Have you had a good meal, Ave?" Matías asked.

"It was wonderful, as always. It's one night a week when I don't have to cook for everyone." She smiled at the three boys standing with them.

Ave and George had been foster parents for many children over the years, and these three boys were their current kids. Ian was fourteen, Benji was twelve, and Jamie was nine. No one knew what their story was except for Ave and George, but it didn't matter. They were being looked after by the best people now.

"I can imagine the amount of food you must go through with these three," Eli said.

"Whatever you imagine, triple it, and you might be there." Ave chuckled. "What are you two doing here?"

"We're having dinner," Matías said, knowing exactly what she was asking.

Eli snorted. "We're on a date, Ave." Eli glanced at him and gave a small shrug as if to say *we might as well get it over and done with now.*

No time like the present, it seemed.

"Well, would you look at that! We won't disturb you any longer. I had heard about you two, but I hadn't been sure until I saw it with my own eyes. I'm so happy for you both. You fit together perfectly." She clapped her hands together. "When did you get together?"

Chapter 6

Eli

"We're a very recent thing, Ave. I met Matías a little while ago, and we're taking things slow. No blowing this out of proportion, okay, Ave?" He narrowed his eyes playfully at her, and she giggled.

"Of course not. Every relationship has to start somewhere. I'm so happy for you both."

"Ave, maybe we should leave them to their meal? I'm sure they want to interact with each other instead of us," George said, sliding his arm around her shoulder.

"Yes, of course. Sorry. Oh, I'm so happy." She covered her mouth. "Okay. We're going. Have a wonderful evening."

Eli watched them go with a smile on his face. He loved Ave and George. They complimented each other in the best way, and he reckoned that was why they had lasted. He transferred his gaze to Matías, finding the man already staring at him.

"Sorry if I was out of order there."

Matías tilted his head. "You realise she's going to blow this out of proportion even though you told her not to, don't you?"

Eli chuckled. "I know, but at least the warning was there."

"True."

"Here are your meals, gentlemen." Rosalia placed the plates in front of them. "Do you need anything else?"

"No, I think we're all good," Matías said, cocking his eyebrow at Eli.

"Yes, I'm good, thanks."

"Perfect. Give us a wave if you need anything." Rosalia smiled and disappeared.

Eli closed his eyes and inhaled. The scents of sea bass, garlic, herbs and vegetables were delicious. He opened his eyes again and caught Matías staring. Eli lowered his eyes to his plate, wanting to hideaway. He didn't mind people looking at him, but Matías took it to a whole new level.

"So, what do we need to discuss?" he asked, laying the napkin across his lap and picking up his knife and fork.

Matías cleared his throat. "Mainly what happened at the suit fitting and when we decided to give us a try, I think. Anything else in between. The 'getting to know you' thing we can do as we go because we can use the excuse we are recently together as you said to Ave."

"Sounds good. At least we don't have to remember a lot of information."

"Yes! It's reminiscent of those fake relationship films," Matías said with a grin. "*The Proposal* eat your heart out."

Eli huffed a laugh. "So, the suit fitting...?"

"The discussion about the colour of it."

Eli narrowed his eyes. "Yes, I distinctly remember you trying to worm your way out of a grey suit everyone else was wearing."

"It didn't match my complexion!"

Eli tutted and grinned. "It doesn't matter. It's what the bride wanted. Have you ever seen 27 Dresses?" Matías shook his head. "You should. It brings a whole new light to the wedding planning business. As does The Wedding Planner."

"There you go. We could say that was what sparked our interest and go from there."

Eli nodded and did a calculation in his head. "It would mean we've been seeing each other for about three weeks?"

"I think it's a good number. With my shift patterns and your busy hours, we can say we've not had much time to see each other. We can work on that as we go."

"Sounds like a plan. Did you ask me out or the other way around?" Eli asked, placing another bite of sea bass into his mouth and barely containing his groan. It was mouth-watering.

"My family knows I'm quite shy when it comes to asking men out, but it doesn't mean I won't. What would you prefer?" Matías appeared to be enjoying his food to the same degree Eli was.

"I would say we keep to the truth as much as possible. You asked me to go for dinner as you did for tonight."

"Agreed." Matías rested his cutlery against the plate and took a sip of wine. "Okay, getting to know you part one. What do you enjoy doing outside of wedding planning?"

Eli chewed, contemplating his answer. He was going to sound boring, but he won't change his answers lest they get caught out. "Being with my family and watching films. That's about it. I spend most of my time organising weddings."

"You own your business, so I can see why it's important to you. You need to make enough money to make ends meet, and if it means long hours, you'd do it without thinking twice."

Eli peered at him. "How do you know that?"

The corner of Matías's mouth curved. "You can be quite intense sometimes, but I understand why. You have a lot riding on your income, and if I had to guess, I would say you have been taking care of your family, too?"

Eli dropped his gaze. How had Matías seen so much of him when he hid from so many other people? He needed to shore up his defences. Matías was already much closer than Eli liked men to get. Although saying that, Eli was on a date with a man. It was as close as anyone had been to him ever. If you exclude in the biblical sense, anyway.

"I didn't mean to make you uncomfortable. If there's anything you don't want to answer or want me to stop talking about, tell me. You're doing me a favour, Eli, and I promise I won't force you to give more information than you're willing to." Matías cleared his throat. "What's your favourite colour?"

Eli glanced at Matías, focusing on his shirt. "Emerald green," he whispered.

He refocused on his food, and they made small talk while they finished. It was comfortable, despite the slight awkwardness from earlier. The food was delicious, the wine was divine, and the company was better than Eli could've hoped for. If he could fall for anyone, he would've chosen Matías. The man was an all-around good guy and loved his family with every ounce of his being. Eli could tell that from the way he spoke about them all. The love shining through his eyes whenever he spoke their names was a beacon to all those who had a similar feeling. Eli could relate. He loved his family with everything in him. He couldn't share the love with someone on the outside. He refused to allow anyone to come into the family and destroy what they had worked so hard to rebuild after his father had left. They were finally on an even keel after so many years, and Eli would not turn his back on that.

"Would you like dessert?"

Matías's words caught his attention, and Eli smiled despite his thoughts. "No, thank you. I'm stuffed."

Matías smiled and held his hand in the air to get Rosalia's attention. Eli saw her nod in their direction.

"After everything we've talked about, are you still happy to go ahead with this?" Matías asked.

Eli crossed his arms and leaned on the table, staring down at their plates. He wouldn't go back on what he'd offered Matías, but their conversation that evening had proven he'd made the right choice. He peered up at him.

"I'm happy."

"If you are one hundred per cent sure, can I arrange for you to come to dinner with my parents?"

Eli's heart thumped, and he breathed deeply to stop the pain of the palpitations. "Sure. When?" He waved his hand between them.

"I'll check with Mum and let you know if that's okay. Is there any day better for you?"

"Weekends are out, for obvious reasons. But usually, Mondays are good. Sometimes, Thursdays, too."

"Perfect."

"Gentlemen, what can I get you?" Rosalia asked with a smile.

"Could we have the bill, please?" Matías asked.

"Of course. I'll be right back."

Eli sipped at his water. He'd stopped drinking the wine after the first glass, knowing he had to drive home. He might indulge in another glass when he was finally behind his own door, though. Their dinner had been enlightening, and he needed to dissect it and figure out what was going on inside his head.

Matías paid and held Eli's coat while he slid his arms in. It was a pleasant feeling to have someone to do little things like that.

"Where have you parked?" Matías asked. Eli pointed in the direction of where his car was. "Can I walk you to your car?"

Eli stared past Matías, not knowing the correct answer to the seemingly simple question. "Sure."

They walked in silence, side by side, not touching apart from the odd brush of their hands. The cool night air sent billowing steam from their mouths on each exhale, but Eli couldn't feel the cold. When they reached Eli's car, he let out a small puff of air.

"This is me."

"Thank you for tonight. I enjoyed it." Matías smiled.

"I did, too."

Eli stared at Matías, not sure if there was anything left to say. He froze when Matías leaned forward and closed his eyes when the man's lips touched his cheek. Disappointment curdled inside of him, and he fought it down. It was only a ruse. They were not real. Eli didn't want them to be real.

It didn't stop him from turning his head as Matías pulled away and brushing his lips against Matías's. Both paused, sharing the same breath, less than an inch between them.

"Practice makes perfect," Matías whispered.

Eli didn't reply. This was a bad idea. They didn't need to practise kissing. Instead, he lifted his head slightly, and Matías took his cue. The man cupped Eli's jaw and rubbed his cool lips against Eli's, the dryness of both letting them slide across unimpeded before Matías pressed harder. Eli's eyes closed, and he let Matías lead. He sipped at Eli's upper lip, then his lower, repeating the action several times and sending Eli's head into a tailspin. Matías stepped closer, their chests touching. Eli gripped at Matías's jacket as the man flicked his tongue against Eli's mouth. Eli tilted his head and opened his mouth a fraction. Matías slid his hand to the back of Eli's head and slid his tongue into Eli's mouth. The heat invaded, and their breathing grew rapid, even though the kiss was still gentle. Eli lost all sense of time as Matías explored.

A wolf whistle drew them apart, both a blessing and a curse as far as Eli was concerned. Their arms loosened, though they didn't let go immediately. Eli stared at Matías, his lips swollen and red, his cheeks rosy, his eyes glassy.

Eli removed his arms and smiled, trying to calm his heart rate. "Thank you for a lovely evening, Matías."

"You're welcome."

Ignoring the hoarseness of the man's voice, Eli climbed into his car and switched on the engine. His body wanted more from Matías, but his heart wouldn't let him. He knew Matías was dangerous to him because, for the first time ever, he tempted Eli to take more.

Eli focused on the list on his tablet. He ran through it one more time before nodding and handing it back to Alex, his new assistant.

"Everything looks ready to go for the evening celebration. Have there been any problems mentioned to you?"

"Nothing at the moment." She glanced at the tablet and fiddled with the case.

"What's wrong?"

Alex grimaced. "One of the groomsmen is being a little too forward in his advances. Doesn't like the word no. He's had a bit too much to drink."

Eli sighed. There was always one. "Who?"

"Adam."

Eli nodded. "I will have a word. If necessary, I will arrange for a taxi home for him."

"You don't need to do that. It's fine."

Eli clasped her shoulders, making her look at him. "No, it's not, Alex. No one has the right to do that when you've told them no. It would be better all-round if he slept it off at home."

"I don't want to cause problems."

"You won't. Remember the discussion we had a few weeks ago? No one has the right to make you feel uncomfortable. Adam is causing you to feel like that, and I'll deal with it." He held up his hand. "I'm not saying Adam will try anything, but wouldn't it be better if we stopped even the possibility? Especially as it would ruin the wedding day if something kicked off."

Alex nodded slowly. "I get it. I hate being the cause of trouble."

"You're not. He is. Let me speak with Della. I'll let her know what's going on."

"Thanks."

Alex exited the room, and Eli blew out a breath. This was one part of his job he didn't enjoy. Telling on family members was never pleasant, but what he'd told Alex had been the truth. He wouldn't want anyone to feel uncomfortable working for him, no matter the cost to his business. Eli stood by his beliefs, and if others didn't like how he worked, they could find another wedding planner.

He finished his green tea, though it was cold and tasted disgusting. He loved green tea, just not cold, but the effects would be the same as if it was hot. Traipsing out of the room they had allocated him, he bypassed many guests in different states of inebriation. The reception was going well so far, and all the speeches were out of the way. The only thing left for this event was the throwing of the bouquet before the newlyweds disappeared into their suite to get changed for the evening celebration.

He paused at the back of the room, trying to locate the mother of the bride, then wandered around the perimeter of the room to the head table where she sat. He crouched behind her chair, making sure he made a noise so as not to startle her.

"Mrs Dixon, could I have a quick word?"

The woman, who couldn't have been more than forty if that, twisted in her chair and smiled. "Of course, Eli! What's up?"

Inwardly, he grinned at her words. She was one of the more easy-going, younger-sounding people he'd had the pleasure of working with.

"I seem to have a minor issue with one of the grooms-men."

Della sighed. "Let me guess. Adam?"

"I'm afraid so. I wondered if you would allow me to call a taxi for him and ensure he gets home with no problems?"

"No need. Michael was supposed to be keeping an eye on him. He can take him home." Della patted his arm. "Thank you for letting me know."

"Thank you for listening." Eli smiled. "We're ready for the bouquet throw whenever you are."

"Thank you."

He rose and continued back around the room, checking with the staff he saw along the way. Everything was going smoothly, which he was glad about because he'd been do-ing this job for long enough to spot problems before they happened, mostly. He returned to the room and pulled out his phone, checking for messages.

He wasn't waiting for Matías.

Not at all.

Eli closed his eyes and shook his head. He was an idiot. He couldn't even explain why he was so interested in helping the man.

"Eli?"

He flinched, whirling around to the door. He hadn't heard Alex come in. "Sorry, everything okay?"

"Yes. The bride is ready for the bouquet throw, and the groom has asked if he can throw the garter to the guests?"

Eli could see Alex's mouth twitching, but she was getting better at removing her thoughts from her expression, as he had taught her to do.

He considered the groom's request and couldn't see a problem with it. "We have time. Do you know if Adam has left yet?"

Alex nodded. "He was leaving as I came here."

"I think it will be fine. Let me speak with Trevor to make sure I understand how he wants to do it."

After finding out the groom wanted to take his bride's garter off with his teeth and throw it to the unmarried guests, Eli couldn't help but grin. This family was amazing. So laid back and willing to try anything. They had been one of the best weddings he'd ever done, and that was saying something as Eli's calendar was booked out eighteen months in advance, and he'd seen many things in all his years.

Eli arranged for a chair to be set in front of the head table, where everyone could see. He let the groom take the lead in the new event and disappeared to the back of the room to observe. Trevor called his new wife forward and embarrassed the hell out of her if her red cheeks were anything to go by. Eli kept his expression blank, but inside he laughed at the antics. Once he'd removed the garter, Trevor called on the unmarried guests, who gathered behind him. One man caught it, though, by his expression, he hadn't wanted to.

Eli removed the chair, allowing the bride room to throw her bouquet. The unmarried guests remained where they were—something else Eli loved about this family was the inclusion throughout; there was no separating them into male and female guests, just everyone. Eli began stacking the chairs against the wall because when they finished this part, they would rearrange the room for the evening dance part of the wedding.

As he leaned down to pick some rubbish off the floor, he felt something hit his back and fall to the floor. He turned and saw the bouquet, then glanced up at the room of guests staring at him.

He cleared his throat. "Sorry, did I get in the way?"

Amy ran up to him. "Yay! You caught it."

"I wouldn't say he caught it. It hit him and fell to the floor. That doesn't count, surely?" someone said.

"Shut up, Viki."

Amy clapped her hands. "It doesn't matter if you caught it or not. It chose you. I wonder if your dream will come true, Eli. Mine has. I'm so happy you could be here. Thank you so much for a perfect day."

Amy hugged him, and Eli stared at the offending object, still on the floor beside him. When she pulled back, Eli said, "It's time for you to head out."

Amy grinned, picked up the bouquet and held it out to him. He couldn't do anything but take it because he knew he would upset her if he didn't. With a smile, which was probably no more than a grimace, he took the flowers.

"Thank you."

He shuffled out of the ballroom and entered his room, leaning against the closed door. Staring at the flowers, he wanted to throw them away, but they *were* pretty. He would give it to his mother when he saw her the following day. There was no way he would keep the damn thing. He would never get married because he couldn't trust the person wouldn't follow in his father's footsteps, and Eli had finally become financially independent, so he didn't need another person to help him pay the bills. His mother hadn't needed someone else, and neither did he.

He pulled out his phone and dialled Jasmine. "You'll never guess what happened?"

"What?"

"I caught the bouquet. Well, I didn't. It kind of hit me, but Amy insisted it had *chosen* me. Bloody hell, Jasmine. It's not funny," he griped when Jasmine's laughter sounded down the phone.

Chapter 7

Matías

Matías had known it would be difficult to see Eli at times because his shifts would clash with Eli's bookings, but it wasn't until he hadn't seen the man in person for two weeks he understood how tedious it might get. They'd kept in touch via messages and phone calls, but Eli had been crazy busy with how many weddings he had, and throwing in the additional business he was helping with, it was a lot of work for him. Matías wanted to help but didn't know a thing about the wedding business.

Finally, he'd convinced Eli to come over to his house so Matías could cook for him. He wasn't quite the chef de cuisine Alejo was, but he could hold his own. Initially, Eli had baulked at the idea, saying no one would know he was there, but Matías had argued his brother would know if Matías never brought Eli home. It was true, but it was also a little white lie to get Eli to relax a little. He'd been swamped, and Matías wanted to help him have an evening off, but he'd been concerned if he had visited Eli, the man would've still been in work mode.

When the doorbell rang, he was elbow deep in washing up suds, but he quickly dried his hands as he strode for the door.

"Hey! You made it."

Eli rolled his eyes. "You're not that hard to find, Matti."

Eli had taken to calling him Matti, and he couldn't stop the smile that formed every time he heard it from his lips.

"Glad to hear it. Come on in."

"Is that..." He sniffed. "Is that bolognese?"

Matías grinned. "My speciality. Would you like a glass?" He held up the bottle Eli had given him.

"Sure, thanks."

"Make yourself comfortable."

Matías left Eli to snoop around and headed for the kitchen. He loved the apartment he and Alejo had found. It wasn't big by any means, but it was comfortable. The open-plan living and dining room took up three-quarters of what Matías called the living area—the kitchen, living room and dining room of a house—and the kitchen the other quarter. Opposite the kitchen door was a hallway leading to two bedrooms and a bathroom. It was the perfect size for the two of them.

He removed the cork from the wine and poured two glasses—tumblers because he didn't have wine glasses. After stirring the sauce, he carried the glasses to the living room and found Eli looking through his DVD collection. Many people were getting rid of DVDs now on-demand had grown so big, but he liked the physical reminders of the films he'd enjoyed.

"Did you find any you like?"

Eli jumped and whirled around, his hand on his chest. "Bloody hell!"

"Sorry, I thought you heard me come in." He held out a glass. "Peace offering?"

"Thanks. And yes, there are a couple I've seen, but I don't get much time to watch films. I was surprised to see a fitness collection, though. I thought you went to the gym?"

Matías nodded. "I do, but I hate going. Some days, I like to change it up, so I'll pick a DVD at random and do it. I have to say, the *Fame* workout is a killer." He groaned at the thought. "I prefer jogging if I had to choose. Do you do anything like that?"

Eli snorted. "I do yoga and meditation. Oh, and be on my feet for many hours of the day when I have a booking. I think that's enough exercise for me."

"You'll have to show me meditation. Every time I try it, I can't let go of the thoughts and end up more annoyed with myself than anything else."

"It's hard in the beginning. You have to persevere, and eventually, you can let the thoughts drift in and out with no problem, but it takes a while to get to that stage."

"Maybe I need to keep trying."

Eli glanced at the window. "I can show you after dinner if you want?"

Matías closed his eyes and grimaced, those words conjuring up something completely different from meditation. "That would be great, but you don't have to." He changed the subject because Eli appeared uncomfortable. "Dinner is almost ready. I need to finish off, but if you want to choose a film, we can put it on after dinner."

"Okay."

Matías returned to the kitchen and adjusted his jeans. He couldn't believe the words "finish off" came out of his mouth when his thoughts were in the wrong place. While he checked everything was ready, he gave himself a pep talk, reminding himself this was a fake relationship and nothing was happening between them. Nothing *would* happen between them because Eli didn't want it to. Matías had to keep his cock under control. No more excuses to touch and kiss Eli. No more trying to find ways of being close to him. It had been a bad idea to invite him over. Matías had wanted to spend time with Eli in addition to giving him a break from his workload, but he needed to stop. Make their "dates" in public places, not private ones.

He plated the food and carried it to the table. Luckily, he hadn't gone so far as to put candles and napkins on it because that would've been too date-like.

"There you go. I hope you like it."

Eli sat with a smile. "It looks delicious."

"Thanks. It's one of the few dishes I can cook." Matías dropped his gaze, embarrassed.

"Well, it's a good one to know. Nothing beats spaghetti bolognese, I hear." Eli winked at him, his words a nod to Matías's confession in Romano's on their first public appearance.

Matías grinned. "Nothing better." He picked up his glass then put it down again. "I forgot the bottle. Hold on."

He fetched it from the kitchen and brought it back to the table, refilling both their glasses. Holding up his glass, he said, "To us, for surviving to…" He paused. "Is it rude of me to ask your age?"

Eli snorted. "Little too late now, but I'm forty."

"Huh, I would never have said that. To us, for surviving to forty and thirty-eight. We've done well."

Eli chuckled. "Idiot."

Matías grinned. "Always."

He touched his glass to Eli and caught his eye, the stare lasting for longer than the second he'd planned. There was something about the man that pulled him in every time they were together. Made him do reckless things. Like wanting to lean over the table and capture his mouth. Like wanting to knock their food to the floor and take him on the table. Matías blinked rapidly and swallowed half his glass in one go.

"Enjoy."

They ate in comfortable silence until Matías broke it with a question, "Did you choose a film?"

Eli shook his head and finished his mouthful. "I couldn't decide. It's been too long since I've seen anything. I like anything but horror, so I'm happy for you to choose your favourite or something."

"My favourite?" Matías widened his eyes in horror. "How can you pick a favourite?"

Eli chuckled again. "All right. One of your favourites. Better?"

"Marginally. I'll have to think." Matías rubbed the back of his neck. "Will you tell me a bit about your family?" Eli visibly tensed. "Never mind. It doesn't matter." He refocused on his food, trying to ignore the uncomfortable silence.

"My mum is called Karen. She's a receptionist at a doctor's surgery. I try to see her when I can, but it's not easy. Most of the time, she calls me and orders me to dinner when she believes it's been too long since she last saw me." Eli smiled. "I don't do it on purpose, but time gets away from me, and before I know it, three weeks have passed."

"I know the feeling."

"I have one sister and two brothers. Opal, Lukas and Robbie or Rob, but he'll always be Robbie to us. All younger than me. Opal is a swimming teacher. Lukas is a mechanic. Robbie is a bartender, though he's a bit of a shit and thinks he's better than others. It's something we tried to knock out of him when he was younger, but I think he got his own way too many times, and now he thinks he can rule the world." Eli snickered. "He's got a rude awakening coming."

"I know some other youngest siblings who are like that." Matías grinned. "I'm one of the lucky ones. Alejo is a decent guy all around."

"Oh, Robbie is decent. He'd give you the shirt off his back if he thought you needed it, but he had a view of the world as black and white with no grey areas. It's difficult for him to read between the lines with anything."

Matías nodded. "It must be hard for him."

Eli's forehead creased. "What do you mean?"

"First, being the youngest is always difficult, so Ave tells me. He would've had the attention of his three siblings and mother when he was a baby and toddler. It's a lot of attention that didn't get taken off him when a new baby came along because one didn't. Is it all bravado? Is he hiding his true self from you?"

Eli said nothing, just moved his food around his plate with his fork.

"I'm sorry if that's wrong. It's my two-pence worth. Feel free to ignore it." Matías felt bad for bringing down the evening. "I've decided what we're going to watch. *Geostorm*. Nothing like the possibility of the end of the world to brighten the evening."

Eli snorted. "Okay. Sounds good."

They finished the dinner with small talk, Matías filling any potential silences with stories about his family and what he got up to as a kid. He could've spent several hours talking and still have days' worth of pranks to get through.

Once they were done, he picked up their plates and returned them to the kitchen. When he came back out, Eli was sitting on the sofa, the bottle of wine on the coffee table and both their glasses waiting.

"I didn't want to presume to start the film because I have no clue about your TV setup. It looks complicated," Eli said.

"It's not once you know how."

He set the film to play while Eli refilled their glasses. They settled on the sofa, but at opposite ends, though Matías brought his knee up onto the cushion, so he faced towards Eli. He didn't want Eli to feel like Matías wasn't open to conversation if he wanted to talk.

"What is this about?"

Matías glanced over. "Basically, Gerard Butler created a kind of satellite web that surrounds the world, but it goes wrong, and he has to fix it before it comes crashing down to earth and kills millions of people."

"Oh, something bright and magical. Wonderful." Eli grinned.

"You'll love it."

Throughout, they talked about the film and other general things, and Matías enjoyed himself immensely. When it ended, Matías said, "What did you think?"

"You're right. It was good."

The wine bottle was empty, and Matías felt light and relaxed. He hoped Eli felt the same, and studying the man, it looked like he was.

"Do you want the meditation lesson now?" Eli rolled his head on the back of the sofa and stared at him.

Matías wanted much more, but he would settle for a lesson if it meant Eli would stay for a while longer. "Sure."

"Okay. On the floor." Eli got up and pushed the coffee table closer to the TV, giving them space next to the sofa. "You sit with your legs crossed and your back against the sofa. It will be easier on you."

Matías followed the instructions, eyes widening when Eli dropped down in front of him, their knees touching.

"So, when I first started, I found it difficult to get the thoughts to stop until someone told me they didn't need to. The idea is if a thought floats through your head, let it in, acknowledge it and let it go again. Don't fight it because you'll tense up."

"Okay."

"Rest your hands wherever is comfortable. Some people rest them on their knees, some on their lap, some link their fingers. Whatever you prefer."

Matías let his hands fall to his lap.

"Now, close your eyes and concentrate on your breathing. Count in for four and out for eight if you can. Let it slow down."

Matías did. Concentrating on the sound of Eli's voice as he gave instructions and counted for them. He could feel every place where they touched because it tingled as if electricity flickered between them. He loved Eli's voice, and the thought made all kinds of images jump front and centre into his mind.

"Let the thoughts float away, Matti. Don't fight them."

"There's too many," he said.

"Okay. Let's try something different."

Matías opened his eyes at the change in Eli's tone. "What?"

Eli inhaled. "Scoot forward and stretch your legs out in front of you." Eli stood as Matías did as he'd asked, then stepped behind Matías. "Bit more."

Matías shuffled forward, and Eli sat behind him, his legs bracketing Matías's hips. It wasn't helping with his relaxation.

"Now, scoot back and lean against me." Matías hesitated but moved back, careful not to go too far. "You won't squash me, Matti." Amusement filled Eli's tone, and Matías grinned, shuffling further back. "Better. Now, rest your head back on my shoulder and close your eyes."

Matías did and instantly felt surrounded by the man. He wanted to turn his head and nuzzle into Eli's neck, but he refrained.

"Relax. Concentrate on your breathing again."

Eli's hands rested on Matías's shoulders and began kneading them in a gentle rhythm as he counted. The air from his soft words blew past Matías's ears, and Matías clenched his fists to stop his reaction. A hand left his shoulder and covered one of his hands, uncurling his fist and rubbing circles on the back of it. Matías's focus had been on the first hand, and he hadn't realised Eli had done the same for his other. Eli smoothed his hands up and down Matías's arms.

Matías could feel himself hardening at the touch, and he wanted to cover his groin so Eli wouldn't see, but his limbs felt heavy. Eli's words still whispered in his ear, reminding him to relax, to let his thoughts flow out, but Matías's thoughts were less than pure.

The next time Eli's hands reached his, the need became too much, and Matías arched into Eli slightly. He felt Eli's movement pause but then resume. Each time his fingers passed over the back of Matías's hands, he pressed his head into Eli's shoulder.

"Let the thoughts go, Matti," Eli whispered. "Relax."

When he arched again, his ass pressed against Eli, and Matías was sure Eli was hard, too. He did it a second time, and sure enough, Eli was as turned on as he was. It gave him the courage to turn his head into Eli's neck, his nose resting beneath Eli's jaw.

Despite loving the feeling of Eli's hands against his own, he slid his hands to Eli's legs, rubbing up and down. He gripped behind the knee, lifted them, widened his own legs, and settled Eli's legs over his own, effectively caging himself with Eli's limbs.

"Matti…"

Matías kept hold of Eli's legs as Matías arched into him again, nuzzling his nose against Eli's skin.

Eli exhaled shakily. "Matti, this is not…"

Matías pecked a kiss on the underside of Eli's jaw and arched again, rubbing his ass against Eli's groin and feeling the hardness. It was unlikely either of them would come this way, but it felt divine if nothing else. They could always do something about it in Matías's bedroom later if Eli agreed.

Eli's hands slid down Matías's chest, his fingers curling into him whenever Matías pressed against him. Eli dropped his head onto Matías's shoulder, leaving his ear right beside Matías's mouth.

"Let go, Eli. Relax. Feel."

He felt it the moment Eli gave into the sensation because Eli's hips moved in time with Matías's, and his hand smoothed down his stomach and rested over the bulge in his jeans. Matías's breath caught when Eli applied some pressure. Not enough to get off, but enough to set his nerve endings alight.

"Matti…kiss me."

He didn't need to ask twice. Their tongues duelled and explored the moment their mouths met in a frenzied kiss. He wanted to hold Eli's head but needed to ground himself with his touch on his legs. Their movements increased, and Matías decided to forgo his hold on Eli's legs so he could drag Eli in front of him and let them both explode in release, but before he let go of Eli's legs, a noise caught his attention.

He pulled his mouth away with difficulty and turned to the noise. His brother stood in the hallway with a grin, dousing some of the heat Matías felt.

"Don't mind me. I'll..." Alejo pointed to the bedrooms and disappeared.

Unfortunately, it was enough to break the moment, and Eli scrambled up from behind Matías.

"I have to go."

"Eli, please."

Eli held out a hand while his other threaded through his hair. "That's not how meditation works. I have to go. Thank you for dinner and the film."

He grabbed his stuff, slid his shoes on and left.

Matías dropped his head back against the sofa and pressed against his dick. "Fuck."

He'd possibly ruined the best thing he'd ever had. And the problem was? It was fake, to begin with.

Chapter 8

Eli

Eli ran his hands through his hair several times while the lift took him to the ground floor. He was sure he looked a mess—or as if he'd been fucked—but he couldn't help it. He needed to get home, where he could breathe and dissect what the hell had happened.

The lift stopped, and he slid through the doors before they were fully open, startling a woman waiting in the foyer.

"Sorry," he mumbled but continued on his way through the entrance doors and down the street to where he'd parked his car. Luckily, it was early evening, and traffic wasn't too bad. He made it home in record time without even having to go over the limit.

By the time he locked his door behind him, his chest was heaving and sweat-soaked into his shirt. He did a quick check of the doors and windows to make sure they remained locked and climbed the stairs to the bathroom. He shed his clothes and stepped under the water as soon as he'd switched the shower on, regretting it when cold water coated him and sighing when the hot water kicked in.

He let the water pound onto the back of his neck while he pressed his hands into the tiles, lowered his head and closed his eyes. The moment he did, he was back with Matías. The diluted scent of smoke coating his skin and hair, the softness of his skin compared to the hardness of his body, the groan he made in the back of his throat as if to withhold it, the taste of tea on his tongue, and the expression of pure lust on his face. It had Eli hard and wanting again.

He could've easily scratched his itch with Matías, but somewhere deep down inside of him, he knew it wouldn't be an itch. If he had a taste of what they would be like together, he doubted he'd have enough, and it scared him plenty. Eli couldn't do anything more than kiss Matías because he knew he would test every limit Eli had placed on himself.

Although he hated to admit it, he could see himself falling in love with the guy, and it couldn't happen.

Ignoring his erection, Eli washed and dried, then wrapped the towel around his waist. He wandered to his bedroom and sat on the edge, staring at the shadow-lined wall. What the hell was he going to do now? Could he still pretend with Matías? He wasn't sure.

He heard his phone ring. It sounded far away, and he followed the sound until he found it in the bathroom, still in his jeans pocket. He wasn't sure he wanted to see who had rung. Instead, he carried it back to his room and plugged it in, then pulled on some pyjama bottoms and slid into bed.

Tucking a hand behind his head, he stared at the ceiling, the only light a red hue from his alarm clock. It was barely ten o'clock, but he'd be no good trying to work, and besides, he had an early morning, anyway. He doubted he'd get much sleep as he lay there with visions of Matías that he kept trying to let float away as his meditation had taught him. The images were stubborn.

He didn't know how long he'd stayed awake trying to banish those images, but he awoke to his alarm clock blaring at him. He'd chosen the most annoying sound he could find because he knew it would get him out of bed.

Groaning, he swung his legs out of bed and rubbed at his face, leaving his alarm to screech some god-awful bird song at him while he worked some energy into his muscles. He stretched as tall as he could and switched off the alarm before stumbling to the bathroom and taking care of the call of nature. He scratched his stomach as he wandered to the kitchen.

Frowning at his herbal tea choices for the first time in a long time, he wasn't sure which would be the best choice for him. He needed something to clear his mind. Maybe a green tea? Or peppermint?

He sighed and hung his head between his arms, which were resting on the counter. If he couldn't decide what type of bloody tea to drink, how the hell was he supposed to run a wedding business—two wedding businesses!

He grabbed the peppermint and ripped it open, throwing it into a cup. He flicked the kettle on and strode for the fridge, where he removed his porridge oats and fruit soaked in yoghurt. He preferred eating his breakfast before drinking his tea; otherwise, his food tasted strange.

Grabbing a spoon, he opened the glass jar and ate it while standing, waiting for his tea to brew.

Once he'd finished, he grabbed his mug and retreated to his bedroom, getting ready for the day while drinking his tea. By the time he entered his office, he felt back on an even keel. He still hadn't checked his phone, though.

He sat behind his desk, switched on his laptop, signed in, and while it loaded up his schedule, he unlocked his phone. The missed call was from Matías, as he'd suspected. There was a message, too.

MATÍAS: *Sorry.*

That was it. Eli sighed, no clearer about where to go from there. Putting the phone aside, he started working. He had plenty of emails to get through because of his evening off the night before.

His phone ringing made him jump, and he cursed at it before checking who it was. Jasmine.

"Hey, how are you doing?" he asked.

"Great, thanks. How are you?"

Well, wasn't that the big question? "I'm good. Checking through the hundred emails in the last twelve hours."

"A hundred!" She audibly gulped.

Eli chuckled. "Okay, not quite a hundred." He wouldn't put her off her dream job by telling her there were one hundred and forty-two emails. She'd soon get to know the nitty-gritty details of wedding planning. "So, what's up?"

"I have the Theobold wedding today, in two hours, in fact, and the mother of the bride is driving me crazy. She's been on the phone four times already this morning."

"Pass her on to Nolan. He's your assistant for a reason."

"I know. I feel bad for siccing her on him."

Eli grinned. "How many times have you had to deal with the mother of the bride when I was working a wedding, Jasmine?"

There was silence before she shouted, "You jackass! I thought you didn't have time to deal with them, not you didn't want to. Asshole."

"Well, think of it as training. You know you can deal with her because you've dealt with the MOBs for years already, and if you don't fancy it, pass her to Nolan. He needs to learn, too." He cleared his throat. "Anything about the wedding today you need to ask about?"

Jasmine chuckled. "I don't think so. The wedding is at eleven o'clock. The photos are being taken in the garden at the reception location before the reception begins at one o'clock. The reception finishes at three o'clock when all the guests go home. They will return to the same location for the evening disco and buffet at six o'clock. That right?"

"Perfect." He paused. "Well done, Jasmine. I don't mean that how it probably sounds." He sighed. "I'm sorry for holding you back. You are more than capable of running your own weddings, and when this is all over with Sarah's business, we're going to have a chat, all right?"

"Seriously?" she whispered.

"I'm serious. I want you on board, Jasmine. You deserve it."

"I don't want to take anything away from you, Eli."

Eli leaned back in his chair. "You won't. It's something I've recently realised."

"Since you've been seeing Matías?"

Eli's heart missed a beat. "Yeah, I suppose. More so because of how you've stepped up to the plate with barely a misstep. You've been ready for longer than I want to admit. I'm sorry about that."

"You have nothing to be sorry for. I doubt I would've felt comfortable taking lead on weddings yet if I hadn't needed to do so for Sarah's business. I enjoy being your assistant."

"Well, you're fired." She gasped, and Eli chuckled. "But only from being an assistant. As I said, when you're finished with Sarah's business, we'll talk terms."

"Thanks."

"You're welcome. Now, go sort out that MOB."

"Yes, sir."

He ended the call, and his shoulders lowered, glad to be free of the burden of holding Jasmine back. They would work well together. He knew it.

His phone rang again, and he winced. "Good morning, Mum."

"Sweetheart, are you free tonight? I'd love to have dinner with you and the others."

He glanced at his schedule, double-checking, although he already knew he could. "Sure. I can make it for six o'clock."

"Perfect. We're having roast beef. Your favourite."

Eli smiled. "I was already going to be there, but it gives me even more incentive."

"I know." Karen chuckled. "See you later."

"Bye."

Normally, he would've kicked up a fuss about it, but he needed some semblance of normality with everything that had been happening. His family wouldn't know about Matías, and Eli could pretend he wasn't in dire straits emotionally. Pretence was the key.

He shook his head. His entire life was pretend at the moment.

"Eli!"

Eli braced himself for when Opal ran and threw her arms around him. "Hey, pickle."

Opal backhanded his shoulder. "How many times have I told you not to call me that?"

"And how many times have I told you I won't stop?"

She narrowed her eyes and wandered off, Eli following. "Mum, Eli's here."

"We heard from the way you screeched," Robbie said from his position at the counter, beer in hand.

"I don't screech," Opal said.

"Lukas, tell her I'm right," Robbie said.

"You...talk loudly, Opal," Lukas said, ever the peacekeeper.

"Mu-um, tell them I don't," Opal whined.

"Opal, sit down and stop your whittling. Robbie, get out of my way; otherwise, you won't get fed. Lukas, grab the plates from the oven, please. Eli, grab yourself a drink and sit down. All of you, shush." She began dividing the food between the warmed plates once Lukas placed them on the counter.

"You wanted us here, Mum. You can't complain when we are," Robbie said, dropping into his chair.

"Robbie..." Eli said, sitting next to him.

"What? I'm right." Robbie leaned back in his chair and folded his arms.

"Give it a rest." Eli stared him down, used to the behaviour of his youngest brother, but for the first time, he wondered what had caused Robbie to become so egotistical. Matías's words circled in his head, but he pushed them aside, not wanting to go further down that road than he needed to when he was in company.

"I—" Robbie stopped when Eli tilted his head and narrowed his eyes. "Never mind."

"I'm glad you're all here," Karen said once everyone had what they needed and was sitting at the table.

She sat at the top of the table and held out her hands. They each joined hands: Karen with Eli, Eli with Robbie, Robbie with Opal, Opal with Lukas, and Lukas with their mother. They were not religious in any way, but from when they were younger, their mother had used their undivided attention to ensure they knew she loved them and they should think about the things they were grateful for.

"My four amazing children. I love you. I'm grateful you're well and thriving in this world. I couldn't ask for more."

She squeezed Eli's hand and let go. Eli spared a moment to remember he would be forever indebted to Xyla for her trust and faith in him. Without her, he wouldn't be where he was. He was grateful to have his family, who had not been broken by their father's departure but, instead, became amazing human beings.

He refocused on the food in front of him. "Thanks for this. I guess I'm hungrier than I thought."

"You're welcome, sweetheart." She smiled. "So, any gossip on the wedding front?"

Eli chuckled. "No. It's all pretty standard. Jasmine has taken over some weddings for a colleague who was in an accident, and I've been helping her and doing mine, so it's been busy. Nothing out of the ordinary has happened, though.

"How am I supposed to live vicariously through you if you can't get the gossip, Eli?" Opal complained.

Opal loved the idea of marriage and weddings. If Eli was a betting man, he'd say she would propose to her boyfriend before the year was out, and they'd get married next year. They'd been together for five years, and it surprised him she hadn't popped the question already. It would be wonderful to organise the wedding for a family member, but he knew she would be a new type of bridezilla.

As for Lukas, he and his girlfriend had been together for a few months, and they seemed well matched. Robbie had one-nighters, and that was about all, as far as Eli knew. He'd always been a troublesome child, and Eli hadn't given it more of a thought than Robbie must be acting out. No thought as to why. He needed to rectify it, though he wasn't sure how. Maybe he needed to talk to Robbie more. The man might open up about his life if Eli tried harder.

They spent the meal discussing random things, and Eli tried dissecting their words, as usual, trying to figure out if any of them needed him for anything without them saying the words. It seemed they didn't, which he was thankful for. He wouldn't have hesitated to step in and help if they needed it, but he was overwhelmed with work that it would've added another stress layer on top. His mother appeared quieter than usual, but he couldn't work out why until after dinner, and she asked them to sit down again.

Fiddling with her bracelet, she stared at the table. "Your father called asking if you'd be willing to see him."

Eli stared at her as if she was speaking a foreign language. She must've been because she couldn't have said what he thought she'd said. Karen caught his eye and winced, making it clear the words were true.

"Why?" Opal asked.

"He says he has some news he needs to speak with you about, but I told him he needed your permission first."

"How long is he here?" Lukas asked.

Karen shrugged. "I don't know."

"We should see him," Robbie said.

He felt their eyes on him, but Eli stared at his mother as a warmth started in his stomach and built until he was shaking with the force of withholding the heat from escaping. He glanced at each of them but couldn't say a word, then he rose and walked out of the room.

"Eli, wait!" his mother called after him.

He couldn't. If he stayed, he'd say things he'd regret. He refused to push his feelings on to his family. They were old enough to make up their own minds, and he needed the space to make up his. Though there was no decision needed. He would rather walk down the aisle than see his father again.

"Eli, please."

Karen had come into the hallway, and Eli turned to her, seeing his siblings behind her.

He bent down and kissed her cheek. "Thank you for dinner. I'll see you soon." He waved at his sister and brothers and left, closing the door firmly behind him. He hadn't reached the bottom of the garden before a voice called out to him.

"Are you going to ruin this for us, too?" Robbie shouted.

Eli spun around. "What?"

"You ruin everything. Mum doesn't dare find a boyfriend because she's worried about your reaction. Opal and Lukas daren't step a foot out of line because they're concerned about your opinion. Well, I don't." Robbie was toe-to-toe with him by the end of his tirade.

Eli cleared his throat, willing his voice to stay strong despite the venom aimed his way. "You can choose to do whatever you wish. I will not be visiting with him, however." He turned away and unlocked his car, his heart pounding with every step.

How could Robbie say those things? What had Eli ruined? His mother wanted a boyfriend? Since when?

Thoughts, memories and questions swirled around his head as he drove home, wishing for the comfort of his bed and the peacefulness of sleep.

Did his father want more money? If so, maybe it would be a good idea for Eli to meet with him. He had some he could give him if he promised to leave Eli's family alone. Paying off his father wasn't the best option because he would undoubtedly be back time and again for more, but if he could keep the man away from his mother and siblings, it would be the better choice. Eli had been fifteen when he'd left, Opal had been ten, Lukas had been eight, and Robbie had been five. They probably didn't remember what it was like.

Despite what he'd said to Robbie, he didn't want them to choose to see their father, but he also couldn't stop them unless he could run the man out of town before he went to them.

Instead of sleeping when he arrived home, he stepped into his office, closing himself inside. He sat behind his desk and pulled a pad of paper towards him. He needed to figure out a plan of action. If he could get to their father before his siblings, he might stop all the heartache he was certain would follow.

Chapter 9

Matías

"Matías!"

Matías weaved in the opposite direction from where he had been going, following Paul's voice. "Yes, Chief?"

"We've received a call from the manager of the Whittaker Hotel. They have guests stuck in a lift and need our assistance. Their maintenance people haven't been able to get them out, and they've been stuck in there for two hours already."

Matías winced. "What took them so long to call?" he asked, poised to press the alarm until the station commander had answered.

"They thought they could get them out." Paul shook his head.

Matías pressed the alarm and ran to the engine. His crew followed, and within seconds, they were on their way. He caught them up with the information Paul had given him. "I didn't ask too many questions because we can find out the rest when we get there."

There was a crowd in the hotel's foyer, and they had to shoulder their way through.

"Thank you for coming." A harried woman came up to Pearce wearing a suit that had once been spotless but now bore several black streaks in various places. "We've tried everything we can to get the doors open."

"Okay, let's have a look at it. Iris, Kai, can you cordon off this area and get the foyer a little emptier, please?"

Pearce stared at them until they nodded in understanding. No one wanted an audience, especially one this big. They followed the manager to the lift while she explained what had happened.

"The lift has stopped between the two floors, but only just. Most of the lift is visible. It's only about five feet off the ground. We don't know why none of the electricity works."

"Has anyone tried to get through the hatch in the ceiling of the lift?" Matías asked.

The manager, named Helen, now focused fully on her to see her name tag, glared across the space at a man in overalls, which Matías assumed was a maintenance guy. "Brayden hadn't fixed the hatch from when it broke several months ago. Apparently, he'd been meaning to and had forgotten."

Matías kept his amusement at her tone from his face. Someone was losing their job.

"What about using the manual override for the doors on top of the lift?"

"What manual override?" Helen asked.

"Never mind. Okay. Let's look."

Matías and Pearce stepped closer. The employees had wedged the foyer lift doors open, but the doors to the lift itself remained closed apart from a small gap at the bottom as if something had got stuck in it.

"I wish they gave all members of staff fire safety instructions," Pearce muttered with a sigh.

Matías moved closer to the lift, looking beneath it and at the front as best he could. "It looks like it's come off its tracks." He pointed. "There's a gap between the doors here that narrows as it goes up. It's as if something pushed the door out of sync with the rest of it."

"Nash, Willow, get up to the next floor and look down from above. Let us know what you see."

"Hello, my name is Matías. Can you hear me?" he called into the lift.

"Yes, we can hear you," a man's voice replied.

"Great. What're the names of the people in there, please?"

"Hayden, Jane and little Claire," the man said with a slight smile to his voice, probably for the child's sake.

"Thank you. We'll get you out of there as soon as we can."

He turned to Pearce. "What's the plan?"

He opened his mouth to speak when Nash radioed in. "Go ahead, Nash."

"There's nothing to show any problems from up here. Do you want me to try the manual override?"

"Yes. Let's try that first. If it doesn't work, we'll get the motorised spreader in here."

"Got it. We'll get the equipment," Nash said.

Several seconds later, Willow came running through the foyer and out the doors, returning with some rope and carabiners. While Nash and Willow got ready with Iris joining them, Matías crossed his arms over his chest. What he wouldn't give to have a few minutes stuck in a lift with Eli at this moment.

He hadn't spoken to him in two days, and it felt wrong. He had messaged and called, but Eli hadn't answered; therefore, he was taking things into his own hands. After he finished work that night, he was visiting Eli, whether or not Eli wanted it. At least if Eli told him where to go, he would know they were over and done—before they'd even begun.

He shook his head and refocused on his job. It wouldn't do to get distracted.

"He's going down," Iris said through the radio.

They waited, and Nash said, "The manual override isn't working. It won't turn at all, which makes me think something is stuck somewhere either in the mechanism or in the door itself."

"Okay, come back up, Nash," Pearce said. "Kai, can you get the spreader?"

Kai jogged out of the hotel, returning several minutes later with the metal jaws. While they set it up, Matías stepped closer to the lift, raising his voice to be heard.

"Hayden, Jane, Claire, we're going to be making a bit of noise out here, but if everything goes well, you should be out of there soon. What I need you to do is stand right at the back of the lift for me, and when the noise starts, cover your eyes so no debris gets in them. Okay?"

"Okay."

Matías received a thumbs up from Kai. "All right. Here's the noise."

He stepped back and let Kai start up the machine. The noise, as he'd mentioned to the occupants of the lift, was loud, but within seconds, the doors began opening under the pressure of the spreader's jaws. When the gap was about twenty inches wide, Pearce called for Kai to stop. There was ringing in Matías's ears when it did. Matías stepped closer to the lift, seeing the occupants for the first time.

He held out his hand. "Come on, let's get you out."

The little girl, Claire, came through first, but she wouldn't let go of Matías when she was clear of the lift, and he and Nash swapped places. Matías held Claire in his arms with her face buried in his neck until they rescued the other people. Jane came over and rested a hand on Claire's back.

"Thank you," Jane said.

"You're welcome. Claire, are you ready to see a paramedic now? They need to check you over and make sure you're feeling okay."

Claire's arms tightened when Jane tried to take her off Matías, and Matías chuckled.

"Pearce?" He waited until he had his watch commander's attention. "I'm going to take Claire to the ambulance." Pearce smiled and nodded. "Come on."

"You don't have to..." Jane said.

"I don't mind."

Despite the girl not saying a word, he knew she understood their words and actions because she tensed and relaxed depending on their discussion. When he arrived at the ambulance, he saw Casey.

"Hey, Casey. How're things?"

"Good, thanks. What do we have here?"

"We have a quiet princess and her...mother?" He glanced at Jane, who nodded. He hadn't thought to ask about their relationship. For all he knew, Claire could've belonged to the man, Hayden.

"Hello, Princess Claire," Casey said. "Would you come and sit on our princess bed so I can have a look and make sure you don't have any bumps or bruises, please?"

Claire's arms tightened. "Claire," Matías said. "It's okay. You're safe now. Casey won't hurt you or your mum. You need to make sure you're well, and once you have, we can arrange for you to visit the fire station." He rubbed her back and prised her away so he could look at her face. "There she is. Hello, Princess Claire. Are you ready to play doctor?" He smiled when she nodded slowly. He turned her towards Casey and pointed. "This is Casey. Do you think you can check him over and make sure *he's* okay?" Claire nodded and loosened her hold. "Good girl. I'll see you soon, okay?"

Jane lifted her from Matías's arms and climbed into the ambulance with her, where Casey began showing Claire all different types of equipment.

Matías smiled and returned to the foyer to see everyone tidying up. "What's the thought?" he asked Pearce.

"The door had been knocked off its track at the bottom, as you said. By this..." Pearce held up a mini colouring pencil. "It must've got caught up and slipped or rotated, causing the door to move as they were going up. The minute the door shifted, the lift automatically shut down. That's what I think, but there's no way of telling for certain."

"I suppose it was better it happened down here and not up there," Matías said, pointing to the unseen top of the hotel, which was fifteen floors high.

"Matías?"

He glanced over his shoulder at the sound of his name, seeing an older man standing behind him. "Yes?"

The man held out his hand. "I'm Hayden. I wanted to thank you for the rescue."

Matías shook his hand. "It was a team effort, but you're welcome. Glad you're doing all right. Make sure you visit the ambulance before you leave, okay?"

"I will. I never expected that when I came to the city for a brief visit, but it's certainly something I'll never forget."

The man chuckled, and Matías copied, wondering why the man seemed familiar. "It'll soon be a dim memory. Cambridge is known for better things than lift rescues."

"I hope so." The man sighed. "Well, thank you again." He wandered off, and Matías frowned. Why did he feel a pull towards the man? He'd never met him before.

"Time to get cleared up."

Pearce clapped him on the shoulder, and they worked as a team to get their equipment stored in the engine before finishing up and setting off for the station. If Matías wasn't mistaken, it was snack time.

After setting the engine to rights for the next call, Matías grabbed a cup of tea and dropped into a chair. He pulled out his phone and saw a message from his mother, asking if he was visiting for dinner that night, and another message from his brother, telling him not to visit that night because Mum wanted to see Eli with him. Matías blew out a breath and ignored both messages. Instead, he opened Eli's contact details and dialled.

He'd finished his tea by the time he closed his phone, deciding not to leave another message when Eli hadn't replied to the other messages he'd left. He rose to refill his drink, shaking his head at his stupidity. He wished he'd kept his libido in check because now it had ruined what they'd possibly had between them.

The rest of the shift was uneventful, which was a blessing and a curse. Matías pointed his car towards Eli's house and ignored the unease in his stomach. If Eli didn't want to see him, he could tell him to his face, and Matías would know where he stood. And if that *was* the case, Matías would deal with it as he always did.

He parked outside Eli's house and jogged up the path, knocking on his door. He didn't have to wait too long before Eli pulled it open.

"What are you doing here?"

And maybe that was his answer. Matías cleared his throat. "I thought we could talk."

"There's nothing to talk about at the moment. I'm afraid I have someone..." Eli pointed to his office.

"Oh, okay. Sorry. Um, before I go, could we arrange—"

"Matías?"

Matías frowned and peered over Eli's shoulder. "Hayden?"

Eli glanced between them. "How do you know each other?" There was a bite in his tone Matías didn't understand.

"I rescued Hayden from a lift today. How are you feeling?"

"I'm good, thanks," Hayden said with a smile. "Small world. I didn't know you knew my son."

"Son?"

Matías stared at Eli, who stared at something over Matías's shoulder.

"Yes. I'm here to speak to him after so long apart."

"Not enough time," Eli said, not even keeping his voice quiet. "I wish you'd take my offer."

Hayden closed his eyes. "I don't want your money, Eli. I want to apologise."

Eli spun around. "Apologise for what? Leaving for twenty-five years? Taking our entire bank account so we had nothing? Not even sending a birthday card or a message the whole time? What are you apologising for?"

Matías slipped inside and closed the door behind him, not wanting Eli's neighbours to hear the argument.

"Everything. I need to explain."

Matías couldn't believe Hayden was Eli's father, though now they were standing in such close proximity, he could see a slight resemblance. He would've loved to stay and talk some more with them both, but he could see Eli was barely keeping it together.

"You can't explain it away. Take the money and leave. Don't ruin their lives again," Eli said, his voice catching on his words.

"I won't. I promise."

"Promise?" Eli snorted and shook his head, averting his gaze and landing on Matías. Eli bit his lip.

"Sorry, I'll go. Please call me, Eli."

"No! Wait." Eli stepped closer and lowered his voice. "Please stay. I can't...I need..."

Matías rested a hand on the back of Eli's neck and put his mouth close to his ear. "Whatever you need, it's yours. I'm not going anywhere. What do you want to do?"

Eli dropped his forehead to Matías's shoulder and wrapped his arms around Matías's waist, surprising him. Eli had said he wouldn't show his family how close they were pretending to be, but here he was, doing just that. Matías's eyes flicked to Hayden, who stared at them with a smile on his face and tears in his eyes. He refocused on Eli, holding him tightly.

"I want him to understand. I don't need him. We don't need him. I need you to help me be strong for my family."

"Whatever you need," he repeated, not quite understanding how Eli wanted to play this.

Eli stayed there for a few seconds longer, and Matías felt him take a deep breath and lift his head. He looked into his eyes and saw a banked fire burning to be free. Matías promised himself once they had sorted this situation with Hayden, he would have a tough conversation with Eli and spill a few home truths.

Eli pulled back, threading their fingers together, and turned to Hayden. "Let's finish our conversation." He walked into the office, dragging Matías with him and settling onto the sofa with Matías at his side.

Matías slid an arm around his shoulders, and Eli scooted as close as he could get and rested a hand on Matías's thigh. Hayden sat on the sofa opposite.

"If I had realised you were so important to Eli, I would've stayed to speak to you more," Hayden said to Matías.

"Or to prise information out of him," Eli muttered.

Matías covered Eli's hand with his free one and squeezed, trying to lend his support. "As you said, it's a small world."

"If you don't want money, what do you want?" Eli said.

"To apologise. I was wrong in so many ways." Hayden clasped his hands together but didn't drop his focus from Eli.

"And it's taken you twenty-five years to realise it?"

Hayden shook his head. "I knew from the moment I did it, but I couldn't turn back. It was too late."

"You left us destitute! I had to get a job to help pay the bills. We didn't have the money for food or clothes or school stuff. You took everything!"

Hayden hung his head, but Matías felt no sympathy for him. He'd had no idea what Eli and his family had been through, but if the man in front of them was responsible for what Eli was saying, then Matías agreed with Eli.

"I will NOT allow you to do this to them again. You leave, with or without the money. You will visit none of them because you will only screw with their heads and set them back on their healing. Twenty-five years is not enough time to forgive."

"I'm dying, Eli."

Matías's heart missed a beat, but Eli didn't appear at all affected. If anything, he tensed more.

"So that's why you came. You want to cleanse your soul to get it ready for departure. Well, sorry, but no. Because all it will do is bring you into their lives for you to leave again."

Eli gripped his hair and leaned forward. "Why would you even think this was a good idea? To arrive and say, 'Hey, I know I left and took all your money, and you don't know me anymore, but I'm here, but only for a little while until I die and leave you all alone again.' How could you do that to us—them?"

"I'm trying to make amends—"

"Yes, I get it, but the only one who benefits from your 'amends' is you." Eli stood. "Please leave."

"Eli—"

"Leave."

Hayden stared at Eli, then Matías, who nodded and tilted his head towards the door. "Okay."

The man paused at the threshold but said nothing, then carried on. They stayed perfectly still until the front door clicked closed, and Matías grabbed Eli as he dropped to the floor. If Matías hadn't caught him around his waist, Eli would've crashed into the coffee table.

"Fuck. Eli?"

Matías turned Eli's face towards him and pain speared through him at the sight of this strong man in tears, shaking as if someone had dealt him a physical blow he couldn't withstand. Matías wrapped his arms around Eli and held him tightly, letting him sob into his chest while he rocked him and said mindless things. His throat closed up at the keening cries coming from Eli.

What a fucking day.

Chapter 10

Eli

Eli inhaled after several long minutes, trying to stop himself from breaking down again. It was so unlike him, and he wished it hadn't happened when Matías had been there. The last thing he wanted to do was show him how unstable he was. Although maybe it was for the best. They could call it quits now, and Matías could find someone better for him.

Not that they were together.

He lifted his head and wiped away the evidence on his face. His eyes were undoubtedly red and his face blotchy, but there was nothing he could do about it now.

"Thanks. And sorry."

Matías's forehead creased. "Sorry for what?"

"My little pity party." Eli climbed out of Matías's lap—how he had landed there and not realised he didn't know. He sniffed and grabbed a tissue from the box on his desk, blowing his nose. "I'm sorry you had to see that. My father and I...have a lot between us." That was an understatement of the year. He glanced over at him. "How did you meet him again?"

Matías pulled himself onto the sofa, which had been at his back while he sat on the floor with Eli. "We got called out to the Whittaker Hotel. Some guests were stuck in the lift, and the manual overrides weren't working. We had to jimmy the doors open so they could get out."

"Was anyone hurt?"

Matías shook his head and smiled. "I had a long hug with a cute girl called Claire, then we finished up."

Eli frowned but snorted, crossing his arms over his chest. "Was she that upset she needed a hug from a firefighter?"

Matías rubbed the back of his neck, his cheeks darkening. "She was about six or seven years old. She was scared."

Eli felt like shit. He dragged his fingers over his face. He'd assumed the girl was older. A lot older. "Sorry. I'm a little out of sorts. That was unnecessarily harsh of me." He shook his head. "Thank you for coming over, but I need..." He rested back against his desk and stared at the ceiling. "It's too much at the minute, Matías. I need space."

Matías stood. "Okay. I get it. Your father being here has thrown you. Can I say one thing before I go?" Eli nodded, his stomach somersaulting with what Matías could want to say. "If you need anything at all, even someone to yell and scream at, call me. Please."

"You don't need me—"

Matías stepped forward, resting his hands on Eli's upper arms and stroking up and down while he stared into Eli's eyes. "Please."

Eli swallowed hard and nodded, unable to say a word. Matías smiled, though it didn't reach his eyes, then pressed a kiss to Eli's cheek and left the room. Eli heard the door close for the second time that evening, but he couldn't move. It was too much. Everything was too much. He felt his walls crumbling again, but he breathed in through his nose and out through his mouth until he'd regained his balance, then stalked behind the desk and dropped into his chair, which gave a resounding protest to being used in such a way.

He stared at the piece of paper he'd offered his father earlier that evening, the five zeros at the end of the number mocking him. What did his father want if it wasn't money? He mentioned dying, but Eli didn't believe him. It was a good excuse to use to get close to them because no one wanted to turn away someone who wouldn't live for much longer. Eli didn't believe a word of it, though. Yes, the man seemed on the thin side, and he looked old for his age, but he was also a manipulative bastard, and Eli wouldn't stand for it. He would protect his family at all costs.

The following day, Eli had two weddings and a reception booked in. For the first time in a long time, he wished he hadn't. He'd decided to meet with his father again and *persuade* the man to leave. He couldn't let him get his claws into the family because there was no telling what he'd do. It would have to wait until later, though.

He and Jasmine had been through her day, which consisted of a full-day event. Jasmine had been worried, but Eli knew she was more than capable of doing it. He'd given her a pep talk and pushed her out of the door. The only way she'd get more confidence was by doing it—he knew it from experience.

After he gathered everything together he needed for the day, he checked his phone as he wandered to the car.

LUKAS: *Mum's acting weird.*

Eli frowned. That said everything and nothing all at the same time. Their mother was predictable in her behaviour, and Eli could only assume it had something to do with their father because it was the only change to their lives lately. That he knew about, anyway.

ELI: *In what way?*
LUKAS: *She's cleaning.*
ELI: *She always cleans.*
LUKAS: *Not like this. She's scrubbed the kitchen within an inch of its life, every surface, every item. Even those we don't use. She's also cleaned the downstairs bathroom—three times!*

Eli paused once he'd switched the engine on. She was behaving as if she was expecting company. Hayden. He didn't reply to Lukas; he'd do it later. Instead, he called his mum, putting it through his car speakers so he could drive and talk.

"Eli! This is a pleasant surprise. I wasn't expecting to hear from you today."

"Hi, Mum. I wanted to check in with you, that's all."

Karen tutted. "Lukas has told you about my cleaning spree, I presume. I'm fine, honey. I hadn't done it for a while, that's all. Might as well get it done while I have the energy." She chuckled, though it sounded forced.

"You only clean like that when you're expecting company, Mum. And you mentioned our father the other day. Does it have anything to do with him?" Eli gripped the steering wheel while he waited for her answer.

"Eli Jackson! What I do with my time has nothing to do with you, young man. But to answer your question, no, it has nothing to do with your father. I have heard nothing from him since I told you about it."

Eli's shoulders lowered, and he exhaled. "I'm sorry. I'm worried he's going to try to weasel his way back into your life. I don't want you getting hurt again."

Karen sighed. "I know you don't, but you're not the parent in this family, Eli. You've done so much for us over the years, and I can't thank you enough, but you need to stop trying to protect us. We all have our own lives now. You have your career, too. You don't need to worry about us."

Eli tensed again. "I will always worry about you. You're my mother."

"As I will worry about you, but you don't need to. I'm more than capable of taking care of myself. I want you to concentrate on your life, Eli. Find someone to share it with. You deserve nothing less than the best."

His mind conjured up Matías, but he shook his head as he answered. "I don't need anyone, Mum. I'm perfectly fine on my own."

Karen sighed again. "I know. You can't stop an old lady from wishing, though."

Eli smiled. "You're not old."

Karen chuckled. "Thank you. Now, go. I'm assuming you're at work."

"Just arriving at the church as it happens." Eli parked in the car park and switched off the engine, slumping back into the seat.

"Have a good day, sweetie."

"You, too. Make sure you don't work too hard."

"I'll do my best. Love you."

"Love you."

Eli cancelled the call and stared at the brick wall in front of his car. Despite what his mother had said, he didn't believe her. She was expecting a visitor, but there was nothing he could do about it. He hadn't taken his father's phone number before he'd left last night, so he couldn't call and tell him to leave the family alone. He had to hope the words he'd spoken the previous evening had been enough to make his father think twice.

He rubbed his hands over his face and climbed from the car. The air was heavy with fog and a light misty rain that was supposed to clear up before the wedding started. Eli wasn't concerned. He had everything he needed in case the rain stayed or got worse, including a pop-up gazebo should they need it.

As he worked through the list of things that needed doing, his mind was not on his job. Images of his father, his mother, his siblings, and Matías flitted in and out of his head all day long. His plan to confront Hayden had to happen that night instead of the following day. It might already be too late if Eli was correct about his mother's need to clean the house, but he had to try. He'd helped keep their family afloat over the years, and dealing with his father would be no different. He didn't know what he could say to get the man to understand. All Hayden could see was his selfish need to lighten his soul before he left his body. He couldn't see the repercussions of his actions, and he wouldn't be around to deal with them, either. It would be Eli who had to pick up the pieces. If it was even true.

He refocused on his job, staying well away from the bouquet throwing since his last mishap. He wouldn't go through that again. Once the reception ended and the guests had gone home, Eli helped his employees with the clean-up before climbing back into his car and wishing he was already home, but he had one last chore to do first.

He pointed the car towards the Whittaker Hotel, his best guess for where Hayden was staying, thanks to Matías's information. As he walked towards the receptionist, he pushed his hands into his pockets and clenched his fists.

"Good evening, Mr Jackson. How can I help?" the receptionist asked.

Eli smiled at the man, having seen him around when he'd done weddings at the venue. "Hi, could you tell me what room Hayden Jackson is in, please?"

The receptionist's smile faltered, and Eli wondered if he'd put the two names together. "I'm sorry. I can't give out room numbers, but I could call up to him and ask for his permission if it would help?"

"It's fine, thank you."

The receptionist moved to the side and picked up the phone. He watched as he spoke quietly into it, then nodded and replaced the receiver.

"Mr Jackson would love for you to join him. His room number is 409. If you—"

"Thank you," Eli said, stopping the man's words. "I know the route."

"Of course."

Eli turned and wandered to the lift. By the time he stood in front of room 409, his jaw ached from how hard he had clenched it. Inhaling, he knocked twice and waited. The door flew open, and Hayden smiled.

"I wasn't expecting to see you, Eli. Come on in."

Eli stepped inside, studying the familiar surroundings with unfamiliar belongings. Clothes were strewn across the chairs, and items decorated the tops of the tables. The TV was on and playing a black and white Laurel and Hardy episode.

"It's one of my favourites," Hayden said from behind him.

Eli tensed and pivoted. "Did you visit Mum today?"

Hayden sighed and wandered to the bed, sitting on the edge. "No. I was going to, but I called and cancelled."

Eli didn't know whether to be relieved or annoyed. "So, you let her down again."

Hayden's eyes flashed. "Not because I wanted to. I thought you might turn up at some point to try to persuade me otherwise." Eli opened his mouth to answer, but Hayden spoke again, "I know you think I want money, Eli, but I guarantee you I don't. I have enough of my own. What I want is to make sure you're all doing okay with my own eyes." He exhaled. "You don't have to believe me, but I am dying. I have testicular cancer, and there's nothing they can do about it now."

Eli worked his jaw and strode to the window, crossing his arms over his chest. He didn't want to believe the man, but it was hard not to. It didn't stop the need to protect his family from Hayden jumping into their lives and leaving them again. Yes, it wouldn't be his fault he left, but he would still leave.

"Does Mum know?"

"No. I was going to tell her today."

Eli whirled around. "Don't!"

Hayden reared back. "What?"

"If you tell her, she'll feel obligated to you. Let them choose on their own terms. Not yours."

"You're giving me permission to speak with them?"

Eli turned back to the window, watching the car lights speeding down the road. Was he? He'd come here to send Hayden packing. What had changed? He glanced at the table. Was it the picture of the six of them he had on there? Was it the need he saw in Hayden's eyes? He didn't know why, and it was enough to change his mind back again.

"No. You don't need to see them to know how they're doing. If you want to hang around and check in from a distance, I can't stop you, but you do not need to sit down and discuss anything with them."

"Shouldn't it be their choice?"

Eli ignored the somersault of his stomach that told him Hayden was right and faced him. "I'm protecting them from being hurt. You can't waltz in and out of their lives like they mean nothing to you." He threw his hands into the air. "Can't you see? You left us with nothing, and we became stronger for it, but not before it almost killed us. Why can't you see the pain and suffering you've caused?"

Hayden hung his head. "I know, and I'm sorry."

"If you're that sorry, don't mess them up now. They have good lives. They don't need you interfering."

Eli strode for the door.

"I'm sorry, Eli."

He didn't stop to find out what he was sorry for. When he reached his car, his hands shook, and his legs felt like jelly. He almost fell into his car. He switched the engine on and sat there, breath heaving. Had he done the right thing? Maybe they needed the closure their father could give them? Or maybe he'd spew more lies to make them forgive him. Although Eli didn't know the right option, he had to believe he'd done the right thing. They would be better off without him.

He drove home, diverting to grab some takeaway first. He felt the need for Thai food that night. Parking in his driveway, he left everything that wasn't essential and carried the rest into the house. He grabbed the takeaway, not even bothering with plates, and sat in front of the TV, flicking it onto a film channel. While the characters on screen fell in love, Eli ate and drank, thinking about Matías. He should apologise for his behaviour. Matías didn't need that crap from him.

He picked up his phone.

ELI: *I'm sorry for last night. You don't need it from me when I'm supposed to be helping you. Do you have another "appearance" in mind?*

He threw the phone onto the cushion beside him and finished his Thai food. Matías would message back when he wasn't busy. Eli switched everything off after he'd cleaned up and climbed the stairs. He undressed and stood under the hot shower spray for far longer than necessary, wishing the heat would seep into his bones. When all he received was shrivelled skin, he gave up and dried off.

He climbed into bed and plugged his phone in on the bedside table. It lit up to show a message.

MATÍAS: *You don't need to be sorry. I don't mind helping with whatever you need. I think we can manage without an appearance while you get your dad situation sorted.*

Eli rushed to reply.

ELI: *No! It's fine. If anything, it would be nice to forget about him. I don't have my diary with me because I've just got into bed, but send me some dates, and I'll see what I can do*
.

MATÍAS: *Honestly, it's fine, Eli. Get some rest. I'll call you tomorrow to see how you're doing.*

Eli clenched his jaw and put his phone down; otherwise, he would've thrown it across the room. He'd told Matías he was fine, but Matías wasn't listening. Maybe Eli needed to arrange something. He had Matías's shift pattern, after all.

Feeling better about the idea, he switched the light off and rolled over, but sleep wouldn't come. The image of his father sitting on his bed, looking frail and defeated, stayed front and centre all night, and when Eli finally gave up at four in the morning, he was grumpy as hell. God forbid anyone pisses him off that day.

Chapter 11

Matías

Matías hadn't received a message back from Eli, so he'd assumed Eli had fallen asleep. He would've loved nothing more than to take Eli out again, but he was under so much stress from running two businesses and helping Matías out that having his father thrown into the mix was too much for him, Matías was sure. He would put their "relationship" to the side for now and make sure Eli was okay with everything else before they started up again. His family would understand once Matías explained.

"Hey, you up for going out tonight?"

Matías faced Nash as the man exited the shower, rubbing his hair with a towel. Matías wasn't a prude in any way, shape or form, but Nash took nudity to a whole other level. He would be at home on a nudist beach the way he walked around with no clothes whenever he had the chance.

Matías rolled his eyes. "I would've thought you had other plans already. Did...Mandy? Mary?...not work out?"

Nash snorted. "If you call planning our wedding on the second date as working out..." He shrugged. "I'm not ready for that yet."

"So, you didn't give her the chance to change your mind?"

Nash shook his head. "Nope. Hence why I'm asking you."

Matías stepped back, rubbing his chest and feigned shock. "Ouch! Second best after being friends all this time."

Nash threw the towel at him. "Fuck off, asshole. You know you're always first in line...after my dates." He winked and opened his locker, thankfully dressing.

"Why don't you try a guy for a change? You haven't slept with a guy for months since..."

Nash held his hands up. "Don't say his name. And anyway, it's the reason I thought we could visit Crush. There's a lot more of the LGBTQ+ community there now that it's known for being so inclusive."

"I'm not surprised, though. With the number of gay couples who are friends with the owner, it would've been a surprise if it hadn't become the place to be. It's everyone's favourite place."

Matías loved the pub, too. The welcoming atmosphere and the friendly staff made it a place where he would always choose to go.

"Are you coming out?"

"Yeah. What time?"

"I'll be there around six because I want food."

Matías chuckled. "I'll get there at the same time. Don't order without me."

"No guarantees." Nash shoved his shoulder as he headed for the door with his bag and coat. "See you later."

When he sat beside Nash after a long snooze ten hours later, he cursed his best friend.

"You said you'd wait." He grabbed a menu and opened it.

"I said there were no guarantees," Nash mumbled with a mouth full of chips. "I was hungry."

"Far be it from you to hold on to your hunger for a few more minutes." Matías huffed. "Do you do this with your dates?"

"Of course not. I have to make a good impression. After the fifth or sixth date, though, no promises." Nash grinned.

"What can I get you, Matías?" Analise stood beside their table with a smile. She had been a bartender and server here for as long as he could remember. She was engaged to a detective, Kade, who Matías had met a few times on the job.

"A San Miguel, and can I have the cheeseburger and chips, please?"

"Of course. Nash, anything else?"

Nash lifted his beer. "Another, please. He's buying." He thumbed at Matías.

Matías rolled his eyes and nodded at Analise, who grinned and headed off. "You should buy me a drink since you started eating before me."

"I'll get the next one. So, how're things in the Matías world?"

Matías fidgeted in his seat. He hadn't told him what had been happening with Eli. He felt bad lying to Nash, the same as his family. He supposed he needed to keep up appearances. "I've been seeing someone, on and off." The words tasted like coal on his tongue. They were a lie, though Matías hoped they one day wouldn't be.

Nash coughed, banging his fist against his chest. He grabbed his beer bottle and guzzled it down. He coughed a few more times and glared at him. "What the hell, Matías? How long has this been going on, and why am I only now finding out?"

"A few weeks."

"Weeks! Why didn't you tell me?" Nash leaned forward, elbows on the table.

Matías shrugged. "It's been a bit up in the air."

"What do you mean?"

Matías smiled at Analise when she returned with the drinks. He sighed. "Eli is working a lot, so we haven't had much time to get to know one another properly. We're going slowly."

"Eli?"

Matías felt his cheeks heat, but he couldn't stop the smile from spreading across his face. "He's the wedding planner Isabella used. We started seeing each other after meeting there." It was the truth and not the truth at the same time.

"How often have you seen him?"

Matías shrugged again. "Not often, but we call and text when we can. He's busy, and my shifts haven't merged well with his time off yet. Not that he has much of it."

Nash's eyebrow raised. "He doesn't get time off? Isn't that slave labour?"

"Not when Eli's the owner." Matías chuckled at Nash's expression.

"He owns the business. How old is he?"

"What does it matter?" Matías frowned.

Nash sat back. "Woah! It doesn't. I was curious."

Matías rolled his shoulders to relax them. "He's forty. He's more busy than usual now because he's running another wedding planner's business, too, at the minute."

"How come?"

"The other wedding planner is in the hospital."

"No wonder you haven't seen him. How has your family taken the news?"

Matías took a sip. "You know exactly how they've taken it. They're probably already planning our wedding."

Nash laughed, drawing attention from people on the table next to them. No one had ever been able to ignore Nash's addictive laugh.

"Good luck with that. Good job Eli likes weddings."

"Yeah, not so much the being married part, though." Matías chuckled and drank some more. It was only when he glanced at Nash he realised his words weren't part of the story they were supposed to be telling people.

"He doesn't want to get married?"

Matías cleared his throat. "Well, um, he's on the fence."

"But you want to get married and have kids, Matías. Why are you with him when you have said no to enough other people who had been interested in you because their plans didn't mesh with yours?"

"Fuck," he whispered, relieved when Analise brought his food.

"Anything else, gentlemen?"

Nash smiled at her. "We need a couple more beers for this discussion, please."

"No problem."

Nash pushed his plate away from him, crossed his arms and rested them on the table, focusing solely on Matías. "Eat and talk."

To delay the start of the conversation and try to figure out how he would play this, he bit into his burger and chewed slowly. What could he say? What Nash had said was entirely true. Matías had turned down other people because they had told him they weren't interested in marriage or kids or both. If he'd met Eli in a bar, they wouldn't have even got together because Matías would've shot him down. He could tell part of the truth.

"I've been hoping to change his mind."

Nash raised his eyebrows. "Why?"

"Because I like him."

Nash tilted his head and narrowed his eyes. "You're not telling me everything."

Matías stared at his plate and methodically ate his food. Nash kept quiet, which was an unusual occurrence, so he knew Nash would give him hell when he finished eating. Would he keep it quiet? He glanced up at his best friend and winced at the expectant expression. Matías sighed and pushed his unfinished plate aside.

"Fine. What I say from here on out is not for anyone else's ears but yours, okay?"

Nash frowned. "Sure."

He leaned forward, lowering his voice. "We're not actually together. We're pretending so my family will give me a break from the never-ending butting in they do."

The crease between Nash's eyes deepened. "Why?"

"I told you why. My family never let up on finding me someone suitable. This gives me some breathing room."

"No, I mean, why is *he* agreeing to it?"

"He said it didn't make any difference to him. He is never getting married, so to pretend for a couple of months wouldn't matter."

"That's very magnanimous of him. What is your family going to say when they find out?"

"They won't. As far as they're concerned, we will break up after my birthday party."

"That long?"

Matías glared at him. "He's a nice guy, Nash." He drank, avoiding Nash's probing gaze.

"You were telling the truth about trying to get him to change his mind." Matías grimaced and stared at the bottle. "Matías, what are you doing?" Nash whispered.

Matías lifted his eyes to Nash's face. "I'm going to try to get him to fall in love with me without realising it."

Nash sat back, rubbing a hand over his mouth before dropping his hands to his lap. "You're crazy."

"Takes one to know one." Matías grinned, though he wasn't feeling it. His phone vibrated in his pocket, and he pulled it out.

Nash shook his head. "You're in way over your head. You know that, don't you?"

"Yep." He lifted his beer in a self-recriminating toast.

Nash knocked their bottles together. "Let me know if you need any help."

"Thanks." He checked his phone.

ELI: *We're going on a date. Monday, 7 p.m. I'll pick you up. Dress casual.*

Matías frowned. He thought they'd agreed to wait until after Eli sorted the situation with his father.

"What's up?"

Matías glanced at Nash. "I'd been putting off making another 'date,'" he used air quotes, "with Eli because he's been having family problems. I was trying to give him some space, but he messaged, saying we're going out on Monday."

"Why's that a problem? Maybe his family issue is sorted."

Matías shook his head. "I doubt it. It didn't seem like something with an easy fix." His phone buzzed again, and he looked down.

ELI: *I'm fine, Matti. Our agreement still stands.*

"Matti?"

Matías glared at Nash's humorous tone. "He heard Rafe call me it, and he took it on."

"Nice. Maybe he's not as immune to you as you think."

The butterflies swarming in his stomach held him on the edge of hope, but he didn't want to step over the line completely. He didn't think he could cope if he fell and was left at the bottom of the ravine by himself.

MATÍAS: *It's a date.*

After they'd finished their drinks, Matías offered for Nash to go back to Matías's place for more, and they stopped by the shop to get some drinks and snacks. When they got back, Alejo was watching a film spread out on the sofa.

"Hey! I wasn't expecting you so early."

"Yeah, it's a Saturday night. Crush was busy."

Alejo sat upright. "And it's a problem, why?"

"Exactly my words," Nash said. "I think he's getting old."

Matías walked into the kitchen. "Those crisps are looking nice."

"Don't you dare! You bought them for me!" Nash shouted, storming into the kitchen and grabbing the shopping bag from Matías's hands.

Matías chuckled. "They're all yours. You know I can't stand them."

"Nothing beats spicy NikNaks," Nash murmured when he found them and wandered into the living room. "What are you watching?" Matías heard him ask Alejo.

"*Daybreakers.*"

"Epic."

"I've already watched *Blade* and *Underworld.*"

Matías groaned. "You're on a vampire binge again?" he asked, entering the room with three beers and bags of popcorn and crisps, the latter he threw on the table. He handed them their drinks and dropped into the armchair.

"When aren't I?" Alejo opened his can and took a sip.

"Nothing wrong with them unless you include some of the newer films, which will never be on my radar," Nash said.

Matías laughed. "I know for a fact you've watched them, no matter how many times you deny it."

Nash narrowed his eyes, and Matías mimed buttoning his mouth shut. He didn't dare push him too far in case he opened his mouth about Matías's predicament with Eli. As they settled in to watch the film, Matías's mind wandered. Everything he'd told Nash had been true, but he couldn't see it happening. Yes, he was falling for Eli, but he knew the guy couldn't—or wouldn't—return the affection. Too many things were holding him back, but now he'd seen one reason for it, he could only understand. Having your father leave you in that situation was heavy for anyone to deal with, but to have to become one breadwinner of the house was overwhelming for Matías to think about, and probably more so when Eli actually lived it.

Eli had built up his business to what it was now, and Matías couldn't be prouder of him. Maybe he needed to let Eli know that.

His mind went to the "date" Eli had organised. Where were they going? Casual dress could mean anything. And why had Eli arranged anything?

He pulled out his phone and opened the conversation thread.

MATÍAS: *How are you?*

He didn't expect an answer straight away, though he wished for one. He kept the phone in his hand and refocused on the TV.

The buzzing of his phone woke him with a jolt, and he blinked open his eyes. The lights were off, except for the blue haze coming from the TV unit, and someone had covered him with a blanket. He noticed someone lying on the sofa. Probably Nash, going by the snoring. His phone buzzed again, and he rummaged around to find where it was. When he found it, he switched it on and squinted at the brightness—he usually dimmed the screen before he went to sleep, so it didn't blind him when he woke.

ELI: *I'm okay.*
ELI: *That's a lie, but I will be.*
ELI: *Why do I keep telling you the truth?*

Matías's heart jumped. Had Eli meant to be so truthful with him? Regardless, Matías felt a warmth growing inside that had nothing to do with being under a too-hot blanket. Were Eli's feelings growing? Was it fair of Matías to hope they were?

MATÍAS: *Yes, you will be. I'm here if you need me for anything at all. Please call me if you need me. I mean that.*

Matías stared at the screen, hoping Eli would reply, but he didn't. As it was three in the morning, he hoped Eli was asleep. He'd be exhausted the following day if he wasn't.

Carefully, he rose from his chair and shuffled towards his bedroom. He couldn't sleep in the armchair all night because he'd end up with a crick in his neck. He put his phone on the bedside table and undressed and washed in the bathroom before returning to his bedroom. All the while, his thoughts were on Eli. He hoped he'd have a message from him the next morning. As he closed his eyes and felt himself slipping away, he thought he heard a beep, but he was being dragged under the cloak of sleep.

Chapter 12

Nash

Matías was a brave man. Nash wasn't a coward by any means, but even he would waver if he was faced with Matías's family and the possibility of them finding out he was lying to them. He could see it was a lost cause with Matías because he was in love with Eli. It was visible whenever he spoke about him. If Nash could see it, others would, too.

After waking up with a sore back from sleeping on the sofa at Matías's apartment, he'd left a note and exited, making sure the door was closed properly behind him. He bundled himself into his coat and stepped out into the brisk, chilly morning air, heading for the place he called home. He wasn't due at work until the following day, and he had plans.

As he walked, he thought about Matías's predicament. There was no way Nash would ever get himself into the same situation, but as for wanting a relationship, he was the same as Matías. What he wanted, he'd yet been able to find, and he was tired of the one-night stands and short-term flings. Cambridge was a big city. Surely, there were enough people to go around.

"What are you doing out so early?"

The voice made him jump, and he spun around, breath heaving. "Jesus! You scared the shit out of me, Maddox."

Maddox grinned and continued walking next to Nash. "I'd say I'm sorry, but..." He winked.

Nash chuckled. "I didn't realise you were a jogger."

"Yeah. It's the only way to get myself going in the morning. Are you heading home or leaving home?"

Nash shoved his hands in his pockets. "Heading home."

"Ooh, big night?"

Nash slapped his shoulder. "Only if you include drinking with Matías and his brother while watching films. I can't even remember falling asleep."

"I remember nights like that."

"I've never really asked...do you have a partner?" Nash always used the word partner, even if he knew someone was heterosexual.

Maddox shook his head. "I was with someone, but we ended it a few months back."

"I'm sorry to hear that."

Maddox shrugged. "It happens. We were married for six years. It's obviously run its course."

Nash gaped. "You were married!"

Chuckling, Maddox ruffled Nash's hair. "Yes. I don't tend to talk about my relationships at work. Even though the station is inclusive, it's difficult to get out of the habit of hiding things." He snorted. "I'm sorry. I'm feeling more melancholy this morning than I realised."

Nash held his hands up. "Hey, no problems from me. I'm happy to chat. We can commiserate together."

"Commiserate?"

"I'm sick of being single. Now that Matías has Eli, I'm feeling the sting of envy, and it doesn't look pretty on me."

Maddox raised his eyebrows. "I'm surprised you're having trouble finding someone."

Nash chose to take it as a compliment rather than a come on. Nothing like a workplace romance gone wrong to make things uncomfortable. "Thanks."

"I hadn't heard about Matías's new boyfriend. How long have they been together?"

Nash grimaced. "Hmm, maybe I shouldn't have said anything. It's still new, and they're still finding their feet."

"I won't say a word. I know what it's like when you have everyone butting in on your business."

Nash laughed. "You and Matías have a lot in common. His family is the definition of butting in."

Maddox checked his watch. "I better get going. I have a meeting soon, and I'm still a couple of miles from home."

"Jeez, Maddox. How far do you run?"

"Five to ten miles, depending on what's chasing me." He grinned and took off. "See you!"

Nash watched Maddox navigate through the other early morning people and refocused on his own issue. How was he ever going to find someone to stay with when they all thought he was there for a night? Even when he tried explaining to one date that he wanted more, all the guy did was laugh and blow it off as something unimportant.

Maybe he should stop dating altogether?

Or take a leaf out of Matías's book.

He wished Matías all the luck in the world because changing someone's mind wouldn't be easy.

Chapter 13

Eli

Eli stared at Matías's message for a long time before he could bring himself to reply. It wasn't because he wasn't grateful to him for his offer, but because Eli wanted to call him. He wanted Matías to hold him as he had done the other day. He wanted Matías to tell him what the right course of action was. He'd never been so indecisive about a situation as he was with his father. Everything he had known before seemed wrong now, but he had no one he could talk to about it.

Matías, however helpful he wanted to be, was someone he couldn't open up to. He was a genuinely nice guy, and for some reason, Eli found himself being completely honest with the man. Even when he tried not to be.

ELI: *Thank you. That means a lot.*

Once he'd sent the message, he put his phone down and stared at the dark ceiling before rolling over and punching at the pillow to get comfortable. He had no idea if Matías would like what Eli had planned for their "date" on Monday, but he thought it would give them a new "audience" to play for. And he hadn't been for a long time, so it was a good excuse.

"Bowling?" Matías said, staring at the building.

Eli smiled. "Do you not like bowling?"

"No, I do. I haven't done it for years. Nothing like a challenge, though." He cracked his knuckles, and Eli winced.

"Does it not hurt?"

"What?"

Matías looked down at himself as if to see what he'd done that could hurt him.

"Your hands. You crack your knuckles. Doesn't it hurt?"

Matías's expression softened, and he quirked one side of his mouth. "No, it doesn't, but I'm trying not to do it because I know people don't like it."

"It does sound...loud. Although my knees make a similar noise when I stand, so I can't complain." Eli chuckled and grabbed his bag from the car before locking it. "Are you ready to get your ass kicked?"

Matías's mouth gaped. "You're on."

Eli slid his arm through Matías's and dragged him towards the entrance. Once they'd paid for their games and handed over their shoes, they found their aisle and sat down.

"I could never remember how to add our names when I was a kid. It used to take me ages. I'm glad they've taken over doing it themselves now," Matías said, tying his shoelaces.

"What size ball do you have?" Eli asked.

"Wow, we've only just got here, and you've already started with the dirty talk." Matías tutted.

Eli's face heated, and he glared at Matías. "You know I wasn't talking about that!" Matías laughed, throwing his head back, and it took everything in Eli to remain rooted to the spot and not closing the distance and licking a stripe up the long, muscled throat.

"I know. I love riling you up."

Eli rolled his eyes and turned to the bowling balls. He picked a fourteen ball and placed it in the rack. Matías chose a different colour after going through a few, but Eli couldn't see what size it was.

"You're first," Matías said.

Eli picked up his ball and stepped forward. It had been a while since he'd last been here, but not as long as Matías. He often came here with his siblings, although it had probably been a few months. He stood straight, holding the ball up, got into position and stepped forward, let his arm drop back, and swung it forward with all his strength. He watched the ball's route down the polished floor and smiled when he took down all ten.

Turning back, he saw Matías's mouth open and close, then he narrowed his eyes and picked up his ball. "It's on," Matías said as Eli passed him.

Eli chuckled. This was what he'd needed. Some time to let go and relax. Forget about everything. Even though one of his problems was standing with his back to him, ass nicely cupped by the light blue jeans he wore and the muscles straining against the tight black T-shirt as he moved through the motions of bowling. Eli's stomach fluttered.

"Eli! I wasn't expecting to see you tonight?"

Eli closed his eyes, the flutters dying out as tension seeped back into his body. He turned and smiled at his sister. "Hey, how are you?" He hugged her.

"Good. Tracey wanted to get out of the house, so we came here. Who are you with?"

"Just a friend," he blurted. "Gets me away from work for an hour."

"I'm glad to hear it. You work too hard." Opal's eye flickered past Eli and widened. "Who's your 'friend?'"

Although she didn't use her hands, he knew she would've used air quotes for the word friend if she could. At least they'd taught her some manners.

Eli turned and pasted on a smile. "This is my friend, Matías. Matías, this is my sister, Opal."

Matías's smile widened. "Nice to meet you."

"You, too." She looked him up and down but spoke to Eli, "I didn't know you had any friends outside of work."

"Opal..." he warned.

She smiled and glanced over her shoulder. "I better go. Tracey is waving at me. Have a good night, you two."

She wandered off, and once she was out of hearing range, Eli groaned. "I'm never going to hear the end of this now."

"Is it a problem?"

"Only that I have a similar family issue to you, except mine doesn't bug me to get a boyfriend. They bug me unendingly when I have a boyfriend. They won't let up if they think I'm hiding you from them."

Matías stared in the direction Eli's sister went. "I can help. It's only fair."

"No. Honestly, you don't want to get involved with my family."

"I'm sure I can deal with it."

"It's fine." Eli brushed past Matías and picked up his ball. "Nice shot, by the way."

They continued playing the game, bantering back and forth all the while. There were flirty touches, which Eli tried to play off, scared Opal would see, but eventually, the game ended.

"Shall we get some food while we're here?" Matías asked.

Eli bit his lip. "How about we go next door?"

"Sure."

They handed in their bowling shoes and headed for the exit, Eli trying not to hurry in case Opal tried to stop them. As they exited, Matías rested his hand at the base of Eli's spine, and Eli stepped closer, unable to stop himself. They entered the pizza restaurant, and Matías asked for a table for two. Eli glanced around and saw several people he knew. His plan to make them more visible had worked, but he hadn't factored in seeing Opal. He was a little more leery of making them too obvious now in case his sister came in, too. He should've offered a takeaway at his place.

"You okay?" Matías asked in his ear as they followed the server to their table.

"Yes. I'm good," he said a little too quickly.

They sat on opposite sides of the table, which gave Eli the chance to observe the man properly. They checked the menu while Eli tried to stop looking at Matías. He was a gorgeous man that anyone would be lucky to have, so why did he not have any luck with relationships? Once they ordered, he asked that exact question.

Matías rubbed at his cheeks as they darkened. "I wish I knew." He stared at the glass of water, spinning it in place with his thumb and middle finger. "Although several of them have said I'm too nice. I've never understood it. Do people want to be treated badly in relationships these days?" Matías shook his head. "I don't know."

"I can tell you that being nice is a good thing, not a bad thing. You've obviously not met the person who can put up with you." Eli grinned as he said it, hoping to make the conversation lighter again.

Matías glared at him and chuckled. "You're right. I have many quirks someone might not like. I need to find that elusive person who can deal with everything I dish out."

Eli leaned forward. "What quirks?"

Matías closed the distance but left enough of a gap no one could accuse them of PDAs in the middle of a restaurant. "I crack my knuckles. I can't cook many dishes. I'm untidy unless I'm at work. I always get too hot when I sleep." Matías stared at him when he said the last thing.

Eli licked his lips, and Matías's gaze dropped. "It doesn't sound too off-putting."

Matías picked up Eli's hand, rubbing his thumb over Eli's skin. He never realised how sensitive the skin between his fingers was until Matías showed him. He stared at their hands, his mouth dry, while he tried to recall why a relationship with him wouldn't be a good idea. At that moment, he couldn't think of a single thing.

Their food arrived, breaking the spell, and Eli cleared his throat, trying to rein in his libido. It might be nice to sate his hunger in Matías, but was it a good idea with everything else they were involved in?

"What has you thinking so hard over there?"

The word "hard" should not be allowed to exit his mouth because it sent too many images through Eli's brain. "Just wondering if the food is as good as it was last time I was here."

The corner of Matías's mouth curled as if he knew what had been going through Eli's mind. "It's pizza. It's rare it can go wrong."

Eli sipped his water. Although they were quiet, it wasn't uncomfortable, even with the underlying tension he could feel buzzing between them. Matías's foot hooked behind Eli's, startling him. He flicked his gaze to him and found a simmering blaze in his eyes. He didn't think he could deny where this evening might be heading.

To douse some of the heat, Eli said, "Are we back at primary school?"

Matías smirked. "If it gives me an excuse to play footsie with you, yes."

Eli moved his legs forward, allowing them both to twine their legs together. It felt childish, but he could feel a sense of excitement flowing through him.

"Tell me about work," he said.

"What do you want to know?"

"Do you enjoy it?"

Matías rested his head on his palm, elbow on the table. "I suppose it depends what you mean by 'enjoy.' I love being able to help people, and the thrill of figuring out the best way to fight a fire is great, but I don't enjoy the relentlessness of some fires or the results."

"What do you mean?" Eli leaned forward, crossing his arms on the table.

"People think we can control fires; therefore, when we try to fight one and fail, we're blamed for the result. We're not trained well enough, or we weren't at our best, or we didn't decide fast enough. What they don't understand is fire is uncontrollable. The fire does what it wishes, and we try to deal with the fallout."

Eli reached forward and covered Matías's forearm with his hand. "You do a fantastic job, Matías. You all do."

He gave a small smile. "We try. It's all we can do." He waved his hand. "Anyway, you didn't ask for me to bring the mood down. I enjoy the people I work with. They're assholes, but they're good assholes." Eli chuckled when Matías's cheeks darkened as the server put their food down. "I apologise for my swearing."

The server smiled and nodded at Matías's apology.

They dug into the food, making conversation between bites until every piece had gone. Eli sat back and patted his stomach.

"That was more than I'd eaten in a week, I think."

"You need to take better care of yourself. You're on your feet for so long. You need to keep your energy levels up." The concern was written all over Matías's face.

"I know, and most of the time, I do. It's just this last week has been..." He couldn't think of a good enough word.

"Unending?"

"Basically, yeah."

"Well, think of this as your week reset. You seem to have Mondays off most weeks, so treat this as your weekend. Tomorrow is another day."

Eli stared at Matías, tracing his features with his eyes. "Yes, it is," he murmured. "Shall we go?"

Matías nodded, and Eli got the server's attention. She brought the bill, which Eli paid for, though Matías complained.

"I offered. My treat." His tone brooked no argument, and Matías fell silent, although Eli could tell he was grumpy about it.

They exited the building, and the cooler air refreshed Eli's energy levels. As they approached the car, he unlocked it and found himself turned and pressed against it. Matías moved closer, warming Eli's front with his body. Eli automatically lifted his arms around Matías's neck.

"If this is the end of the evening, I would like to leave you with a reminder of an amazing night."

"And if it's not the end of the evening?" Eli whispered.

"I would like to give you a tease of what is to come."

Matías lowered his head, their lips meeting, chaste at first, then firmer. Matías licked Eli's bottom lip, and Eli opened for him. His hands speared into Matías's hair, gripping tightly as Matías explored his mouth, leaving tingles in the wake of his tongue. Eli sucked Matías's tongue, mimicking what they might do later, and arousal flooded Eli's system. He moved his hips, trying to find some friction, but Matías had a tight hold on him. He groaned into Matías's mouth, and Matías moved his hand to the back of Eli's head, holding him where he wanted him as his mouth and tongue plundered and took whatever he wanted.

Eli's head spun, barely able to catch any thoughts as he lost himself to the kiss. Eventually, he needed to breathe, so he tore his mouth away and dropped his head back, gasping cold air that seared his lungs. Matías's mouth trailed down his jaw and neck until he couldn't go any further, forcing him to reverse his path.

"Home. Now," Eli said.

Matías pulled back but stayed close. He dropped another kiss on Eli's mouth and stepped away, Eli shivering when the cold invaded his body. They stared at each other for several seconds before Matías rounded the car and climbed inside. Eli stayed, breathing heavily for a minute, then cleared his throat and got in.

Without looking over at Matías, Eli started the car and aimed for his house. They hadn't agreed to anything, but if Matías didn't want this when they arrived, Eli would take him home.

When he parked in his driveway, Eli didn't get the chance to say anything before Matías was climbing out and slamming the door shut. Eli watched him drift to the front door and lean against the wall of the house, staring back at the car.

Eli was torn. He wanted this. He *really* wanted this, but was it the right thing to do? Matías didn't move from his position, giving Eli time to decide, which he appreciated. He smiled, making his mind up. If this ruined their friendship, he'd be upset, but it would be better to find out now than later. He wasn't sure they could get through their fake relationship without caving to what he now knew was inevitable.

He climbed out of the car and hit the button to lock it. The orange flash of lights lit up Matías's face for a brief second, and Eli's breath caught in his chest. Matías had looked feral.

Eli shuffled up the path and stopped beside Matías, not looking at him. He inserted his key to unlock the front door and pushed it open, leaving it wide so Matías could enter. The door closed and locked behind him, and Eli's eyes closed. They were doing this.

Hands rested on his shoulders and smoothed down his arms, and even though he still wore his coat, he could feel everything. When Matías reached Eli's hands, he tugged at the sleeves of his coat, and Eli shrugged it off. Matías disappeared for a moment, then pressed against his back, his hands roaming across Eli's stomach and lower until Matías reached his feet. He tapped each foot, and Eli lifted them obediently while Matías removed his shoes. Matías stood, and warm air covered Eli's ear.

"Are you sure?"

Eli's eyelids fluttered at the husky note, and he dropped his head back onto Matías's shoulder and whispered, "Yes."

Matías sucked his earlobe, the sounds indecent in Eli's ear. Matías's hand cupped his throat, tilting his head to the side, and nibbled his way down the column of Eli's neck. Eli's breathing increased when Matías's other hand covered the bulge in his jeans. The man did nothing more than rest his hand over it while he played with Eli's neck.

Eli's hand, of its own accord, covered Matías's on his dick and pressed down as his hips canted forward. He hissed as pleasure fired outwards.

Matías tutted in his ear. "Patience."

Eli dropped his hand and relaxed his body, swallowing hard and feeling his throat move against Matías's hand. Matías removed his hand from Eli's groin and began walking forwards, nudging Eli with his hips—or rather, his bulge—all the while focusing on Eli's neck. Eli had never realised it was such an erotic place on his body.

Eli's eyes snapped open when his feet hit the bottom step of the stairs, and Matías spun him around.

"Last chance."

"I'm sure," Eli said, panting.

Matías gripped the back of Eli's thighs and lifted him. Eli squeaked and grabbed onto Matías's neck, wrapping his legs around his waist.

"Where am I going?" Matías asked as he climbed the stairs.

"First door on the right."

When they reached the door, Eli fumbled with the handle to open it, and Matías kicked it shut behind them. He stopped at the bed, and Eli moved to drop his legs, but Matías tightened his hold. Matías rested one knee on the bed and scooted onto it before carefully lowering Eli onto the covers.

Eli stared up at him, wishing he knew what was going through his head at that moment.

Chapter 14

Matías

He was so fucking beautiful.

Matías traced a finger from Eli's forehead, down his cheek and along his jaw until he reached his lips. He dragged his finger against the lower lip, showing his teeth, and Eli flicked his tongue out, catching the end of Matías's finger. They both froze, staring into each other's eyes. The green of Eli's eyes was bright, even in the dim light of the room—the only light coming from the streetlights shining through the open curtains.

Matías lowered his head, pressing a kiss to Eli's mouth. Eli lifted his chin, giving Matías more access while Eli's hands reached for Matías's T-shirt. He pulled on the fabric until it bunched beneath Matías's arms. Matías rose and yanked it over his head before falling back over Eli and bracing himself on his hands.

Eli wore a dark grey shirt, a mockery of the suit they had made Matías wear at Isabella's wedding.

"What?" Eli's mouth curved. "Why are you smiling?"

"The grey shirt."

He didn't need to say more because Eli chuckled. "You'll like grey, eventually."

"I doubt it. Although on you, it looks great."

Eli's cheeks darkened, and Matías sat on his knees and reached for Eli's buttons. He couldn't remember ever seeing Eli without a shirt—no T-shirts or anything like that. As the buttons came undone, Matías paused, unbelieving of what he saw. He glanced up at Eli, who smirked at him.

"Someone has secrets," Matías murmured, continuing with his job.

When the last button was free, Matías spread the halves of the shirt, giving him a view of the intricate ink patterns decorating his torso. He vowed to trace every inch with his tongue the moment they were both naked, but he noticed something else. The patterns didn't stop. He raised his eyebrows at Eli, who shrugged.

Matías pulled the shirt off Eli's arms, fascinated by what he'd found and amazed by how far the designs went. From cuff to collarbone to waist and possibly beyond, Eli was tattooed, and Matías loved it.

"Is it on your back, too?" he asked, torn between wanting to check it out and wanting to taste Eli.

Eli nodded. "It stops at my waistband."

"Why?"

Eli bit his bottom lip. "I haven't decided what I want there yet."

"We're going to be here a long time," Matías murmured.

"Why?"

"Because I need to taste every swirl of ink on your skin. Every peak and valley. Every soft and hard area. Every inch."

As Matías spoke, he lowered himself to his forearms and pressed a kiss to Eli's lips. Then he began, teasing his tongue along Eli's collarbone, following the black lines around every curve and corner, down his arm and back up again. He kissed across Eli's chest to his opposite shoulder and down to his wrist and back again.

"This will never get old," he whispered.

While he worked his way down Eli's torso, Eli rested a hand against Matías's head. His fingers gripped and relaxed, depending on what Matías did with his mouth and tongue. Matías paid attention to his belly button, noticing the ink making a circle around it.

"God, Matti."

The breathlessness of his tone had Matías growing harder beneath his jeans, and he finished his expedition at Eli's waistband. His eyes grazed the path he had taken and locked onto Eli's face, the flush high on his cheekbones, his bottom lip caught between his teeth, his pupils dilated so much no colour could be seen. Matías kissed Eli's abdomen and unbuttoned his jeans, dropping another kiss on the new expanse of skin. With every notch he lowered the zipper, he kissed and licked, tasting more and more unique Eli taste.

It was only when he felt the heat of Eli's cock he realised Eli had gone commando. His eyebrows rose, and he pulled his gaze away from Eli's face, smirking when he found the shaft trying to escape. Matías licked his lips and pulled the zipper down fully, letting Eli's dick free from its constraints.

Unable to stop himself, he yanked Eli's jeans off his legs, throwing them behind him, and lay between Eli's legs, his mouth in line with the deep purple shaft. He blew a stream of cool air across it, and it pulsed, straining.

"Fuck, Matti. Please!"

Matías grinned and licked a stripe up the underside of his cock, stopping at the sensitive bundle of nerves and flicking his tongue repeatedly over it.

"Holy shit! Ah, fuck!"

Matías held Eli's hips as he swallowed Eli's dick, taking him straight to the back of his throat. He lifted and dropped several times, lubricating his way, then kept Eli in his throat and swallowed.

"Fuck, fuck! Jesus!" He panted when Matías pulled off. "You do that much more, and it'll all be over."

Matías chuckled and climbed off the bed. "Well, we can't have that now, can we?" He stood at the foot and watched Eli squirm as he removed the rest of his clothes. "Where're your supplies?"

Eli blinked several times, and Matías could see the struggle it was for him to raise his eyes from Matías's cock. "What?"

"Supplies? Lube? Condom?" Matías pressed his tongue into his upper lip to stop his smile.

"Oh! There." He pointed to the bedside table.

Matías opened the drawer and picked up the tube and packet, throwing them beside Eli. He slid the drawer shut again and returned to the foot of the bed.

"You're divine," he whispered.

Eli's flush deepened. Matías crawled onto the bed, Eli spreading his legs as Matías drew closer. He braced himself with his hands beside Eli's shoulders and stared down at him.

"What?"

Matías smiled and dropped his mouth to Eli's, taking in his gasp of surprise. He lowered himself a little so their cocks could touch, and he rolled his hips to increase the pressure. Reaching for the lube, Matías pulled his mouth away, earning a mewl from the man beneath him. He rested back on his heels and opened the tube, squirting some lube onto his fingers. He focused on his prize: the tight rosebud Eli was giving him access to.

Glancing up at Eli to check he was with him, he met the turbulent green eyes and knew Eli was with him at this moment. Matías dropped his gaze to his destination and rubbed a finger against the pulsing entrance.

"God, yes." Eli rolled his head on the pillow, canting his hips to get more, but Matías wouldn't let him and drew back. "No!"

"Patience."

"You are Satan's spawn!" Eli panted, and Matías laughed.

"It'll be worth it."

To prove his point, he pressed harder, letting the tip of his finger breach the ring of muscle. He massaged where he could reach and gently pushed further in. Eli's hands reached behind him and gripped the headboard. Matías concentrated on stretching the man, using one finger, then two and scissoring before attempting three. When he crooked his three fingers and grazed Eli's prostate, the man bowed from the bed with a bellow. Matías loved that Eli wasn't quiet.

"God, please. Please, Matti."

Matías removed his fingers to Eli's protest but picked up the condom and tore it open. After he rolled it down his straining length, he slicked it and braced himself over Eli once more.

"Are you ready?"

"I've been ready for ages!"

Matías raised his eyebrows. "Are you ready?" he repeated, not wanting to continue until he'd received Eli's complete consent.

"Yes! Yes, I'm ready. Please, God, Matti."

Matías lowered himself to his forearms and caged Eli's head with his hands. Eli wrapped one arm around Matías's waist, and the other hand cupped his jaw.

Eli locked gazes with him. "I'm ready. I promise."

Matías held his cock against Eli's hole and pressed forward, meeting resistance he knew would eventually give way. Eli's eyes rolled in the sockets, his mouth opening as he panted. They both gasped when Matías pushed through the barrier, sliding inches deep. He paused, gritting his teeth at how tight Eli felt. It took all his will to stay still until Eli nodded. He withdrew and pushed forward again, gaining more access with each forward thrust.

He dropped his forehead to Eli's when his balls met Eli's ass, and they breathed each other's air while both calmed. Matías didn't want to rush this. He wanted to remember every minute of being with Eli, whether or not he was inside him. No time spent with Eli was wasted, but Matías couldn't tell him that. Not yet.

Fusing their mouths stopped him from revealing his secrets, and when their tongues met, he began moving. Eli's hands gripped him, his legs wrapping around Matías's waist while Matías thrust his hips. He could feel himself slipping down the path of his impending orgasm, so he changed his angle, and Eli shouted. Matías stroked Eli's cock in time with their movements, and within seconds, Eli was done. Hot spurts of come coated both their chests and Matías's hand, and the contractions pulled Matías's release from him.

He bit down on his bottom lip as he held himself deep, dragging out the pleasure for as long as he could stand it. He kissed Eli gently because the man had slumped to the bed, all limbs akimbo, his eyes closed. Matías smiled but winced when he pulled free, the sensitivity a little too much. Throwing the condom in the bin beside the bed, he laid on his back beside Eli and rolled his head to look at him.

His chest, neck and cheeks were stained red, his lips rosy and wet. He looked completely debauched, and Matías should clean him up, but he looked so content. No care for his state of undress or cleanliness. Matías should've licked up Eli's come—he wanted to know what he tasted like, but it would have to be for another day. Matías didn't like it when it was cold and sticky.

"Make sure my mother doesn't know how I died, okay? That would be so embarrassing." Eli's words and tone had Matías cracking up, and he threw his arm over his head.

Comfortable silence ensued, and Matías felt himself drifting until Eli spoke again.

"This changes things," he whispered.

Matías didn't like the tone he used, so he tried to make light of it, "Not really. We could have a fake relationship with real benefits." He hated the idea, but it was too early to show his hand. Eli would pull away faster than a runaway bride if Matías told him about his plans for them.

"Hmm."

Matías's heart sank. "Tell you what. Think about it. I know it's going to be a tough couple of months because you won't be able to go out and get laid by anyone. After all, if people saw, they wouldn't take too kindly to the appearance of cheating." He wasn't above putting thoughts into his head for him to think about. "So, why not take what you can get while we're 'together,' and everyone wins?"

"Okay. I'll think about it."

It wasn't the answer Matías wanted, but it was better than an outright decline. He inhaled. Eli didn't come across as someone who allowed hook-ups to stay the night; therefore, he swung his legs over the bed and gathered his clothes together. When Eli didn't protest, he knew he'd made the right choice.

"Do you mind if I use your bathroom?" he asked.

"Sure. It's the door opposite this one."

"Thanks."

He shuffled to the bathroom, wanting a shower but not wanting to overstay his welcome. He wet a flannel and wiped his stomach clean as best he could then dressed. He hadn't planned on sleeping with Eli, but he was glad he'd experienced it. If he hadn't been falling for him already, this would've started the journey because Eli was so expressive, so unreserved. It was a shame he didn't have the same emotions for the other aspects of his life.

Matías rubbed at his face and exited into the chilly hallway, finding Eli standing there with the sheet wrapped around his body.

"I've thought about it." Matías's heart pounded. "Real benefits sounds good."

Matías grinned and stepped closer, crowding Eli into the wall. "I'm glad because you're right. It does sound good." He gripped Eli's chin and took his mouth, slowly but deeply. "I'll let you get some sleep." He pecked him on the lips once more and wandered down the stairs to the front door. He put on his coat and shoes, waved at Eli, who was still waiting at the top of the stairs, and left the house.

It was only when he got outside he realised Eli had picked him up that night. He chuckled and shook his head, pulling out his phone. He dialled.

"What time do you call this, asshole?" There was the Nash he loved.

"Can you give me a lift home?"

"Why?"

"Because I'm stranded."

"What happened?"

Matías sighed. "Get in the car and pick me up, and I'll explain." He gave him the street and began walking to the end of the road.

"You owe me. I've been asleep for two hours already."

Matías winced and went to apologise, but Nash had ended the call. He'd make it up to him. Although why was he already asleep? It wasn't that late. He tugged the collar of his coat up to give him some respite from the cold air and shoved his hands deep in his pockets while he waited.

When a car pulled up, it wasn't Nash's, and Nash wasn't driving. His station commander was. Matías climbed in the back, frowning.

"I wasn't expecting you. Not that I'm not grateful."

Paul chuckled. "Nice save. Nash was at our house. I thought it would be better if I drove as he was still half-asleep."

"Thanks, and sorry for making you come out this late."

"Not a problem."

Nash turned in his seat to see Matías. "So, spill. You told me you'd give me the dirt." He glanced at Paul and shook his head, but Nash either didn't see him or didn't care. "Did you go out with Eli? Are people still seeing you together?"

Matías didn't want to have this conversation when Paul was in the car, but Nash was like a firefighter racing for a shower at the end of a shift. Nothing would stop him. "Yes, I did."

"Don't you think two months is too long? You're already getting feelings for him. What if he never feels the same for you?"

Matías swallowed. "Then he doesn't. And two months isn't long."

"Long enough for him to be comfortable with your family, and then you're going to throw him away?"

Matías glared at him. "You know that's not what I'm going to do."

"Sorry. It's his idea. I remember now."

"Nash, come on."

Nash held his hands up. "I'm sorry. I don't like the idea of pretending. It doesn't make any sense to me."

Matías chanced a look at Paul and noticed a frown on his face. "It doesn't need to make sense to you. It's my life."

"But it's not just yours it affects. It's Eli's. It's your family's. Don't you think they're going to be upset?"

"Nash, enough," Paul's voice brooked no argument. "Nash has had a few too many drinks tonight, and I think his brain is still swimming in tequila."

"Tequila." Matías groaned. It made a lot more sense now. Nash didn't do well with tequila. Or rather, tequila didn't do well with Nash.

They reached Matías's apartment building in silence. Paul idled the engine, but when Matías climbed out, so did he. He braced himself for something, though he didn't know what.

"Tell me if I've got this straight," Paul said, leaning back against the car and crossing his arms. "You're pretending to be in a relationship with Eli." Matías averted his gaze but nodded. "Why?"

The answer seemed so juvenile now, but he had never been anything but honest with Paul. "I wanted a breather from being hounded about being single. Eli offered, and I accepted."

Paul stayed silent, and Matías glanced at him, seeing the strain in his features. The disappointment. Matías's stomach churned.

"It's not my decision to make, Matías, but think long and hard about the consequences of this. You're playing with people's lives. You're pretending to be something you're not. If anyone is likely to get hurt by this ruse, I suggest you rethink it."

"The only one who's likely to get hurt is me, Chief." He cleared his throat. "Eli told me right from the beginning he didn't want an actual relationship and never would, but..." He trailed off, not wanting to admit how stupid he was.

"But you've fallen in love with him." Matías shrugged. Paul sighed and came to stand in front of him. "This was a reckless move, Matías. One I would never have thought you would make. It's been done now, though." He rested a hand on Matías's shoulder. "Love is not to be trifled with. If Eli doesn't return your feelings, you need to let him go at the end of the day. Can you do that?"

"If I have to," he said, his throat closing with the thought.

"What happens if your family finds out the truth?"

"They won't."

Paul raised his eyebrows. "So you say." He squeezed his shoulder and let go. "I need to get Nash back. Think carefully, Matías. Call me if you need anything."

"Thanks for the ride."

Paul smiled. "You're welcome. Have a good night."

Matías watched the car disappear down the street, then stared a little longer. The lightness of an hour ago had been weighted down by the home truths Paul had given him. He knew Paul was right, but he didn't know if he could stop. He needed Eli, and though this was not the best way to do it, he would try anything.

Chapter 15

Paul

Paul concentrated on the road as he drove through the streets after dropping Nash at home. Nash seemed to be drinking himself to an early grave more than usual lately, and Paul wasn't sure how to go about changing it without getting an earful from the man.

As for Matías... Paul sighed. The man was in a predicament. Paul hadn't ever believed Matías would get himself into such a situation, but his men surprised him all the time.

By the time he pulled into his driveway, he was exhausted, but he needed to talk things through with Quinn because Matías might need his help, but he had no idea how he could. His husband was always better at working through problems than Paul was unless it came to work problems. Emotional problems? Well, Quinn was king.

He let himself into the house and locked it quietly behind him. He shouldn't have bothered, though, because Quinn was sitting at the kitchen table, cradling a mug of something hot.

"Everything okay?" Quinn asked.

Paul nodded. "Just my boys being idiots."

"I think someone needs to intervene with Nash before he does something stupid."

Paul stepped behind Quinn and rested his chin on his shoulder. "My thoughts exactly. I need to talk with him because he's not mentioned anything that points to why he's started drinking so heavily suddenly."

Quinn covered Paul's hands when they slid around his waist. "Has anyone asked him?"

Paul's heart jumped. "I haven't. Idiot that I am. I'll speak to him. See if he'll unload on me."

"If he doesn't, send him my way."

Paul chuckled. "Trust me, I will."

"What happened with Matías? How come he needed a ride?" Paul sighed and settled into the seat next to his husband. "Actually, hold that thought. Let me get you a drink."

Quinn stood and pottered around the kitchen until the scent of hot chocolate seeped into the air. He always knew how to make Paul feel better. When he had the mug in his hands, they transferred to the living room and the comfortable sofa, and Quinn repeated his question.

"Matías is in a fake relationship with Eli."

Quinn gaped. "He what? His mother will go mental when she finds out."

Paul nodded. "I know his family pushes him to find a boyfriend, but this isn't the way to stop them from interfering."

"Did he say what his plan was?"

"No, but the idiot has fallen in love with Eli. I warned him to stop things before they got too far, but he said it was too late. I'm worried Matías won't manage when the relationship, as it were, ends. I don't think he'll be able to walk away without getting hurt."

Quinn snuggled into Paul's side. "What made him decide to do it?"

"He said he'd had enough of his family badgering him to find a partner, and Eli had offered." Paul exhaled. "Matías is going to get hurt."

Quinn hummed. "Possibly. Unless Eli feels the same way."

"I don't know."

"It's his choice, my love. Matías is a grown man, and he needs to make his own decisions. We need to be there for him if he needs us." Quinn sighed.

"I never realised having a station meant dealing with another twenty-four kids."

Quinn chuckled. "And you love it."

"That I do."

He rubbed Quinn's arm and kissed his forehead. "Do you ever wish we'd had more kids?"

"Maybe in the beginning. Now, though, no. I'm glad we stayed with two. You?"

"Nah, two is more than enough."

They finished the drinks in silence, except for the ticking of the clock. Paul lost himself in the memories of his station and how far they had come since the beginning. He wouldn't change the crew members he had now for anything. They had worked hard to get the station as inclusive as possible.

"Come on, love. Leave their troubles for another day."

Quinn pulled him to standing, and they made their way to bed. Paul had to believe everything would work out. He hated seeing his boys upset or struggling, but all Paul could do was lend a hand. He hoped it would be enough.

Chapter 16

Eli

"So, who was your 'friend' last week, Eli?" Opal asked once they'd sat down at the table, ready to eat.

Eli closed his eyes and glared across at her. "He is a friend. Nothing more."

"You haven't mentioned him before."

Eli had known the minute Opal had seen him and Matías, this would be the result. She was the nosiest bitch in the city. Perhaps the country. "He's a new friend. I met him through one of the weddings I did."

"Ooh, at least you know he likes weddings." Opal waggled her eyebrows, and it was all Eli could do to keep his cutlery in his hand rather than sending it hurtling over the table.

"Who is this you're talking about?" his mother asked.

Opal leaned forward. "His name is Matías."

"Matías?" Karen frowned down at the table before meeting Eli's gaze. "You *are* the Eli Sofía was talking about. I didn't think it was you. I denied it to her face. Why didn't you tell me?"

Eli stared at her. "Tell you what? That we're friends?"

Karen narrowed her eyes. "You know exactly what I'm talking about, Eli Jackson. I was speaking with Sofía in the supermarket the other day, and she told me her son, Matías, had finally met someone called Eli. She said they'd met at her daughter's wedding, and Eli has been to several family events, introduced as Matías's boyfriend. I thought it was a coincidence about the name."

Eli lowered his gaze. This was why he hadn't wanted to tell anyone about their arrangement. The moment his family thought he was in a relationship, they would expect to meet the guy and give him the third degree. Especially as Eli had always been so against a relationship. He could tell them the truth, but his mother would be angry they were deceiving Matías's family and insist they end the ruse. He could agree it wasn't nice of them to do so, but she didn't know what his family was like. If he defended his choice, he would disappoint Karen. No, he'd need to keep up the pretence for a while longer.

"I'm sorry I didn't tell you." He licked his lips. "It's still so new, and I'm trying to reconcile being in a relationship when you know I haven't ever wanted one. It's tricky for me." All of that was the truth in some form.

Karen's expression softened, and she reached across to pat his hand. "I can understand it. I still wish you had told me. I'm going to look like a fool when I next see Sofía."

"I didn't realise you knew her."

Karen smiled. "She's the dentist in the building next to where I work. We often see each other when we go to the bakery to fetch lunch."

Wonderful. Now, when he broke up with Matías, his mother's friendship might be on the rocks, too. He focused on his food, though it tasted like a week-old cake. His family chatted around him, thankfully, leaving him to his thoughts. When they'd finished the main meal, and Karen was dishing out ice cream, there was a knock at the door. Karen wiped her hands.

"Robbie, can you finish dishing these up, please?"

She didn't wait for an answer. Robbie grumbled but finished spooning the ice cream into bowls and giving them to everyone, including putting a bowl full in front of Karen's place.

Eli heard his mother's voice growing louder as it came closer. When she entered the kitchen, she was wringing her hands, and her gaze went immediately to Eli. He knew why. Even before the man stepped into the room, Eli knew what she'd done.

"Everyone, this is Hayden Jackson. Your father," Karen said in a shaky voice.

Eli stood, scraping his chair across the floor. "Thank you for dinner, Mum. I'll see you soon."

"Eli, please...?"

Eli kissed her cheek and ignored her requests, saying goodbye to his siblings and striding for the front door. He paused to slide on his coat.

"Eli, wait." Eli glanced over his shoulder at Hayden's words but continued zipping up his coat. "Can we talk this through as a family?" Hayden asked.

Eli clenched his jaw. "You are not part of this family, so don't pretend you are. I will speak with *my* family when you're not here. By all means, though, talk to them, twist their memories, get them on your side. But you will *never* be part of my family."

He yanked the door open and slammed it shut behind him. Driving away, he shook his head, feeling a headache coming on. He knew he was out of paracetamol and aimed the car for the nearest shop, which happened to be a supermarket. He grabbed two boxes and, annoyed his father had stopped him from having his dessert, visited the frozen aisle and chose a tub of cookie dough ice cream. Far more extravagant than he usually bought, but he needed the sugar. Picking up some strawberries to go with the ice cream, he turned when he heard his name and came face to face with Matías and Rafe.

"What are you doing here?" he asked.

They hadn't seen each other since the night they slept together because they were both busy, and Matías had worked an extra shift when a firefighter had called in sick. They'd messaged every day and chatted on the phone a couple of times.

"Nice to see you, too, sweetheart," Matías said, raising his eyebrows.

Eli blinked and shook his head. "Sorry. Rough night. Let's try that again. Hi, Matti. Hi, Rafe."

"Right back atcha. Looks like you're having a cosy night in," Rafe said, pointing to the basket in Eli's hands.

Eli glanced at the basket and back at Rafe. "Yeah. The family dinner didn't quite go to plan, and I missed out on dessert."

"Everything okay?" Matías asked, stepping closer and resting his hand on Eli's elbow.

Eli waved his hand. "It's fine. Nothing that won't sort itself out." It was funny how he could lie to Matías when there were other people around, but not when he was alone.

He could see Matías didn't believe him, but the man didn't push.

"Well, we can help with that, can't we, Matti?" Rafe nudged Matías. "Invite him."

Matías winced, the apology already in his eyes. "Rafe owns a club, as you know. He holds a couples night every month, and tonight is one of those nights. Would you like to come? It's a regular club with a bar and dancing."

Rafe gasped and held a hand to his heart. "A regular club! You wound me with your words."

Matías rolled his eyes, and Eli chuckled. "Sorry. It's a highly sought-after club with amazing bartenders and the ultimate music experience. That better?"

Rafe grinned. "I should get you working on my advertising campaigns."

Eli chuckled again, glancing between the two men. "Do you know what? Yes. I'll go. I need to go home and get changed first."

"You don't need to. You look amazing as you are," Matías said.

Eli tilted his head and smiled. "As much as I thank you, I've been in these clothes all day. I need something fresh."

"Can I pick you up?" Matías squeezed Eli's elbow.

"No, you go ahead with Rafe and work on his campaign." He winked at Rafe. "I'll meet you there."

"Okay. It starts at nine o'clock." Eli nodded. "I'll let you get back to your shopping," Matías said.

Eli felt the loss when Matías removed his hand and moved away, but within seconds, he was back, cupping Eli's jaw and joining their mouths for a desperate but brief kiss.

"Sorry. I know I said I'd let you instigate it, but I've missed that this week," Matías said.

Eli said nothing but watched Matías wander off. Pulling himself together, he finished getting what he needed and checked out. By the time he arrived home, he had regretted agreeing to go. He wasn't sure he was in the mood for dancing and drinking, but he remembered his father interrupting their meal, and he threw caution to the wind. Eli had already slept with Matías. What was dancing and drinking going to do? Make things worse? He wasn't sure it could. He didn't have long to get ready, so he reluctantly put the ice cream in the freezer, vowing to eat some when he got home later that night, and climbed the stairs. A quick shower, followed by several long minutes of deciding what to wear, and he was ready.

He chose tight black jeans, a dark purple shirt and a black waistcoat. He loved wearing suits; it made him feel like he'd made an effort, and they were comfortable. His wallet and phone went into his pocket, and he kept hold of his keys to lock the house. He wouldn't be drinking because he had to work the following day, so he threw a coat over his clothes and left the house. Matías had mentioned the club Rafe owned when they had been at Sofía's party, but he'd told him the name again before they'd left. Zoo sounded about right if Rafe was anything to go by. The place was probably all about showing off what a person has and others watching. It's what normal clubs are like.

Eli chuckled to himself when he thought about it. No doubt Rafe would curse him for calling it normal. He parked in the car park across the street from the club. It was manned twenty-four hours a day, so he felt happy about leaving his car there for a few hours. He checked his phone.

MATÍAS: *When you get here, go to the bouncer and tell them my name. It'll get you in quicker. I've told him to expect you.*

Eli hated the idea of it, but he also didn't like the idea of having to wait in line for ages. He inhaled, shoring up his confidence, and strode for the door.

"Can I help you?"

"I'm here with Matías Lopez."

The bouncer smiled. "You must be Eli. Nice to meet you. Go on in."

Eli smiled back and exhaled as he opened the door. It was unexpectedly quiet, but he realised why when he stepped into a foyer.

"Hello. Welcome to Zoo. May I take your coat?"

Eli wandered over to the woman who had spoken. "Thanks." He slipped off his coat and handed it over, receiving a ticket in return, which he slid into his pocket.

"Go through those doors, and it will take you to the main club."

"Thank you."

The moment he opened the door, the noise accosted him. A deep bass vibrated through his body, and he gritted his teeth against it. It wasn't his type of music, but the ambience of the place was undeniable. It had a large, open-plan room with booths, tables, chairs and stools scattered around the perimeter and stairs leading to upper levels. If he excluded the music, it had a warm feel to the place with ambers, browns and oranges on the walls. It wasn't as dark as he'd expected. There were lights placed around the room, casting a warm yellow glow over everything.

"What do you think?"

Eli spun around at the voice in his ear, hand on heart. "Jesus! You scared the crap out of me!"

Matías laughed, though the music swallowed up the sound. "Sorry. I don't think there was any way I couldn't have scared you. You wouldn't have heard me coming either way."

"The music is a bit loud for me, but it looks great."

Matías held out his hand. "Want to go somewhere a little quieter?"

Eli nodded and slid his hand into Matías's, following when he tugged. They weaved through the crowds, down a small hallway and up a flight of stairs. The further they moved, the quieter it became. Matías opened a door and stepped inside, closing it behind them and locking away most of the noise.

"Is this better?" he asked.

Eli sighed. "Yes, thanks. I don't mind loud music, but a deep bass song has never been my favourite." He wandered to the full-height windows that looked out onto the main dance floor area they'd just been in. "There has been a lot of thought put into this place."

Matías stood behind Eli and rested his hands on Eli's shoulders. "Yes. Rafe spent months planning the layout before spending a penny towards it. He wanted it to be perfect. A haven for those who needed it."

"He's done a good job, from what I can see."

Matías slid his hands down Eli's arms and wrapped them around his waist, dropping his chin to Eli's shoulder. "Why don't you show off your tattoos?"

It hadn't been what Eli had expected him to ask. "I don't want you mauling me." He chuckled and squirmed when Matías tickled his ribs.

"Why really?"

Eli sighed and leaned back against him. "Because they're for me, not anyone else. I didn't get them to show off to other people. I got them because each and every one of them meant something to me."

"I got my tattoo because I loved the design, and it called to me. I'm getting a similar layout to yours, eventually. It'll take me a while to catch up, though." Matías nibbled on Eli's ear. Eli tilted his head and rested it against Matías's shoulder. "Can't wait to trace every inch again," he whispered.

The door opened, and Eli lifted his head, almost cracking heads with Matías. He glanced over his shoulder to see Rafe enter with a tray of drinks.

"Glad you made it, Eli. The party will get underway soon."

Eli frowned. "Is it not already?"

Rafe chuckled. "No, this is a normal night." He checked his watch. "In nine minutes, it will turn into couples' night. You'll see a lot of people leave and just as many arrive."

"What is different about it?"

"The music, for one. It's softer. More romantic. It's for all those people who don't want to admit they love romance. Here, they can enjoy it with no ricochet."

Eli stared at Rafe while he arranged the drinks. "You like it."

Rafe glanced up. "Of course I do. Wouldn't do for me to admit it outside of these walls, though."

"Why not?"

Rafe stepped closer. "There are sharks around. If they think I'm soft, they'll try to take over my club."

"Very mafia-like," Eli deadpanned.

Rafe and Matías laughed. "Yes, but unfortunately, also true." Rafe held out a hand towards the drinks. "Let's watch the couples' night unfold before you join their ranks."

Matías led Eli to the chairs where they could watch the main floor. Rafe had brought him a choice of alcoholic and non-alcoholic drinks, which Eli was pleased about. He found it easy to be around both men and relaxed quickly. Matías retained hold of Eli's hand, their fingers threaded together.

"So, Matti tells me you have a thriving wedding planning business."

Eli smiled at Matías. "Yes, I do. It's going to expand over the next few months as well, I hope."

"Have you spoken to Jasmine?" Matías asked.

"Briefly. I fired her as my assistant and said I would rehire her as my partner once this other situation is resolved. She seemed pleased."

"I think it's a good choice. She won't let you down."

Eli knew she wouldn't, though his stomach still tied itself in knots when he thought about the future of Devoted Weddings. It was his cross to bear, though.

"How is the station doing, Matti? I saw Quinn the other day, and he mentioned the firefighter calendar had gone down well. They're thinking of making it an annual thing."

Matías glanced at him, his cheeks darkening, and it immediately intrigued Eli. "Calendar?"

Rafe stared between the two of them, and his grin grew. "Has Eli not seen your photos, Matti?"

Matías rubbed a hand over the back of his neck and dropped his head, groaning. "It was under duress!"

"Don't talk shit. You were happy to do it." Rafe leaned forward. "The fire station took part in a firefighter calendar last year to raise money for the homeless shelter. They ended up with two calendars, a male one and a female one. Matti, here, was on two months."

Eli peered at Matías. "Really? I wish I'd heard about this. I would've grabbed one."

"Do you want to see the pictures?" Rafe asked, a glint in his eye.

"Rafe!"

"Eli?"

"I can't say no to seeing pictures, now, can I?" Eli teased Matías, squeezing and patting his knee in commiseration. "Might as well get it out of the way now."

Matías dropped his head into his hands and groaned again. "Rafe, you're a dead man."

Rafe handed Eli his phone after pressing on it a few times. "Here he is in all his glory. Well, almost all his glory."

Eli stared at the photo. Matías stood with three other men, his feet braced apart, firefighter boots on, helmet on, and the hose wound around him like a snake coiling around its nest. There was no telling if he was naked beneath it, but the implication was there. He raised his eyebrows at Matías, who flushed a dark red.

"Swipe left for the second one."

Eli swiped and almost swallowed his tongue. "I need copies of these."

Rafe laughed. "I'll send them to you."

"I think it's time we went downstairs," Matías said, standing. He held out his hand to Eli, which Eli had noticed he did a lot, and pulled Eli up. "Ready to dance the night away?"

Eli would be willing to do a lot of things with Matías. Some things he shouldn't. He'd seen the man naked in his bed, but there was something about the photo that made it just as sexy. He wouldn't be getting the image out of his mind any time soon. Maybe Matías would dress up if he asked.

"A couple of hours, anyway," Eli said, reminding himself he needed to sleep before he had to work the next day.

"More than enough time to spend with you."

Matías dropped his head and kissed Eli, soft and brief but overwhelmingly sweet. It was a good job he had hold of Eli because Eli's knees were like jelly. His heart pounded, and he wanted nothing more than to be wrapped around the man. Eli was in trouble.

Chapter 17

Matías

Having Eli all to himself for a couple of hours was better than anything else Matías could imagine. Focusing on him and not on their fake relationship. Matías wanted it to be real for tonight, at least.

He pulled Eli onto the dance floor and spun him into his body so their chests were flush. Matías slid his arms around Eli's waist and began moving to the sensual beat of the Latin-style music that was currently playing. It wasn't too loud; they could converse if they needed to, but it was enough they could pretend to be in their own little bubble and ignore everyone around them.

Eli's arms held onto Matías's neck, gripping the short strands at the base of his head. Their foreheads were resting together, their eyes locked. The music changed and slowed down, and Matías pulled Eli tight against him, removing any space between them. He could feel Eli, hard against his thigh, the same as he must be against Eli's lower stomach. They swayed, and Eli closed his eyes, dropping his head to Matías's shoulder.

"This is nice," Eli murmured.

"Mmm-hmm."

Matías wanted the night to last forever. They swayed and danced through another three songs, then Matías dragged Eli to the bar.

"God, I needed that," Eli said once he'd drained his bottle of water. "I didn't realise how thirsty I was. It's been..." He tilted his head. "It's been far too long since I last went out like this."

"I'm glad I could help." He ordered two more bottles.

"I see you, Matías. What? Couldn't stand the pace on the dance floor anymore?"

Matías laughed and hugged Jason. "I don't see you still out there."

"I'm getting old, man. I need to keep this body in prime condition for many reasons." Jason grinned at Harry.

"I don't want to know, thanks. Eli, this is a colleague of mine, Jason, and his boyfriend, Harry. In case you are still obsessed, Harry was the photographer for the firefighter calendar." Matías slid an arm around Eli's shoulders when he stepped closer to him.

"Nice to see you, Harry," Eli said. "You did good work with the calendar."

Harry dropped his head. "Thanks. It wasn't hard to make this lot look good, though."

"They didn't make it easy for you, Harry. I was there. I saw their shenanigans."

"Eli, this is Oliver, the owner of Nourris Moi."

"Nice to see you again, Oliver." Eli elbowed Matías. "I already know them. I've worked with them before for weddings."

"Sorry. I'm assuming you don't know anyone."

"I suppose I should be grateful you're introducing me at all." Eli smiled.

Matías tightened his hold.

"Where's your other half?" Jason asked.

"Toilet break." Oliver chuckled. "For about the tenth time. I don't think he's used to drinking so much. Water that is. Not alcohol."

"Did Paul say whether he and Quinn were coming?" Matías asked. Paul hadn't treated him any differently than usual at work, but he was concerned Paul would be different socially.

"No. They're staying home with the boys tonight."

"Ah, here he is." Oliver slid his arm around Dean. "Dean, this is Eli, Matías's...boyfriend."

The pause had been slight, but there all the same, and Matías was sure it was because he hadn't announced anything about them at work.

Dean shook hands with Eli and Matías. "How long have you been here?"

"Only an hour or so. We have a carriage and pumpkin situation here." Matías grinned at Eli, who elbowed him again.

"I have to get my beauty sleep. It takes work to look like this," Eli said with a wave of his hand down his body. "We don't all come out of the womb looking like gods."

"Aw, thanks, honey." Matías kissed his temple.

"So, how did you two meet?" Harry asked.

Matías stared at Eli, who answered Harry, "We met at Matías's sister's wedding. I was planning the wedding, and Matías was a guest who didn't know I was right, and he was wrong."

"I still don't agree."

"Have you seen the photos? You look great."

"Yes, I have, but I don't know. I still think you did it to make me squirm."

Eli smirked. "Maybe."

"Did what?"

Matías shook his head. "We had a disagreement about the colour of the suit for the wedding. Isabella wanted us in grey suits, but I don't think grey works for me. Eli told me to shut up and get over it. It was love at first sight."

As soon as he said the words, he wished he'd kept his mouth shut. Eli tensed in his arms, and Matías rubbed at his biceps to apologise.

"Well, nothing like a wedding to make people fall in love, eh, Eli." Harry grinned.

"Ain't that the truth."

"Right, well, we're going back for a boogie. We'll catch you later," Dean said, walking backwards and pulling Oliver with him.

"I suppose we should, too," Jason said, arching an eyebrow at Harry, who nodded. "Have an amazing night, you two. We'll see you in a bit."

Jason bent down and picked Harry up in a fireman's lift and jogged to the dance floor.

"Harry has a lot to put up with," Matías said.

"They look happy. Both couples do."

He glanced at Eli, who had what Matías thought was a wistful expression on his face, but it was gone within seconds, so he couldn't be sure.

"Do you want to sit down for a bit?"

"Yeah."

Matías pointed to a booth along the back wall, and they made their way through the crowd. He slid in first and caught Eli's hand, tugging him to the same side as he was in. Purely selfish reasons, obviously. He rested his back against the wall and bent his knee across the seat, and let Eli scoot in front of him, resting his back against Matías's front. Matías draped his arm over Eli's shoulder.

This. This was what he wanted. The ease at which they fit together, talked, handled things was beyond anything he imagined he could find. He would've been happy with someone who had no similar interests, but he'd been shown that he and Eli could work very well together. He needed to figure out how to convince Eli of the same.

Eli looked up at him. "You're quiet. Is everything okay?"

Matías smiled. "Everything's perfect." He kissed Eli's temple. "Are you enjoying yourself?"

"Yes, surprisingly. I've never been one to visit clubs, but this has been great."

"Maybe we can do it again sometime?"

Eli stared at him for a minute before saying, "I'd like that."

"What time does the carriage become a pumpkin?" He grinned when Eli rolled his eyes.

"I have to be up at seven o'clock tomorrow morning, so I think maybe eleven. We'll see how we go."

Matías tightened his grip on Eli and kissed his head again. Eli threaded their fingers together, and Matías's heart sang when Eli brought their joined hands to his mouth and kissed them. Did he feel the same pull Matías did? If he said anything, would it push Eli further away or bring him closer?

Matías was concentrating so hard on where they touched he hadn't noticed Eli slide a hand between them and cover Matías's cock. He went erect in seconds, and Eli chuckled.

"Jesus, Eli. You can't do that here."

"I'm feeling up my boyfriend. Nothing no one else doesn't do."

It sounded fantastic. The boyfriend thing, not the feeling him up thing. Although that sounded good, too.

Matías dropped his head forward, hiding his closed eyes and gaping mouth in Eli's neck. He panted against Eli's skin, the scent of lavender reaching his nose. He wanted more. He *needed* more, but not here. Not with an audience of over a hundred people.

"Eli…"

He gritted his teeth when Eli let go.

"I'm not teasing you." He smirked. "Well, maybe a bit." He chuckled and slid around in the seat so he faced Matías. "Do you want to dance some more?"

"I might have to sit here for a few minutes before I get up there again."

Eli shrugged. "It won't make any difference. The way we dance, we'll both be hard within seconds."

Matías grabbed the back of Eli's head and slammed their mouths together. He pulled back immediately, worried he'd been too rough. "I'm sorry—" Eli fused their mouths again, and Matías forgot what he was going to say. Eli straddled his lap and slid his arms around Matías's neck once more. It seemed to be his favourite position. Matías took everything Eli gave him, wanting nothing more than to give him everything right there and then. He had to be patient, though. He didn't think Eli was ready for that yet.

Eli slid his hand to Matías's chest and pulled back, panting. "We need to dance."

"This is not the place I will have you, however much I want to. When I get you home is when I'll take my time with you."

Eli paused, and something flashed in his eyes, but he smiled. "Let's go." He dragged Matías from the booth and to the dance floor, turning and moulding his back to Matías's chest again. Matías slid his hands down Eli's arms and clasped their hands. Sweat beaded on their skin and ran down their foreheads, but neither let go.

"I wish we could stay like this forever," Matías whispered, knowing Eli wouldn't be able to hear him over the music.

Eli, though, tensed and stepped away. He faced Matías with an expression twisted into pain. "This is not a forever thing, Matti."

"Fuck! I know, Eli. I know it's not. I wish...I wish..." He couldn't say it. He couldn't risk losing the best thing he'd ever had in his life. If he said the words, Eli would run. Matías knew he would.

"You wish what?"

"I wish things were different for us. That's all." It wasn't the whole truth, but it would have to do.

Eli stared at him for several long seconds, the dancers around them either oblivious or uncaring about the potential drama unfolding. Eli shook his head, and Matías saw him mouth the words, "I have to go."

He didn't know if Eli had said the words aloud or not, but Matías couldn't let him leave without trying to fix what he'd done. He followed him to the foyer doors, holding the door for him when he reached it. When they blocked out the music—which was worth the expense for soundproofing as far as Matías was concerned—he tried to talk to Eli again.

"I'm sorry. I know that's not where our relationship is going. Sometimes, it's hard to let the feelings go when we've been so close already. But I know where the line is. I promise I do."

Eli stared at the floor with his hands in his pockets. "Maybe this is a bad idea, Matti," he whispered, not looking at him. "As you said, we've already been close, perhaps too close, and it won't gain us anything because it's only pretend." Eli sighed. "I can't give you what you need."

"I know. You're already giving me a lot. I'm sorry. I really am. Don't let this ruin our friendship, Eli. Please."

Eli crossed his arms over his chest and stared at the wall. "I need time to think. Tell your family I have a busy schedule, and I'll come and visit when I can. Give me time." He met Matías's gaze. "I can't guarantee my answer will be the one you want—to keep going with this ruse—but I will give you an answer."

Matías's heart was in his throat, and he couldn't speak. He nodded as he held back the emotion he knew wouldn't help the matter at hand. "Please keep in touch. I want to make sure you're okay."

"I will."

Eli turned to the wardrobe staff member, who had kindly been ignoring them and pretending not to hear. He passed over his ticket and retrieved his coat. Matías took it from him and helped him into it. When they were facing each other again, Matías couldn't help but cup Eli's jaw and stare into his eyes.

"Please forgive me."

"There's nothing to forgive, Matti. I need to think."

Matías pressed a kiss to Eli's forehead and stepped back. He wanted to tell him he loved him but knew it would be better to run into a burning building than say the damning words. He watched as Eli left the building and dropped into the vacant seat, holding his head in his hands.

What had he done? He hadn't meant anything by the words. At least not on the surface. Maybe Eli had read as much into them as Matías had meant for them. Maybe he hadn't been as sneaky and smooth as he thought he'd been.

"What's wrong?"

Matías closed his eyes and sighed. Rafe. He lifted his head. "Nothing. A disagreement, nothing more."

Rafe raised his eyebrows. "You were so happy. What did you do?"

Matías stood and slashed his hand through the air. "Nothing, all right! We'll be fine." He approached the wardrobe staff and handed over his ticket. "I'll speak to you soon."

Matías threw the coat over his shoulders and stalked to the door.

"Matti." He paused. "You'll win him over. You're both perfect together. I can see it. Your family can see it, and I'm sure you can see it when you get your head out of your ass. Maybe Eli needs a little push in the right direction."

Matías pivoted on his heel and stared at Rafe. What the hell? "How did you know?" he whispered.

"I wasn't certain, but I overheard some of what you said."

"Are you mad at me?"

Rafe smiled and shook his head. "Nah. If I'd thought about it, I would've done the same. Family expectations are not for the ill at heart."

Matías snorted and stepped away from the door. "I don't know how to do it."

"To do what?"

"Make him fall in love with me."

To Matías's surprise, Rafe laughed. "That is not the problem."

"What do you mean?"

Rafe squeezed his shoulder. "If I'm not mistaken, he's already in love with you, and it scares the shit out of him. Your problem is how you're going to make him realise it's not the bad thing he thinks it is."

Matías stared, mouth open. "When did you figure all this shit out, and where was I when you were doing it?"

Rafe chuckled. "I enjoy watching people. You can learn a lot through that hobby." He sobered. "So, what are you going to do?"

"I'm going to give Eli the time he asked for. It's the least I can do after everything he's already done for me."

"Don't let him go too long without hearing from you, though. You don't want to lose the momentum you already have with him."

Matías nodded. "Thanks." He pulled him in for a hug and clapped his back. "I'll see you soon. Don't work too hard."

"As if I would."

Matías caught a taxi from outside the club and stared out of the window, not noticing the passing scenery. He was back in the foyer, but his words were different, and Eli's responses were different. If only. He was supposed to have invited Eli to dinner at his parents' house, but he'd have to make an excuse now. Why couldn't he learn to keep his mouth shut? He was always running headfirst into relationships and ruining them. Hadn't he learnt from all the other times he'd given people his heart, and they'd thrown it back in his face?

Granted, Eli hadn't done that because it wasn't supposed to be where they were headed, but Matías couldn't help it that Eli was an amazing person, inside and out. He wished he could get Eli to see exactly what he did for those around him.

Matías closed his eyes and shook his head. He'd completely forgotten to ask Eli about his father. What had he decided to do about him? Had he left already? Did Eli have to deal with this on his own as well?

So many questions he didn't have answers to because he had to open his mouth and let his secrets out. Maybe he should stop the whole ruse and start fresh with Eli. Woo him. Fight for him.

He couldn't accept he'd ruined things with Eli. He couldn't. There had to be a chance for them. There had to be.

Because Matías had never felt like this about anyone he'd ever been with before.

Chapter 18

Eli

Eli managed to block out Matías's words in the daytime. He threw himself into work, making the weddings the best they could be, training Alex as his assistant, and helping with the business side of things for Sarah's business. But at night, it was a different matter.

I wish we could stay like this forever.

The words had made Eli flinch at the time. Not because Matías sounded so honest, but because Eli's initial reaction was to agree. It had shaken him enough to pull away. Every night, though, he replayed the words, the atmosphere, the company, and he let himself believe it could happen. In the bright light of the morning, he reminded himself why it couldn't.

Matías had kept his promise and hadn't hounded Eli about getting together again. He had, however, messaged him every day, asking how he was, making sure he was eating and drinking enough. Matías had started his shift pattern again, so Eli's calendar told him, and he found himself keeping a closer ear on the news to make sure nothing big had happened.

Luckily, because he was so busy, he had little time to think about anything other than work, especially that weekend. Both he and Jasmine were full for the next three days, each having two or three weddings a day.

Eli had spoken to Sarah the previous morning, and she was a lot better. She had asked if Jasmine could continue for another couple of weeks, and then Sarah would take the reins back. Jasmine had agreed. Sarah had also said she would pay them for their help, and although Eli argued, she wouldn't be dissuaded.

His father was still around, too. That hadn't helped Eli's mood. His mother had called him several times, and though he'd answered, he refused to talk about Hayden. He'd also spoken to his sister and brothers, who confirmed they'd had a conversation with the man. Eli hated their mother had forced them into it. They should have had the choice, but his mother had taken the choice away from them. It would only end in tears, and he was saving himself from the pain.

"Everything is ready to go," Alex said, breaking into his maudlin thoughts.

"Thanks. Let's go."

Glad for the diversion, he threw himself into it, not stopping unless it was to grab a cup of tea or to eat. By the time he arrived home, it was nearing ten o'clock in the evening, and all he wanted to do was drop into bed and sleep. He wandered up the path, rummaging through his bag for his phone when a noise caught his attention. His gaze snapped up and met Matías's, who immediately stood and held out his hands.

"I'm not here for anything other than to bring you some food. Mum knew you've been busy and wanted to send something for you in case you hadn't had time to cook." He held up a bag. "I didn't want any animals to get into it, so I waited."

Eli wasn't sure what to say. "Thanks."

He continued up the path and took the bag, pausing for a second. He couldn't think of anything to say that would make things easier between them because Eli was still as confused as ever. His scent sent Eli's eyelids fluttering as he brushed past. There was just something about it.

"Sorry again," Matías whispered.

Eli unlocked the door and turned to invite Matías in, but he was already striding to his car. Eli's heart raced with the need to call him back, and it was for that reason he didn't. He watched Matías climb into his car and drive off. Closing the door with a soft click, he locked it and shuffled to the kitchen. He flicked on the lights and put the bags on the table. Opening the one from Sofía, he smiled when he saw spigola alla griglia—the meal he'd had when he went out with Matías for the first time. Had Matías requested the meal, or had it been purely coincidental?

He put the food into the microwave, not missing the part where it came with a container he would have to return, and emptied his work bags while it was heating. The scent of garlic filled the air, and Eli felt lighter than he had for several days. He pulled out his phone, hesitating before typing a message.

ELI: *Thank you for the food. I was hungrier than I thought I was. I'll return the dish as soon as I can.*

He wasn't sure what else to say, so he sent it as it was, hoping Matías would understand the underlying meaning behind his words. Eli was still no closer to figuring out the best course of action, but he was trying. Matías made him want things he couldn't trust, and that was thanks to his father.

The microwave pinged, and Eli brought out the food, inhaling deeply. He sat at the table and devoured the meal. When he finally took a breath, he patted his stomach and groaned. It had been delicious, but he'd eaten too much. He doubted he'd have trouble sleeping that night.

His phone chimed, but it was not who he wanted to speak to.

MUM: *Please give Hayden a chance to talk to you. You may not get another chance. I love you and will support your choice, but please think about it. I don't want you to regret missing out on the opportunity to speak to him. I love you. x*

Eli stared at the message and sighed. He didn't understand how *she* couldn't understand why he wouldn't speak with Hayden. The man had left them with nothing, and now, they expected him to forget all that and forgive him for his sins. Not going to happen.

ELI: *I love you, too. Get some sleep. x*

No promises, no anger, just sweet ignorance of what she'd asked. There was no other way to deal with it.

Eli put the dish in the sink and filled it with water, leaving it to soak, and headed for bed. Tomorrow was another busy day, and he had an early start. Unfortunately, his brain wouldn't switch off, and memories of him and Matías circled as he drifted off.

Eli entered the farmer's market and smiled at the atmosphere. He loved visiting this place but didn't get to go very often. It had been a busy week, but he'd had an impromptu day off when a wedding had been cancelled at the last minute. The couple had split up the previous day, though Eli didn't know the reasons for it. It meant he had a day to catch up on other things, but mainly, a chance to visit this place.

His mother had brought him to the farmer's market every month when he was a child. He remembered the liveliness of the people they met, the bright colours of the fruit, vegetables and other items. Despite the name, this market wasn't just about food. The organisers allowed people who sold their own creations to be there, too.

He slid his hands into his pockets and started down the first aisle. The vegetables were of good sizes and smelled amazing. As always, he refrained from buying the produce until the end. He wandered around, looking at the gift stalls.

He found a stall that had woodwork designs and noticed a wooden key on a keyring. Some of the other products had patterns burnt into the wood, and it gave Eli an idea.

"Excuse me? Would you be able to put some writing on this key? Is it big enough?" he asked the owner.

"Hi. It depends how many words there are."

"I want Devoted Weddings on it."

The man nodded. "Shouldn't be a problem. Would you like me to do it now for you?"

Eli's eyebrows raised. "You can do that?"

The man smiled. "Sure. If you can give me half an hour, I'll have it done for you."

"Brilliant." He paid for the item and carried on moving.

While he was here, he could look for something for his mother and Robbie's birthday because they were coming up in a couple of months, and he didn't know when he'd get the opportunity to come here again. With a plan in place, he checked out every stall. He found a snow globe for his mother, which had an ocean scene inside—kind of a contradiction because he didn't think it could snow in the water, but it looked amazing all the same.

Robbie was another matter. He was difficult to buy for. He found the perfect item when he saw a metal bottle opener with letters UCKER etched onto it and a dial in front of the letters with several letters on it. He could move the dial and change the word depending on the letter he chose. The letter choices were F, S, P and M. He thought all those words could describe Robbie at some point.

He headed back towards the woodworker but stopped when something caught his eye. There was a picture frame that had several pictures within it. Each picture was of a unique part of a firefighter's equipment or uniform but moulded into the shape of a letter. A rolled-up hose made the O, a crane made an R and many others. It was well done, and Eli couldn't get the idea out of his head. It was Matías's birthday in a couple of weeks, and though they hadn't seen each other since the night Matías brought him food, they had been messaging.

"Can I help you?"

"Yes. Can these be made to order?"

"Sure can. I usually say a week, but I can get it done sooner if necessary."

Eli smiled. "A week is perfect. Can I have the name Matías?"

The stall owner took his order, and Eli paid for it, then turned when he heard his name.

"Sofía! How nice to see you."

Sofía hugged him and held him by his arms. "It's been so long, Eli. I thought you'd emigrated."

Eli chuckled. "No. I've been really busy. With the two businesses, it's a bit hectic."

"I can imagine. Are you eating properly?"

"Yes. And thank you for the food the other week. I will return your dish. Promise."

Sofía waved her hand. "Don't worry. I have plenty more. What brings you here?"

Eli glanced around. "I love coming here. I used to come with Mum when I was younger, but when I got busy, I couldn't find the time. I only managed it today because a wedding was cancelled."

"Oh, that's terrible."

Eli shrugged. "It happens. Rarely, I might add, but it happens."

"Does that mean you're free tonight? Will you come for dinner? Say six o'clock?"

Eli could've slapped his forehead. Why had he told her he wasn't working? He could hardly decline the invitation now. "Sure."

"Wonderful!" Sofía glanced at the stall. "I've been trying to think of something to buy Matías for his birthday, but he's so difficult to buy for."

"My brother is the same. It takes a lot of thinking to find something."

"It does. What are you buying him?"

Eli cleared his throat. "I've actually just bought him one of those." He pointed to the picture frame.

Sofía covered her mouth with her hand. "It's beautiful. He'll love it."

"I hope so." Eli's phone rang, and he was grateful for the reprieve because, despite the fact he liked Sofía, she could be a bulldozer when she wanted to be. "I have to answer this. I'm sorry."

"Don't forget! Six o'clock!"

"I won't," he called back as he answered the phone. "Devoted Weddings. How can I help?"

He moved off to the side so he wasn't in anyone's way and answered the questions of the lady wanting to speak about what was involved in hiring him. When he finished ten minutes later, he ordered a herbal tea from a stall and wandered back around the market, checking on the fruit and vegetables. By the time he'd been through every stall, bags weighed him down. He'd remembered to go back to the woodworker and pick up the keyring. He couldn't wait to give it to its intended recipient.

He packed them away into the boot of his car and dropped into the driver's seat, exhaling. It wasn't even lunchtime, and he felt like he could sleep for a week. When he got home, he carried everything into the house and set about putting it away. He hadn't had the time to cook himself anything for a long time, and typically, he wouldn't that night either. Everything would keep, and he could do it another night. He needed to make an effort to cook for himself instead of relying on sandwiches or takeaway. He used to love cooking.

His phone chimed when he'd settled into his armchair to drink his tea.

MATÍAS: *Good morning, how are you?*

ELI: *I'm good, thanks. Just got back from the farmer's market with far too much food for me.*

MATÍAS: *There is no such thing as too much food, just not enough time to eat it.*

ELI: *Ha ha. Says you.*

MATÍAS: *I do. How are things with your father?*

ELI: *I've not seen him. I know he's still around, though, because Mum keeps messaging me to listen to him.*

MATÍAS: *You don't have to do anything you don't want to.*

ELI: *Thanks. I've been wondering lately if I should cave in and listen to him, but I don't want to hear his lies.*

The phone rang in his hand. Matías.

"Hey," Eli said.

"Hi. I thought it would be easier to talk this way. Is this okay?"

"I wouldn't have answered if I didn't want to talk to you."

Matías chuckled. "I'll remember that."

Eli laughed. "That's not what I meant."

"I know." Matías exhaled. "You don't have to listen to him if you don't want to. You have every right to be annoyed at him. He left you in a bad situation without any care in the world. Has he said why he's back?"

Eli huffed. "He says he's dying and wants to make amends. As if words can make up for what he did."

"How has your family taken it?"

"They've all spoken and visited with him. They all tell me I'm too hard on him, but I can't..." He cleared his throat. "I can't."

"Then don't. It's as simple as that. You need to do what you can live with. If talking to him is going to cause you to regret it, don't do it. If not talking to him is how you can be happy living your life, then don't. You do what's best for you. Everyone else will do the same."

Eli's throat closed up, and he battled with the need to cry. "How come everyone else is so much wiser than me?"

Matías laughed. "I'm not wise, but you're too close to the situation that everything is blurry."

"Harry would like the analogy."

Matías chuckled again. "He would." Eli heard some noise in the background. "Sorry, I'm going to have to go. I'm helping Rafe move some stuff, and he's a taskmaster."

"I can imagine. Have fun."

"I will. You take it easy."

There was silence, and Eli took the phone away from his ear to see if the connection had ended, but Matías was still there.

"Look, Eli…I'm sorry for everything that's happened. You're going through so much. You don't need my crap on top of it. I'm seeing my family tonight. I'll tell them we broke up."

"No! Don't. I'm good, Matti. We're good. I need to get my head around it."

Silence again, and Matías said, "Okay. I'll wait a few more days. See you soon."

"Bye, Matti."

Eli didn't know why he hadn't told Matías he would be at his family dinner that night. Was he hoping to talk himself out of it? Did he want to talk himself out of it? No, he didn't. He missed Matías; that much was true, but he was concerned if he let this carry on too long, he would cave to his desire to stay with Matías, and they would both end up hating each other. He refused to do it to him, but he would keep his promise and give Matías a reprieve until his birthday. It was the least he could do.

He spent the afternoon catching up on emails and returning phone calls, then showered and dressed to get ready for dinner. When he got to Sofía's, there were several cars already there, including Matías's. He grabbed the dessert he'd made—a lemon meringue pie—and rang the doorbell. He could hear voices inside, and he smiled, knowing what he would find.

The door opened, and Matías stared at him.

"Surprise," Eli said with a shrug.

"I didn't know you were coming."

"Your mum invited me earlier today. We bumped into each other at the farmer's market."

Matías narrowed his eyes. "And you didn't tell me when we spoke earlier because..."

Eli grinned. "You didn't need to know."

Matías chuckled. "Come on in. Mum would have my hide if I left you on the doorstep."

Eli juggled the dessert while removing his coat with Matías's help and followed him through to the kitchen.

"Eli!" Sofía came over and kissed his cheek. "I'm so glad you could make it."

"Thank you for inviting me. Here." He handed her the dessert. "It's nothing special, but it's my mum's favourite recipe."

"Ah, pollito. Gracias. You didn't need to, but thank you."

"Now, I understand why there was an extra table setting," Matías whispered in his ear, and Eli shivered. "Are you sure you're okay doing this?"

Eli nodded. "Yes."

Matías pressed his lips to Eli's temple, a move he'd noticed Matías liked to do. "Come on. Sit with me."

Following Matías was no hardship. He wouldn't have been able to change directions if he tried.

Chapter 19

Matías

Matías pulled Eli into the seat beside him and grabbed hold of his hand. He hadn't expected Eli to turn up, but his plea earlier that day now made sense. Eli fit in with his family. There was no awkwardness, no uncomfortable silences. Just cheerful banter and conversation. He had to let go of Eli's hand when the plates were handed out, which was a shame, but he could find another excuse to touch him later. They were, after all, still pretending.

"Eli, Matías tells us you've been busy. Are you going to be able to make it to his party next month?" Diego asked.

Eli smiled. "It's already in my diary. I have a wedding that day, but the evening is free."

"Wonderful. If you thought the members of the family you met at the party for Angelique were bad, you wait until you see a birthday party." Diego winked.

"Don't scare him, Dad," Matías said. "He might change his mind."

Eli covered Matías's hand. "I won't change my mind."

They locked gazes, and Eli seemed to be saying more than what the conversation was about. Was he giving them a chance? Eli refocused on his food, and Matías was more confused than ever.

"Alejo, what news do you have today?" his mother asked.

His brother shook his head. "I have nothing good to say. We took away several children from their parents. One had severe trauma and was hospitalised. It's been a tough week."

"I'm sorry, hijo. Not every week is like this, though. Soon, things will be better."

"I know."

Matías leaned closer to Eli, whispering in his ear, "Alejo is a social worker."

"Isabella? What about you?"

"Mum goes around to everyone at the table and asks them to find something good in their week to talk about," he said, moving back.

Isabella sighed. "Well, we got in a supply of the medicine we'd been waiting weeks for. It's a shame it won't last very long. There are so many people waiting for it."

"But many people will be healthier now because of it," Sofía said. "Justin?"

"I finalised a deal to merge two companies. It's been a work in progress for months."

"Congratulations," everyone said.

"Matías?" Sofía asked.

He put his cutlery down and twined his hands in his lap. "We saved a brother and sister from a house fire, and Nash didn't burn the food."

"I'm so glad you were able to save them, hijo. And hallelujah." Sofía threw her hands in the air. "What did he cook?"

"Spaghetti bolognese."

"Tell him good job from me, okay? Diego, do you have some good thoughts this week?"

His father steepled his fingers and stayed silent for a moment. "This week, we have a new addition to our table, and nobody tried to rob the bank."

Everyone laughed.

"Does it happen a lot?" Eli asked. "People trying to rob it?"

Diego chuckled. "No, luckily. The only time someone tried was about five years ago, and they got caught quick enough to not get a penny."

"I don't think I could do that job."

"Dad scares everyone," Alejo said.

"I do not." Diego smiled. "Okay, only those who should be." He clapped his hands. "What about you, my love?"

Sofía stared at the occupants of the table in turn and smiled. "I see my family growing, falling in love, getting married, having wonderful careers, being healthy, being kind. I can't ask for a better family."

From the corner of his eye, he saw Eli put his fork down and twist his hands in his lap. He reached over and covered his hands, but Eli pushed him away. He knew their fake relationship was weighing on his mind. Matías decided once dinner was over, he would tell Eli the truth. All of it. He hoped it would be enough to get Eli to see how good they were together.

"Eli, would you like to say something?" Sofía asked. "You don't have to, but I didn't want to leave you out."

Eli licked his lips, and Matías stared at his profile.

"I'm grateful for a new friend who has recently come out of hospital. She had been in an accident, but she's gaining strength every day."

"I'm so glad to hear that." Sofía clasped her hands to her chest. "So many things to be thankful for."

They continued to eat, although Eli at a slower speed than before. Matías felt ashamed for having taken advantage of the man, even though the idea had been Eli's in the first place. Matías should've said no. It was too hard on Eli, and Matías wasn't being fair to him. He focused on his food and tried to keep his hopes up as the meal drew to a close.

Alejo and Isabella were on dish duty, so Matías took Eli to one side and asked to speak with him. He led him into the living room and closed the door.

"What's wrong?" Eli asked.

Matías wet his lips, unable to meet Eli's gaze. "There's something I need to tell you." He rubbed the back of his neck.

"Okay." Eli sounded confused, which was understandable.

Matías wasn't sure where to start. "I'm in love with you." Blurting it out might not have been the best option.

Eli stayed quiet, and Matías eventually lifted his head. The colour had left Eli's face, and Matías could see a tremble in his limbs.

"Shit. Sit down, Eli." He guided him to the sofa. "Sorry. Fuck. I shouldn't have said it like that."

Eli dropped his head into his hands. "This was not supposed to happen," he murmured.

"Do you…" He paused, not knowing what to say. He rolled his eyes. He'd already blurted out the L-word. He might as well go out with a bang. "Do you feel anything for me? Could you feel anything?"

"Jesus. Fuck. Shit. Damn." The curse words kept coming from Eli's mouth, which Matías took as a bad omen.

"I wanted you to know—"

"So, I'd feel like shit when I tell you no, I don't," Eli said, standing from the sofa. He moved to the other side of the room.

"No! I never want you to feel like shit."

"Well, you're out of luck." Eli shook his head and huffed a non-humorous laugh.

"I'm sorry. I thought we'd grown closer over the last few weeks. I can't help how I feel. You're an amazing man, Eli. Anyone would be lucky to have you."

"But don't you get it. I don't want anyone. I told you that. It's why I agreed to this in the first place."

"I know. I thought maybe…"

Eli snorted. "You thought you could completely ignore the words I said in the beginning and try to change who I am."

Matías held out his hands. "No. I would never change you. You're perfect as you are."

"But you want me to love you. I told you I would never be with anyone in a relationship. I told you what my father did. I told you how broken and depressed my mother was. I told you what we went through when he left. Why can't you understand I will *not* let that happen to me?"

Matías swallowed through the lump in his throat. "I do understand, but I thought we were different."

Eli dropped his head back and stared at the ceiling. "We are different, Matías." The use of his full name was like a bullet slamming into him. "You're capable of love. I'm not."

"That's not—"

"That's *my* truth." Eli stared at him. "That's *my* reality." He exhaled. "I guess that's where we leave it. I assume you'll tell your family we broke up."

Matías clenched his jaw and nodded, wanting nothing more than to scream and shout until Eli changed his mind, but that was the problem, wasn't it? Eli had hit the nail on the head with his words. Matías *had* tried to change Eli; he just hadn't realised it.

"Thank you for everything," Matías said. He didn't move closer, worried Eli would pull away. He didn't think he could take any more refusals.

"You're welcome. I apologise about missing your birthday."

Matías nodded. "Can I walk you out?"

"Yes, thank you."

Making sure to keep plenty of distance, Matías led the way to the front door, handing Eli his coat. He kept his body tense, not wanting to let on how distraught he was.

"Goodbye, Matías."

"Goodbye, Eli." His voice cracked on the words as he held the door open.

Eli exited the house, and Matías closed the door, unable to watch him leave.

"Matías? Where's Eli going?"

Matías rested back against the door and slid to the floor, dropping his head to his knees. The tears he'd held back broke free, and he sobbed.

"Oh, Matías! What happened?" His mother knelt beside him, rubbing his hair as she used to when he was a child.

"It's over," he whispered. "We're over."

"What! Why?"

"He doesn't love me."

Sofía gasped. "That's a load of rubbish if ever I heard it. Of course, he does. I can see it as plain as day in his face."

Matías lifted his head. "You're wrong." He stood. "I have to go."

"No, Matías. Stay here for a while." She reached up and cupped his face. "Stay with us."

Matías shook his head. "I need to go. Please say goodbye to everyone."

"Matías..."

"No, Mum. I have to go."

He pulled on his coat and shoes, and with a small smile for his mum, he left, climbed into his car and drove. With nowhere in mind, he drove, knowing he couldn't go home because Alejo would go straight there when his mum told them what she'd seen. Up and down roads, over roundabouts, under bridges, until he stopped the car outside a house. He stared at the shadows behind the curtains, lit by a light from behind, not sure if he wanted to be seen or not.

Matters were taken out of his hands when the door opened, and a man strode towards him. Matías wound down the window.

"Are you coming in?" Quinn asked, crossing his arms over his chest, no doubt to keep the cold at bay.

"I don't know." His voice sounded wrong.

"We have cheesecake." Matías remained silent, his thoughts numb. "And Paul is trying to play Twister with the kids. It's not going well."

Matías turned off the ignition and raised the window, climbing out of the car to stand beside his chief's husband. Quinn threaded his arm through Matías's arm and tugged him towards the house.

"When I left them, Paul was twisted up like a pretzel. I bet he's on the floor by now. I'm not convinced Twister is supposed to be played by adults."

Matías was glad for the continued one-sided conversation. It meant he didn't have to say anything in return. They entered the house, the heat trying valiantly to warm Matías, but it couldn't reach where it was needed most—his heart.

"We'll give them a few more minutes while I brew some tea."

Quinn deposited him on a stool at the tall table in the kitchen, and Matías stared at his hands. How could he have been so stupid? He honestly thought Eli returned his feelings. Had he been projecting his feelings onto him? He ran through some of their dates, and he couldn't see when he fell for him. It wasn't one thing Eli did that made Matías realise. He'd slowly fallen in love with the amazing man, but he couldn't have him. He could see times when he thought Eli seemed happy, but did happiness mean he had feelings?

Quinn placed a cup in front of him and squeezed his shoulder before disappearing. Matías watched the steam rising, unsure of his next actions. He felt adrift, and it was his own fault. He'd poured so much hope into him and Eli as a couple and had kept nothing back for himself.

Matías glanced to the side when someone sat beside him.

"How are you holding up?" Paul asked, sipping his tea.

Matías dropped his gaze to his cup again. "I've been better." They sat in silence, but Matías felt fidgety. "You can say I told you so."

"I wouldn't do that to you. Everyone walks their own path. Others can give advice, but the person walking it chooses the route. No one can foresee how the other path would've worked out because it's not viable anymore."

"I honestly thought he might feel the same."

"Maybe he does, maybe he doesn't. Whatever he feels doesn't matter, unfortunately. You have to listen to what he's saying. No means no. It doesn't matter if his actions show otherwise."

Wasn't that the truth of the matter? Eli could love Matías and deny it until his dying day, and Matías could do nothing about it.

"I'm worried about him. He has so much going on; he's going to burn out if he's not careful. I wanted to help him."

"Help him by listening to him. If he changes his mind, he'll come to you."

Matías glanced at him. "How do you know?"

Paul smiled. "Because love is worth risking everything for. You should know that."

"I do." Matías lifted the tea to his mouth and drank. He didn't feel better about leaving Eli to deal with everything by himself, but he couldn't ignore what Eli had asked for.

Their goodbye had been their last words to each other. Now, Matías had to live his life, but he'd never give up hope that Eli might come back to him.

"Thanks, Chief."

"Thank me by helping me beat these kids at Twister."

Paul twisted on the stool and stood, taking both their empty cups to the sink. When he turned back, he had a smile on his face.

"Those kids are going down."

Matías chuckled for what felt like the first time in months and followed Paul into the living room. Three people were tangled up on the floor, and Matías couldn't help but laugh.

"What made you agree to this?" he asked.

Paul narrowed his eyes at the tangled heap. "The kids said I was getting old."

Matías shook his head, hiding a smile. "No way, Chief. You could give every crew member at the station a run for their money." He had an idea. "Hey, it could be a charity event. The crew against the boss." Paul stared at him, and Matías lowered his head. "Or maybe not."

"Get the idea out of your head right now. I *am* too old for that crap. Why do you think I'm the station commander now and not a firefighter?"

"Because you're damn good at your job?"

Paul laughed. "Nice sucking up, but it doesn't get you out of this." He waved a hand towards the now fallen heap of bodies. "Matías's turn."

"Oh, thank god," Quinn said, crawling from the pile. "I love you, dear husband, but you have some shitty ideas sometimes."

Paul threw his head back and laughed. "You're right, but that's why you love me."

"Always." Quinn kissed him and focused on Matías. "You're up."

Matías held out his hand. "I don't think I'm bendy enough."

"Neither am I. Have fun," Paul said.

Matías sighed. "Okay, fellas. What's the deal here?"

Eddie grinned. "Papa said there was no way we could beat him at Twister. We've proved him wrong several times, but he keeps trying."

Toby threw his arm around Eddie's neck. "He did better than I expected."

Paul and Quinn's adopted twin boys had certainly grown up fast. Paul had shared their background with the crew members because he didn't want them to inadvertently say something that might trigger them, especially with how often the crews visited their home. After everything the boys had been through, finding Paul and Quinn had been the best thing for them because Matías could see how happy they were. The darkness that had been there had slowly diminished, and now all that was left was happiness. Both Eddie and Toby were at university, and although they could have stayed at the housing on-site, they chose to stay home. Matías knew Paul and Quinn didn't mind.

He clapped his hands. "Okay. Let's give this a whirl." He could fake being content as much as the next person.

He spent the next hour laughing so hard he thought his sides would bruise. Contorting himself into positions he never thought he'd be able to was unexpectedly hilarious, especially when the kids were doing the same. He was surprised none of them had broken bones by the end with how hard they fell sometimes.

Paul called time, and they relaxed with another drink before Matías stood to leave. Quinn pulled him into a hug.

"You know you're welcome here whenever you want or need us." Quinn tapped his cheek gently.

"Thank you." He said goodbye to the kids, and Paul walked him to the door. "Sorry to turn up and bust in on your family night."

Paul backhanded his shoulder. "You're family, too. You don't need to apologise for needing someone."

Matías smiled, small though he knew it was. He didn't like the idea of going home because he knew Alejo would be there to grill him about the evening.

"You can stay here if you want."

Matías shook his head. "No point burying my head in the sand." He hugged Paul and left, wishing he'd taken Paul up on his offer, but his words still held true. The longer he left facing his brother, the harder it would be. At least he would have work to keep him occupied in a couple of days.

He braced himself before he entered his apartment but found it empty and a note from Alejo on the fridge.

Thought I'd give you some breathing room. I don't know what happened, but I know you'll be hurting. If you need me to come back, I'm a phone call away. If you don't, that's fine. I'll be back tomorrow evening. Don't lose yourself. A x

The love and affection in the note gave Matías the strength to get through the night and the following day. With each hour that passed, he grew stronger, despite not wanting to. Would he ever see Eli again? It was something he couldn't predict. It wouldn't stop him from remembering what they'd been through together. It wouldn't stop him from remembering how Eli felt wrapped in his arms while they made love. That's what it had been for Matías, regardless of how Eli saw it. Matías wouldn't belittle his feelings. He was in love with Eli, and he'd have to live without him.

Chapter 20

Eli

Eli threw himself into his work after leaving Matías. He barely slept four hours a night, but he was so productive he found himself wallowing in the spare time he never usually had. He spent time creating a business plan for when he took Jasmine on as a partner, developing new ideas for weddings and sourcing new companies and locations. All things he would never have had the time for before.

However, his mother had been on his back for the past five days. Every day, she called, asking him to meet with Hayden. Every day, he had declined. His sister would call and talk about Hayden as if the man had never left them. He was finding himself getting angrier by the day. Angry at his mother, his siblings, his father, Matías. He wished they would leave him in peace.

To make matters worse, he'd received a call from the photographer who'd created the picture frame for Matías's birthday, saying it was ready for collection. Eli had asked him if he could keep hold of it, for now, to which the man had agreed. Eli had no idea what to do about it, so he pushed it from his mind.

"Devoted Weddings. How can I help?" he asked when he answered his phone.

"Good morning, Eli. How are you today?"

He closed his eyes. "Hello, Mum."

"Are you free for dinner tonight?"

"I'm sorry, I have plans."

"Hayden won't be there in case you were worried."

Eli snorted. "And why would I believe you when you set us up last week?"

"Eli!"

"It's true, Mum. You didn't let us permit you to introduce him. You had no right."

"I'm your mother. I have every right."

Eli inhaled, trying to keep hold of his temper. "No, you don't. If we were kids, possibly. Now, though, we're adults and have the right to make our own choice. You didn't give us the option. You threw him at us and expected us to bend to your will."

"I did what I thought was right."

Eli's temper cracked. "Exactly. You did what *you* thought was right with no consideration for us. You knew I didn't want to see him. I haven't kept my disdain for him a secret over the years."

"You need to see how he's changed."

He was done. "I don't give a fuck how he's changed. All I care about is what he put us through. He has no right to come swanning back into our lives and expect us to drop everything and welcome him with open arms. He's a thief. He's a liar. He's a coward."

The silence on the end of the phone was complete until he heard a sniffle, but he wouldn't cave. She had no right to choose for him, and he wasn't backing down.

"Okay."

Eli frowned. "Okay?"

His mum sniffed again. "Yes. Okay. You're right. I sometimes forget how old you were. How much responsibility you had to take on at fifteen. I've pushed all those painful years into a box and shut the lid, trying to keep my head above water because I had you kids to look after. I haven't allowed myself to open the box yet. I thought it would be better if I kept it locked away, but…I need to face it."

"You don't need to face it, Mum. Let us choose if we want him in our lives."

"I'm sorry for pushing, Eli. I'll stop."

Eli chuckled. "No, you won't. It will be about something else instead."

Karen giggled. "Probably. Which reminds me, how are things with your boyfriend?"

Eli's happier mood plummeted. "It ended."

"I'm sorry. What happened?"

He picked up a pen and tapped it on the pad of paper in front of him. "He wanted more than I was willing to give."

"Oh, Eli. Don't let your father ruin your relationships. Not everyone is like he was."

"It's fine. I'm sorry I can't come for dinner. I'll sort out when I'm next free and let you know."

She sighed. "Okay. Love you."

"Love you, too."

When the doorbell rang, he dropped his phone and rubbed a hand over his face. He contemplated ignoring it but thought better of it.

"Sarah! Wow, I wasn't expecting you. Come on in." He stepped back, opening the door wider. "How are you?"

"I'm doing much better now, thanks. I thought I'd come and discuss things with you if you have time."

"Yes, actually. I rarely book weddings on Mondays, and the one you have booked, Jasmine is taking care of."

"She's an angel."

"She certainly is." He stopped outside his office. "Would you like a drink?"

"Coffee would be great if you have any."

"Sure. Make yourself comfortable in the office, and I'll get it brewed." He pointed to the door and left her alone.

He hadn't expected Sarah to be up to discussing business for a few more days, but it was a grateful distraction for him. Anything to get his mind off the troubles in his life. He made a coffee for Sarah and a peppermint tea for himself and carried them into the office on a tray, complete with some biscuits.

He handed Sarah her coffee, and she inhaled deeply. "I've missed coffee," she said. She must've seen Eli's confusion because she laughed. "I've only just been allowed to have it again, and I'd forgotten how much I loved it."

Eli smiled and sat on the opposite sofa. "Are you back to full strength now?"

"Coffee? Yes. Body? Almost."

Eli chuckled. "I'm glad."

Sarah sat forward. "I cannot thank you enough for stepping in, Eli. It had never occurred to me I would need a backup plan in case something happened to me. Working alone has its perks, but it also has its downfalls, as we've found out."

"Definitely. Are you still determined to take over again next week?"

Sarah smiled. "Yes. Definitely. I'm going stir crazy doing nothing all day."

"I can imagine. I can't remember the last time I had nothing to do."

"Exactly. So, I thought I would start getting my hands dirty again with the administration side of things if you're ready to let them go."

Eli smiled. "I'm happy to go through everything with you. Make sure you're well enough, though. I don't mind holding onto all or some of it while you find your feet again."

"Thank you."

Eli stood, putting his cup on the coffee table. "Let me move this chair, and we can get you behind the desk with me so you can see what's happening in your world."

He spent the next two hours going through all of Sarah's upcoming bookings, making sure everything was in place. By the time they'd finished, she had a to-do list the length of a church aisle, but she seemed brighter and happier than when she'd arrived.

"I can't believe you kept taking bookings for me. I was sure I was going to have to start from scratch again. You're amazing, Eli. Thank you so much."

"You're welcome. I'm glad I could help."

"Few people would've done what you did."

Eli waved her away. "It worked in my favour, to be honest."

"What do you mean?"

"Well, Jasmine has been my assistant for years, and she's amazing at it. When I decided to help you, I knew I couldn't do all the weddings myself. It's why I asked Jasmine to do it. I knew she was more than capable, and it gave me the kick up the backside I needed to fire her and take her on as a business partner instead. I don't know when it would've happened if I hadn't taken on your business, too."

"Well, I'm glad something else good came out of it. Jasmine is an excellent wedding planner."

"She is."

"Right. I'll let you get on with your own work. I've monopolised your time enough." Sarah stood. "Thank you again, and don't let this be the end of our conversation, Eli. Don't be a stranger, okay?"

Eli smiled. "You got it."

He showed her out and headed for his kitchen to get some lunch. It had been nice to talk business with someone else. With Jasmine being so busy with Sarah's bookings, they hadn't had as much time to chat as they used to, and Eli missed it. Hopefully, they could start again once Jasmine was back with him full-time.

He'd bitten into his sandwich when the doorbell rang again. Cursing, he strode to the door and flung it open, wishing he'd ignored it this time.

"What do you want?"

His father stood on his doorstep, hands clasped in front of him. "I'm going to be leaving soon, and I wanted the chance to talk to you once more before I go."

"I have nothing left to say to you."

"I have a few things to say to you, though."

Eli considered shutting the door in his face, but his mother's pleas circled his head. He opened the door wider, allowing his father in. Leading the way to his office, he sat behind his desk and crossed his arms, waiting.

"I know you hate me for what I did. I hate myself for it, and I know there is nothing I can do to stop the past pain I've caused. You don't need to forgive me. I don't want you to, but I want to ease some of the burden I've placed on you." Hayden held out an envelope, which Eli took with trepidation. As he looked at it, Hayden continued, "This is in no way a bribe for forgiveness. As I said, I don't expect it, but I would like to pay for any grandchildren you four may have to have a chance at university. I have placed this amount into a fund you and your mother can access at any time. I have no access to it, and I have placed everything in your names." He cleared his throat. "I am extremely sorry for what you went...for what I put you through."

Hayden turned and walked out of the room and the house without another word.

Eli's gaze was stuck on the contents of the envelope. He had transferred the fund into their names, as Hayden had said, but Eli couldn't stop staring at the figure. One point two million pounds.

Despite his hatred for the man, Eli felt a weight lifted from his shoulders. He'd been concerned about how he could afford to pay for any kids they had to go to school. He knew he would've figured it out, but with this, and hopefully, no strings attached, he didn't have to worry.

But then he got angry. Although Hayden had said it wasn't a bribe, it certainly felt like one. What had he offered the others for their forgiveness? He threw the paperwork onto his desk and focused on the screen of his laptop. Nothing had changed. He wouldn't accept a penny from that man.

"What happened with Matías?" Jasmine asked when she arrived. "Jason told me you broke up."

Eli snorted. "You could say that."

"What's that supposed to mean?" She dropped her bag to the floor and dropped into the visitor's chair. The chair he hadn't offered his father seven days ago when he'd arrived with the bribe.

He refocused on Jasmine, trying to remember her question. "It was all fake, Jasmine. We were pretending to be together to give Matías a break from his family breathing down his neck about his lack of relationship." He stared at his laptop.

"What? No way! There's no way you could fake that."

Eli raised his eyebrows. "Why not?"

"I saw you two together. There's no faking how you feel about each other."

Eli stood, picking some papers he needed to put in the filing cabinet. "It was fake, Jasmine," he repeated. "Believe what you want to believe, but it was a ruse that has now ended." He flicked through the folders, buying as much time as he could before he had to face her.

"Why would you agree to it?"

Eli rested his arms on the cabinet and paused, thinking back to the pain in Matías's voice that day at his sister's wedding. Matías's mother and aunt had both been trying to figure out why Matías couldn't keep anyone for longer than a few weeks, and every word they said had hurt Eli, even though they weren't about him. Matías's dejected look didn't help. Eli couldn't even remember walking across the space between them. Only the touch of his lips against Matías's cheek and the warmth of his hand.

"Eli?"

Eli blinked and cleared his throat. "He seemed upset, and his family wouldn't leave him alone. I wanted to help."

"Why?"

"Does it matter? It's done now."

Jasmine stood, crossing her arms over her chest. "Yes, it matters."

Eli moved from one filing cabinet to the other. "I told you, I wanted to help."

"But why him, Eli? I'm sure there are many people out there who could do with similar help, and you've not offered it to them. Why Matías?"

"What do you want me to say, Jasmine? I felt sorry for him. It wasn't fair how they were treating him." He slammed the drawer shut and glared at her, then moved towards the coffee table, ready to tidy it.

"Eli, sit down!" Jasmine shouted.

Eli immediately sat because Jasmine never raised her voice in that tone. It was only ever in jest. She sat beside him on the sofa and took his hand.

"You need to stop."

"Stop what?"

"Just stop. How many hours have you worked this week? Eighty? Ninety? More?" She shook her head. "You won't be any use to the business if you're burnt out."

"I'm fine."

"No, you're not. You're grieving."

Eli pulled his hand free. "I'm not."

Jasmine sighed. "You're grieving the loss of your father again, even though he's not dead. You're grieving the loss of the close connection you had with your family, even though it hasn't gone away. You're grieving the loss of control."

"I haven't lost control of anything." Eli glared at her, clenching his jaw and wishing he'd never told her anything about his father or Matías or his family.

"You've lost control of your heart, Eli. You fell in love with Matías and have done everything you can to deny it, but nothing can stop the heart from wanting what it wants. Your words might deny it, but your heart won't allow it."

"I'm not...He's not..." Eli felt his heart racing and his stomach churning. The denial on his lips wouldn't come. He closed his eyes. "I can't love him. What if he leaves me?"

"What if he doesn't?"

"What if I've ruined everything with him?"

"What if you haven't? What if he's waiting for you? What if he's giving you time? What if you allow yourself to love?

What if you live happily ever after? So many what-ifs, Eli, and none of them are bad."

Eli leaned forward and dropped his head into his hands as sobs wracked his body. What had he done?

Jasmine's arms came around him, and he leaned into her. She had been completely right about everything, but he didn't know if his mind could go after what his heart wanted. His brain was mixed up, battling between what he thought was right and what his heart said was true. Matías said he loved him, but did he? Had he seen all the darkness in Eli, the need to be in control, the need to take care of people, the need to interfere where it wasn't always welcome? Could he love someone like Eli?

He wiped his face and pulled back, inhaling deeply and blowing it out shakily. Glancing at Jasmine, he caught her smile. "Sorry."

"I've been worried about you for a while, Eli. You take on so much by yourself and don't let people help. You don't have to carry the world on your shoulders. Let others share the load."

"I think I've ruined things with him."

Jasmine lifted a shoulder. "You won't know unless you speak to him."

Eli frowned. "It's his birthday in four days. I don't want to ruin his party."

Jasmine grinned. "I don't think you could, but what a great time to show him how you feel."

Eli shook his head, eyes widening. "I couldn't do it in front of all his family. What if he turns me down?"

"There's that what if again. What if he doesn't?" She smiled. "If you're worried, why not have a conversation with his mother? You said she seemed nice. She might help."

"She might also stab me with a knife because I hurt her son."

She laughed. "There is that, too. What have you got to lose?"

"Other than my life? Nothing, I suppose."

"Then get on the phone."

Chapter 21

Matías

"Come on, Matías. Cheer up. It's not the end of the world," Kai said. Willow backhanded him. "What?"

"Leave him alone. He's broken up with someone. Give him a few weeks to mourn the loss," she hissed.

Kai shrugged. "They weren't even together properly."

Since he'd broken up with Eli, he'd told the members of his crew and a few other firefighters what had happened and that it was all pretend. They'd commiserated with him, and a couple had said he was an idiot for doing it in the first place, but most of them supported him. Not that it mattered because it was over.

He hadn't told his family the truth, only that they'd broken up and weren't talking, but maybe they could get back to being friends again, eventually. He didn't know what else to say to them, and they'd blissfully left him in peace. It wouldn't last. His mother had already rung asking when he was next coming for dinner. As if he could face their house when it was the place he'd lost hope.

Nash brought him another beer and dropped into the seat beside him. They were all at Paul's house for a spring barbecue because the weather had turned so good. Some members of Green Watch crew had already left to take over from White Watch, some of whom were supposed to be visiting after they'd finished their shift. As for Matías's crew, they were all here, as were Red Watch. For the first time in a long time, most of the firefighters of Cam Fire and Rescue had attended.

"Burgers should be ready soon. Do you all have drinks?" Paul asked from his position in front of the grill.

"Yes, Chief," Jason called. "All set up for the pre-puking game."

"Hey, speak for yourself," Kai said. "I never puke after drinking."

"Yeah, after drinking coffee. It's another thing when it's alcohol." Iris laughed. "I remember the last time we went out. Wasn't a pretty picture."

"I mixed drinks. You know no one should ever do that. What did you expect me to do?"

"I expected you to aim for the floor, not my shirt." Iris raised her eyebrows.

Everyone jeered at Kai.

"Burgers are ready. Come get 'em," Paul said.

"You want one?" Nash asked, standing.

Matías shook his head. "I'm good."

He watched his friends and co-workers grab a burger each from the rapidly diminishing pile. Paul already had another batch cooking on the barbecue with hot dogs as well this time.

"How are you feeling?" Quinn asked from beside him.

Matías rolled his head on the back of the chair where it rested and smiled. "I'm fine."

"Is the distraction working?" Quinn gestured to the people around them. Matías grimaced. "Didn't think so. In which case..." He held out a tumbler of what smelled like whiskey. "Here's to getting rat-arsed drunk."

Matías took the glass. "Why are you drinking?"

"No one drinks alone in my house." Quinn grinned. "Plus, Paul is in charge tonight."

They clinked glasses, and Matías sipped the drink, wincing at the strong burn in his throat. It wasn't his usual choice, but he wouldn't turn down the opportunity to be blissfully numb.

"Are you looking forward to your birthday? It's only a couple of days away now, isn't it?"

Matías nodded. "Yeah, two days. I could do without it if I'm honest, but Mum insisted since we'd already invited everyone."

"Here's to family's being a pain in the ass." Quinn clinked their glasses again, and Matías dutifully drank.

By the time he'd finished the whiskey, he felt more relaxed than he'd been in weeks. After a couple more, he was the jolly drunk he always was, singing and dancing with the rest of the crews. When he'd finally got tired, someone showed him to a bed, and he promptly passed out.

Bright light piercing his retinas and skull woke him, but he could tell immediately he shouldn't move. Even scrunching his eyes up to reduce the amount of light getting through made him queasy. He tried to recall anything, but it was a blur of music, laughter and eating. He had a feeling he hadn't eaten. It might account for the tenuous hold he had on his stomach.

The problem was he needed to pee. He inhaled through his nose and didn't recognise the scent of the sheets, so he assumed he was still at Paul's house.

Slowly, things cleared up, and he remembered Quinn plying him with whiskey, and a vision of him on the picnic table, singing *Come On, Eileen*. If that image was true, he wished he were dead.

Someone knocked, and the sound ricocheted through his head, and he groaned. A door opened.

"I assume from that noise you are awake and regretting your choices."

Matías grunted, giving the only answer he could muster.

Paul chuckled. "Well, you have a clear run for the bathroom now everyone is up and out of the house, so if you need to go, go now."

Matías tentatively rolled to his back, stopping when he got there to breathe through the nausea.

"May I suggest you get up and go to the bathroom quickly? I have a feeling your drink will reappear in...three, two, one..."

Matías bolted from the bed and barely made it to the toilet before he threw up. The stench made his stomach worse, but once he'd cleared himself out—for this bout at least—he felt better. He grabbed some tissue, wiped his face and flushed the toilet, sinking to his ass on the floor next to it and leaning against the bath. Paul passed him a cup of water, and he sipped at it.

"Thanks," he croaked. His throat was on fire.

"No thanks needed. It's the least I can do when my husband made you like this." Paul wet a flannel and rolled it, sitting on the edge of the bath and holding it against Matías's nape.

Matías closed his eyes. "It's not his fault. He gave me what I wanted."

"What was that?"

"To forget for a while."

Paul removed the flannel, refolded it and placed it back again. "Has it made it any easier?"

Matías didn't answer. He didn't need to. It hadn't done a damn bit of difference. His stomach churned again, and he rose to his knees.

By the time his stomach had settled, Paul had brought him two bacon and egg sandwiches and a large glass of water, and once he'd finished it all, Paul had sent him back to bed. This time under the covers with fewer clothes.

When he woke the second time, he felt much better. He had no idea what time it was because there wasn't a clock in the room, and his phone was somewhere amongst the clothes he pulled off earlier, but the sun was still shining, so it couldn't be that late.

Testing the waters with his stomach, he slowly rose and swung his legs off the bed. Other than his body being a little shaky, he felt okay. He saw a pile of folded clothes on the chest of drawers and headed for them. A note told him he could use them after his shower, so he grabbed the clothes and headed for the bathroom. Paul had told him he could use the shower before he left, and Matías had no intention of letting the opportunity go when he knew he smelled like a brewery.

As the water pounded down on his back, he closed his eyes and let the heat do its trick. He wished he could wash away everything, but his emotions were there to stay. He hadn't seen or heard from Eli in the two weeks since they'd been at his parents', and he hoped the man was all right. He could've asked Jason to check in with Jasmine, but he didn't think either Jasmine or Eli would be happy about that. Plus, he didn't even know if Jasmine knew their relationship had been fake. He didn't want to out Eli if he was keeping it quiet.

Once he was washed, dried and dressed, he gathered up his own clothes, pulling out his phone, and wandered down the stairs.

"Hello?"

There was no answer, so he aimed for the kitchen, which was where someone would usually be in this house. When he found no one there, he almost turned around before he saw a folded piece of paper on the table with his name on it. He picked it up and checked who it was from before reading the words.

Matías

Help yourself to anything you want. I've had to go into the station, so if you need anything, give me a call. Otherwise, make yourself comfortable. You're welcome to stay as long as you want to. I should be back around five o'clock, but Quinn will be home about three o'clock. It's pork chops for dinner if you're staying. Remember to stay hydrated.

Paul

Matías grinned. Paul and Quinn were the best of the best around here, and he was extremely grateful for their help, but he needed to get home. He jotted a quick note back and let himself out, posting the keys back through the door after he'd locked up.

His birthday wasn't until tomorrow, but he needed to get himself organised. His family was known to descend on his apartment at the crack of dawn, and he needed to tidy up. Sofía would cry if she saw the state of his bedroom. He almost did when he arrived home and saw the state of the room. Shaking his head, he got to work.

His birthday, as predicted, dawned bright and early with a chorus of the birthday song as he woke. His family sur-rounded his bed, which made him grateful he didn't have someone sharing his bed and that he'd tidied up.

"Happy birthday, hijo!" Sofía gushed, leaning down to kiss his cheeks.

"Thank you, Mum."

"Come! Birthday breakfast is almost ready."

They all filed out of his room and closed the door so he could get dressed in peace. He closed his eyes and rubbed his face, wishing he could fast forward to tomorrow. He'd made so many plans for this day, but that was before things had ended with Eli. He couldn't even think about doing any of them now.

He allowed himself another minute of feeling sorry for himself, then slapped his cheeks, none too gently, and climbed out of bed. He pulled on some jeans and a T-shirt and stopped with his hand on the door handle. Resting his head against the door, he breathed deeply. They were only his family, but he knew how the day would go. He would be lucky to go an hour without someone mentioning either Eli or Matías needing to find a boyfriend. Maybe he should make a bet on which one would be first.

He loved his family, but he wished they would let him live his life. Once he'd had the thought, he backtracked because that way of thinking had taken him on the journey with Eli, and though he wouldn't change it for the world, he couldn't do it again.

Opening the door, he strode into the living room, seeing his immediate family waiting for him. He smiled when his mother presented him with a plate full of pancakes. Birthdays in his family were all about traditions, and ever since his fifth birthday, when his mother had asked what he wanted for his birthday breakfast, he'd replied with the same thing: pancakes with syrup. She had stopped asking several years ago but continued making them.

He sat at the head of the table—another tradition—and everyone joined him, their own breakfast in front of them.

"Happy birthday, Matías," they said.

"Thanks."

They all dug in, chatter and banter being thrown back and forth. Matías kept up with his side of the conversation, trying to keep a smile on his face. When they were done, Sofía sent Alejo and Isabella to the kitchen to clean the dishes, and his father went to the sofa, switching on the news. His mother came to sit beside him.

"You still miss him, hijo?" she asked.

Matías smiled but stared at the table. "Yes. It'll go. It will."

She cupped his cheek. "The heart knows the right path, Matías. Have faith."

He expected her to add something about finding another person sooner rather than later, but she didn't. Instead, she stood and fetched a gift.

"I thought we weren't exchanging gifts until later," he said.

Sofía sat again, caressing the wrapping of the gift she'd yet to hand to him. "This is something I got before you and Eli broke up. I probably shouldn't give it to you because I know you're hurting, and this might make it worse, but I also think you need to see it. I'm not trying to upset you, though, hijo, and if you'd prefer not to open it, I understand."

Matías swallowed hard and thought about what she'd said. Yes, he would be sad if it was a reminder of his and Eli's time together, but it would also be something he could remember fondly in time. He wouldn't erase their time for anything, and he didn't have much to show for their time together.

"I'd like to see it." He nodded in encouragement.

She handed it to him, then rose and sat beside his father, who wrapped his arm around her shoulders and kissed her temple. Matías refocused on the present and turned it over to unwrap it. When the paper fell away, he barely contained his tears. It took several deep breaths before he could look at it again.

There, in black and white, was a picture of him and Eli, arms encircling each other with Eli smiling up at him and him returning the expression. Such happiness radiated from the picture, and he wondered who had taken it. He covered his mouth with his hand and stared at it, wishing he could go back. Wishing he could do something different and get a different result.

He carefully wrapped it back in the paper and left it on the table. Wiping at his eyes, he stood and rounded the table to the sofa. He leaned over the back of it and kissed his mother's cheek. "Thank you."

When his siblings had finished cleaning up, they all trooped out of the apartment and headed for their parents' house. Everyone was meeting them there in a few hours, and the party would begin at lunchtime. Sofía always made a buffet-style lunch so guests could help themselves to food during the afternoon, and there would be a barbecue—weather permitting—at four o'clock, which would turn into a music festival, otherwise known as the disco, after dinner. There would be games of all kinds, too. It would go late into the evening, and people would come and go throughout the day.

Matías often wondered how everyone managed to be here every time one of them had a birthday, but everyone seemed happy to be there. He supposed those who weren't didn't attend.

Matías was worn out by the time the barbecue was ready, but he kept smiling and chatting with everyone.

"Matías! Come here, hijo!" his mother called.

He went in search of her, aiming for where he thought her voice had come from and found her at the dining table.

"I'm here."

"Ah, good. Stand here. It's cake time!"

Matías smiled. This was the one thing they always kept a secret from him. Each year, he had a different decoration on the cake. His mother carried out a box and placed it in front of him, calling for everyone's attention.

"Open it."

Matías lifted the lid off the cake and laughed when he saw a firefighter's helmet. It was huge and looked so real. "This is amazing. How did you get it to look so real?"

"I have to admit I didn't make it this year, hijo. I had someone with insider knowledge get me the best cake decorator because I knew exactly what I wanted."

"It's great, Mum. Thanks."

She clapped her hands. "Let's light the candles." She took the lighter off his father and began lighting them. Luckily, she had given up putting one for every year, and now they usually had five, one for each of their family. Someone must've miscounted, though, because there were six this year. His mother must've added Justin into the family this time.

"Ready?" Matías nodded. "Remember to blow them out and make a wish."

He stared into the flames and knew exactly what to wish for. He inhaled and blew out the candles, closing his eyes as the singing began, and wished with everything he had in him. When the singing stopped, he opened his eyes and smiled.

"Thank you for being here, everyone."

Matías frowned when everyone's gaze went behind him, and he spun, mouth opening, when he saw Eli standing there with his hands in his pockets and a dark flush on his face.

"Happy birthday, Matti."

Chapter 22

Eli

Eli hadn't been sure if Sofía would help him out or not. She hadn't been happy when she'd found out the truth about Eli and Matías's relationship, but Eli hadn't felt comfortable asking for her assistance when he had been lying about them. He did make her promise not to mention anything to Matías—at least until after his birthday.

Only Sofía knew what Eli had planned, and she was over the moon about helping him once she'd moved past her anger about their lies. It wasn't as if Eli was asking much. He only wanted to arrive slightly late to the party and hide the gift at her house prior to the day. Before she had agreed, he'd had to tell her his entire life story, and it gave him a bit of pleasure to see her anger at his father.

After Sofía had agreed to his requests, Eli's stomach had swooped, and nerves had set in. The "what-ifs" began circling again, and he wasn't sure he was doing the right thing, but he trusted Jasmine and her advice.

When the time came for him to get ready to go, he spent an ungodly amount of time in front of the mirror, trying to decide what outfit to wear and how to style his hair. In the end, he could've saved himself plenty of time because he'd chosen his usual fare of jeans and a shirt with his hair down.

The drive to Sofía's house took less time than he'd hoped, and before he knew it, he was standing at the door. Sofía had told him to let himself in because the door would be unlocked for those that needed to come and go throughout the day. She'd told him to arrive at four o'clock because that was when she planned to give Matías his cake. She had told him, "*I know Matías will wish for you, and when he opens his eyes, you'll be there.*" He hoped it would be a pleasant surprise.

As he weaved through the guests, most of whom had no idea who he was, he felt his cheeks warm and his hands shake. He stopped behind Matías and caught Sofía's eye as she said to Matías, "Ready? Remember to blow them out and make a wish."

Eli licked his lips as Matías did as his mother instructed. The guests sang happy birthday, and Matías thanked them before going quiet and whirling around, mouth gaping.

"Happy birthday, Matti."

It felt good to use his nickname again. He'd started calling him Matías again to try to give himself some distance between them, but the nickname sounded much better. At least, it would if Matías had said something in return.

"What...? How...?" Matías closed his eyes and opened them again as if he was checking Eli was still there. "Why are you here?"

Not quite the response he wanted, but he could work with it. "I wanted to celebrate your birthday with you." He cleared his throat, flicking his gaze to Sofía and back to Matías. "I have a few things I want to say if you'll let me?"

Matías nodded. "Here or somewhere private?"

Eli wished he could go somewhere private, but he'd agreed with Sofía that Matías needed to hear it straight away. "Here is fine." He glanced at the floor and lifted his gaze again. "I was wrong, Matti. Completely wrong. My life hasn't been easy, and I blamed that on the wrong person, but it became a shield for me. A barrier to stop me from being hurt. A way to keep people at arm's length. You broke through every single one of them, and I got scared and ran. It was the last thing I should've done, and I hurt you in the process. I'm sorry for that." He inhaled. "I love you, Matti. If you'll still have me, I'd love for our relationship to become real."

Silence descended, and Eli's heart raced. He wouldn't blame Matías if he told Eli to take a running leap off a cliff, but he hoped he wouldn't. Matías's eyes roamed Eli's face, and he stepped closer, lifting his hands to Eli's jaw.

"It always has been real." Matías lowered his head and joined their mouths in the softest but most heartfelt kiss Eli had ever encountered. "I love you."

A cheer sounded from the guests, and Eli glanced around before ducking his head, resting it on Matías's chest. Matías laughed, the sound rumbling through his body, and Eli slid his hands around his waist. He couldn't believe Matías had forgiven him so easily.

"Hijo! I knew you would be happy again." Sofía rested her hands on their shoulders, and Eli peered up at her. "You and

I, though, have to have words later." She glared at Matías, then smiled.

Matías laughed again. "Okay, Mum."

"Barbecue is ready! Come get your burgers and hotdogs!"

The crowds dispersed outside, and Eli was left with Matías. "I am really sorry. You don't have to forgive me so easily. I know I'm a pain, and it's unlikely I will change, but I—"

Eli's mouth was soon busy with Matías's, and he forgot what he'd been saying. He slid his arms around Matías's neck and succumbed to the pleasure of being close to him. It ended too soon, as far as he was concerned.

"I forgive you. It's done, and now we're where we should be. Together. That's all I need to know. We can discuss everything else later. It's my birthday."

"Oh, that reminds me. I have a gift for you." He glanced around, disentangling himself from Matías. "I need to find your mother, though."

Matías frowned. "Why do you need to find Mum?"

Eli smirked. "Because she hid your present here for me."

He raised his eyebrows. "Have you been in cahoots with my mother?"

Eli's cheeks heated. "Maybe."

Matías chuckled. "All right. Let's get some food, and we'll do presents after."

"Are you sure you don't want to open it now?" Eli wasn't sure if he wanted an audience when Matías opened it in case he didn't like it.

Matías kissed him. "Stop worrying. You think I won't like it. I will love it. I know I will."

Eli still hesitated. "I still don't understand how you can act like everything is normal."

Matías slid his arms around Eli's waist and pulled him close. "Because everything that's happened has led us here. Do I understand why you did what you did? Yes. Do I wish you hadn't? Yes. But it doesn't change the fact I'm so happy you're here. That you love me. That you're willing to work for us. We can talk about the future, the past and the present another day. Today, I'm celebrating you being here with me."

Eli wasn't someone who caved to emotion, but the words had him hiding his head in Matías's chest and choking back a sob. He gripped the back of Matías's shirt and breathed deeply.

"I might whip your ass for squealing on us to Mum, though."

Eli chuckled. "Understood."

Matías placed a finger under Eli's chin and lifted his head. "Let's eat."

Eli nodded.

When they joined the rest of the guests, there was a cheer, and everyone settled down. Eli's stomach was still somersaulting, so he picked at the food, not hungry but not wanting to offend anyone. Matías scooted closer and rested his arm on the back of Eli's chair.

"Are you okay?" he whispered close to Eli's ear.

"Mmm-hmm."

Matías snorted. "Once more with feeling?"

Eli coughed and covered his mouth. "Hey!"

Matías chuckled, then sobered. "What's wrong?"

"I'm wondering what my family will say."

"Did you not tell them what you were planning?"

Eli shook his head. "I didn't want to get their hopes up in case you said no."

Matías palmed Eli's cheek, turning his head. When their gazes locked, Matías said, "I could never say no to you."

Their lips met, and Eli's stomach settled, his heart expanding with the amount of love he never thought he'd be able to feel. How had he thought he could live without Matías? From this moment forward, Eli promised to make Matías the happiest man alive.

"Time for presents!" Sofía called, and an army of people followed her from the house, carrying wrapped presents.

"Are these all for you?" Eli asked.

Matías's cheeks darkened. "I have a big family."

Eli grinned. "You're so spoilt."

Matías kissed him on the cheek and wandered over to his mother, doing the same to her. One by one, his family approached him, offering their gift, and Matías opened them with a flourish, smiling, laughing and joking with them as he thanked them. Eli was in awe of how relaxed and confident Matías was. He had something to say to each of them as if he'd taken an interest in their lives, which naturally, he would because they were family. Eli couldn't put his finger on it, but Matías seemed...complete.

"Eli?"

Eli blinked and focused on Sofía. "Yes?"

"Your turn." She smiled, gesturing to the last gift she held.

The butterflies returned, but Eli strode over, pretending he wasn't as shaky as he felt. "Thank you." He took the gift from her that the photographer had helpfully wrapped for him and faced Matías. "Happy birthday."

Matías smiled. "It's big. Can you hold it while I unwrap it?" he asked.

Eli nodded. He watched Matías find the tape and carefully undo it. With the amount of tape the photographer had used to wrap it, they'd be here all day. "Rip it," he said.

Matías eyed him, then grinned and yanked at the paper, tearing it to pieces. Eli manoeuvred the frame out of the paper and held it between them so they both could see it. He frowned when he saw an addition to the frame he hadn't asked for. Each photo depicted a letter of Matías's name, but there was one on the end that was empty. Eli hadn't bought anything to add to it. He hadn't asked for it either. He'd have to find something to put there.

"I love it. Thank you." Matías leaned forward and kissed him. "I'll have to find the best place to put it."

"I didn't know there would be a gap at the end. We'll have to find something to go there," Eli said.

Sofía cleared her throat. "I think you'll find, Matías, the present I gave you earlier will fit beautifully." Eli frowned again, and she lowered her head. "When you told me what you were buying him, I asked the photographer to add the extra space and make the photo I've already given Matías. It was supposed to be a surprise for you both. When you broke up," she narrowed her eyes, "I wasn't sure what to do with it until you contacted me."

Matías took the frame from Eli's hands and wandered inside, Eli following. He placed the frame on the table and pulled something from some paper. Eli stopped beside

Matías and saw the photo of them, almost bursting into tears.

"It was supposed to be a fake relationship," Eli whispered. "It doesn't look fake."

Matías slid an arm around his shoulders. "No, it doesn't. I think we were both in denial, to begin with, and with everything you were dealing with, it was too much for you. Especially when I threw my declaration at you, too." He pulled him closer, resting his lips against his head, and Eli wrapped his arms around his waist.

"I'm glad Jasmine talked some sense into me."

Matías laughed. "I wondered what had changed your mind about us. It makes sense now."

"I owe her everything."

Matías pulled back and reached for the frame. "Let's see if this fits." He checked the back and pushed the photo onto the square block in the frame. Once situated, he stepped back. "It's perfect."

"Where are you going to put it?"

"Near my bed, so it's one of the first things I see in the morning and at night."

Eli sank into Matías, closed his eyes and enjoyed being held. He'd never felt as secure and loved as he had at that moment—if he excluded his family. This was a different kind of love, though. A love, he hoped, would last a long time.

"Will you come home with me tonight?" Matías whispered.

"Definitely."

Eli looked up at him, and Matías fused their lips. What started as a slow kiss turned into something heated as they sipped, nibbled and explored each other. Eli's hand raked through Matías's hair, and Matías's hands held tight to Eli's ass and back. Eli lost his balance, and he bumped Matías back into the wall, immediately grateful for the position because it meant he could grind his hard cock against him.

A throat clearing had them releasing each other as if burnt, and Alejo laughed. "Don't stop on my account, but Mum wanted you to know that dessert was ready." He chuckled and left the room.

Eli covered his mouth with his hand, touching the tingling skin. "Why is it always Alejo who interrupts us? You're a bad influence on me."

Matías ran his fingers through his hair and stood from his lean. "Same goes for you. Let's finish dessert, and Mum might let me go early."

Two hours later, Matías slammed Eli back against the wall of his apartment after kicking the door shut. Hands grabbed and pulled as they both fought to get free of their clothes without losing the connection of their lips. Matías growled when he had to pull back to yank his T-shirt over his head. Eli's hand reached for Matías the moment the item was gone, and they stumbled down the hallway to his bedroom and fell onto the bed with a laugh.

"At least we hit the bed," Matías mumbled as he reached for Eli's mouth again.

Eli pushed at the waistband of Matías's briefs, wanting them skin on skin. "I don't care where we are. Just fuck me, Matti."

"Gladly, although you're returning the favour later." Matías kissed down Eli's neck and across his collarbone and chest, paying special attention to his nipples.

Eli couldn't focus enough to understand Matías's comment, so let it float away for later. When Matías reached Eli's briefs, he mouthed at the wet patch before pulling his shaft free from its confines. While Matías licked around the head of Eli's cock, he dragged the underwear free and threw it away.

Eli gripped the sheets at his hips and closed his eyes, biting his bottom lip to keep quiet.

"Let me hear you," Matías said and sank down on his cock again.

Eli couldn't help the whine that escaped when his dick hit the back of Matías's throat. Each time he lifted and lowered, Eli's body shivered and shook and cursed.

"Fuck, yes, right there," he gasped when Matías flicked his tongue against the bundle of nerves beneath the head of his cock. "No!" he shouted as Matías pulled away.

"You're coming when I'm inside you."

Matías's words heated Eli's blood further. The man reached for the bedside table and threw a condom and lube on the bed. Matías rolled the condom on straight away, then slicked it and focused on Eli. Fingers, slippery with lube, found his hole and massaged it. Eli's eyelids fluttered.

"Eli?" Matías whispered.

The moment he caught Matías's gaze, Matías breached the ring of muscle. Eli's mouth gaped, and he panted. Yes, it burnt. Yes, he felt full, but by God, did he need more. His hips twitched, pushing to get Matías inside faster. One finger became two, and two became three until Eli was squirming on the bed and chanting for Matías to fuck him.

Matías rested the head of his cock against Eli's entrance and paused. Eli knew what he wanted, and the instant Eli looked at him, Matías pressed forward. Eli bore down, making the entry easier on them both. Matías withdrew and thrust in small increments, gaining distance each time until he was fully seated with his balls against Eli's ass.

"Fuck, yes," Eli said. He wrapped his legs around Matías's waist and his arms around his neck and pulled him down for a kiss. The position pushed Matías deeper, and Eli groaned. "So good."

Their tongues tangled while Eli adjusted, and Matías lifted his head. "Ready?"

"Always."

Matías smiled and withdrew, then slammed home. "This is going to be quick."

"Don't care. Need you."

Matías gripped Eli's waist and snapped his hips forward, burying himself deep over and over again. He cruised past Eli's prostate each time, barely grazing it until he slid his knees closer and settled Eli's hips higher. The position became Eli's favourite because Matías hit his prostate dead centre with each thrust.

Eli reached above his head and gripped the headboard, pushing back against Matías. His eyes rolled into the back of his head, and he came, hands- free, with no warning.

"Fucking hell, Eli." Matías groaned, thrust a few more times and held himself deep inside Eli. "Fuck." He caught himself on his hands before he crushed Eli.

They panted, and Eli pulled Matías down to cover him, wrapping his arms around his back. They were still joined intimately, and Eli wished they could stay that way, but Matías moved his hand between them, and Eli felt him grip the end of the condom and withdraw. Eli felt the loss and almost whimpered.

"Give me a few minutes, and we'll go again," Matías chuckled.

Eli huffed, his eyes closed. "I don't know if I can."

"You can. This time, it will be slow and long." Matías kissed him and crawled off the bed.

Eli shivered but couldn't move to pull the cover over him. When Matías returned, he cleaned Eli's stomach and climbed into bed, dragging the covers over them. Eli snuggled into Matías's embrace and sighed.

"This is everything," Eli whispered.

"Sleep if you want. I'll wake you soon." Matías kissed his head and tightened his grip. "I'm not going anywhere."

"Neither am I," he mumbled, already sinking towards slumber.

He had never believed he could have this. This complete lack of worry that someone might take everything he had. He knew Matías wouldn't do that. Where his confidence came from, he didn't know, but he knew it with everything inside him. His heart sang for Matías, his body reached for him, his mind focused on him. He hoped they had a relationship as good as Matías's parents had. If they managed it, Eli would be ecstatic.

Chapter 23

Matías

"Don't be scared," Eli said. "They're just people."

"'They're just people,' he says." Matías exhaled. "They're your family."

"You've already met Opal." Eli manoeuvred the car through the streets towards Matías's doom.

"And she seemed super inquisitive." Matías rubbed his hands over his thighs. Nothing had ever made him nervous before—unsure, uneasy, worried, but not nervous—but the idea of meeting Eli's family had him wanting to run for the nearest airport.

"My family is no different from yours. If anything, mine are more relaxed." Eli grinned and reached over to pat Matías's leg.

Matías sighed. "Have you heard any more from your father?"

Eli had updated Matías on what had happened with his father. Hayden Jackson had left after giving Eli the paperwork for the fund, and no one had seen him since. Eli kept expecting him to turn up unannounced at some point, but Matías believed he was truly gone.

Eli shook his head and gripped the steering wheel tighter. "He's disappeared. Again. Like I said he would."

"Has no one else heard from him?"

"No. Or at least, they're not telling me they have."

"What did your mum say about the money?"

Eli blew a raspberry, making Matías laugh. "Nothing. I gave her the papers, she nodded and changed the subject. I can't decide if she knew about it or not."

"Did you ask her?"

"I didn't think it was wise."

"That's surprising." Matías bit his lip, withholding his smirk.

Eli was quiet for a moment. "What's surprising?"

Matías let his smirk free. "That you didn't do something because it wasn't wise. It never stopped you before."

Eli backhanded his shoulder. "I can let my family loose on you, you know. All I need to do is say the word, and they'll hound you like a pack of hyenas."

Although he knew Eli would never do such a thing, Matías shivered with the idea. He needed Eli to be on his side to weather Storm Jackson with him. Matías's mother had told him not to worry because she was friends with Karen and had said she was a nice woman. It hadn't helped ease Matías's mind.

"I take it all back, my love."

The warmth that spread through him from being able to audibly acknowledge those words was enough to chase away the chill of Eli's threat. They'd had almost a week between their words of love on Matías's birthday and the dinner with Eli's family. A week of stolen hours, random meet-ups and mashed-up breakfasts and dinners, where Eli was eating breakfast, but Matías was eating dinner because of his shifts. The good news? They'd slept beside each other for three nights out of six. It was a prophecy of what was to come, but he didn't doubt they could weather it.

"They'll love you as I do," Eli whispered.

"So, remind me again who's going to be there?"

"Mum, Opal, Lukas and Robbie. Just us six. You'll be fine," Eli stated again, this time with heat. "You have no more time to worry, either. We're here..." Eli's voice trailed off, and he squinted at the house they'd pulled in front of. "Weird."

"What?"

"There are more cars here. I don't recognise them." Eli switched off the engine and sat back. "I wonder if they're for a different house."

Matías gazed at the cars, and his heart dropped at the same time as his stomach fluttered. "That's Dad's car. And Justin's car."

They glanced at each other, climbed out of the car and met at the front.

"Do you think this is a party again?" Eli asked, his voice weary.

Matías chuckled and wrapped his arm around Eli's shoulder. "We can leave before they see us." He knew the answer before Eli even opened his mouth.

"Too late."

The front door opened, and Opal ran out. "You're here! Come on. Everyone's waiting."

"And who is everyone, Opal?"

She grinned. "You'll see."

Eli sighed. "Let's get this over with. You do realise this was supposed to be a small family dinner, so you could get to know Matías?"

"It is." Opal paused with her hand on the front door. "Just take away the 'small.'"

She pushed inside, and the moment they entered, a cheer went up. Matías shook his head as he spied his family mixed in with Eli's family. He wasn't against them being together, but he could bet his annual wage his mother had something to do with this.

Eli tugged Matías straight for his mother and hugged her, then turned to him. "Mum, this is Matías. Matías, this is Karen Jackson."

"Nice to meet you. Eli has told me a lot about you all."

Karen side-eyed her son. "I bet he has. I would say it wasn't true, but it probably was with all the tricks these four got up to when they were younger." She pulled Matías in for a hug. "You're very welcome, dear."

"I apologise if my mother pushed too hard to make this a party instead of a small dinner." Matías winced.

Karen laughed, a light tinkle of sound that got lost in the surrounding conversations. "Oh dear, no. This wasn't Sofía's idea. This was mine."

"Mum!"

She waved Eli away. "I thought Matías would be nervous meeting us for the first time on his own. So, I brought some backup for him. It's nice to meet your family as a whole, and it gives me the opportunity to cook for a large family again. I miss my days of working in a kitchen."

Matías frowned, and Eli hooked his arm through his. "Mum used to work at a cafe as the cook. She'd spend hours and hours cooking, then come home and do it all over again for us. She loved it."

"What made you stop?"

Karen's smile was small, her gaze distant. "Life interceded, and we needed the extra money from a better-paid job."

Matías wished he hadn't asked. "I'm sorry."

"Oh, don't be. I love the job I have now, and though I don't do it often, I batch cook a lot of things for the kids to take home with them. It keeps me going. One day, though, I will consider hiring a cleaner." She chuckled.

Matías laughed. "I agree with you there. It would be money well spent."

"Anyway, visit with your family while I finish dinner. You can meet Lukas and Robbie before we sit."

Eli kissed his mother's cheek. "Do you need any help?"

"No, thank you, sweetheart. You keep Matías company."

They watched her leave the room, and Eli rested his head on Matías's shoulder. "See. It wasn't that bad."

"She's like Mum."

"Two peas in a pod."

They glanced at each other and laughed.

"What's all this laughter about? This is a party. Not a comedy show."

Matías spun around and wrapped his arms around his best friend. "How come you were invited?"

Rafe polished his nails against his shirt. "I happened to be in the room when Eli's mother extended the invitation."

"What were you doing at my parents' house? You usually only go when I'm with you," Matías asked.

"Not strictly true," Rafe said, a gleam in his eye. "Your dad has been giving me pointers for the security issues I keep having. He's been great."

"What security issues? You haven't told me anything about that."

Rafe held up his hand. "It's nothing big. Get your panties out of the twist before it becomes uncomfortable. We've had a couple of break-ins over the past few months. I wanted a second opinion about what my security firm was suggesting."

"Jesus, Rafe. Did you lose a lot?"

Rafe shook his head. "That's the thing. They took nothing. It was as if they wanted to see if they could break in. It's weird."

"Well, let me know if I can help with anything. You know I'll do what I can."

"I know, thanks."

"Gentlemen, sorry for interrupting, but I thought I'd come and say a quick hello."

Eli hugged Jasmine. "You're always welcome to interrupt. I didn't expect you to be here."

Jasmine smiled. "Your mother called and insisted I come because I was part of the family. I couldn't resist."

Matías leaned forward and kissed her cheek. "You are definitely part of the family."

Eli had told him what Jasmine had said to him a few days before Eli's appearance at Matías's birthday. If it wasn't for her, Eli didn't think he would've turned up at all. They might never have become anything other than a memory if she hadn't kicked his ass.

"Aww, you're sweet." She shifted her gaze to Rafe. "And who might you be?"

"Jasmine, this is my best friend, Rafe."

Rafe took Jasmine's hand and kissed the back of it, eyes never leaving hers. Eli tugged on Matías's arm, making him lean down so Eli could whisper, "I think we have a winner!"

Matías chuckled, and Eli continued, "Jasmine was so unsure of herself before she took over Sarah's business for those few weeks. I've never seen her so confident and sure of herself as she is now. It makes my decision that much easier."

"Does she know?"

"Yes, but I haven't made it official yet. I was waiting for her to rest after all the work she's been doing. I'm hoping to get the contracts back from the lawyers early next week. The second I get those, I'll set her up."

"You're a good man, Eli." Matías waited until Eli looked at him and kissed him chastely.

An echoing "Aww" sounded from the occupants of the room, and Matías laughed, breaking away.

"Shut up," he said, his cheeks and neck heating. He rubbed the back of his neck to chase away the embarrassment.

"Let's get the crap out of the way," Eli said and excused them from Jasmine and Rafe, who didn't appear to notice, and went over to his brothers.

"Lukas, Robbie, this is Matías."

Both men stared at him. Lukas had a smile on his face, but Robbie had a scowl.

"Say hello." Eli's voice firmed.

"Nice to meet you, Matías," Lukas said, holding out his hand. Matías shook and smiled.

"I've heard a bit about you."

"Likewise. If you ever need someone to check over your car, let me know."

Matías grinned. "Will do. Good to know there's a mechanic on hand." He turned to Robbie and held out his hand, which Robbie ignored. Matías clenched his jaw and dropped his hand to his side.

"Robbie!" Eli hissed. "Get over it."

Robbie glared at Matías, then Eli, and stalked off. In the distance, Matías heard the front door slam.

"I'm sorry about him. He's never been able to get his head around the idea that men can like men, and women can like women and everything in between despite knowing I'm gay. He's a black and white type of guy." Eli shook his head. "No idea where it came from."

"It's fine. He might come around eventually." Matías hoped so for Eli's sake more than his own. It couldn't be easy having a brother who detested his lifestyle choices.

"Dinner's ready, everyone," Karen called from the doorway.

Matías and Eli let everyone else go first and followed at a slow pace. "This is going to be our usual dinners now, isn't it?" Matías said.

Eli nodded. "I believe so. We've officially become a large family."

Matías chuckled as they entered the large kitchen. Eli gasped. "What?"

"We used to have a table that seated six. Where did she get this from?"

Matías glanced at the table, noticing it was a twelve-seater table. "It's as big as the one in Mum's house."

"Eli, Matías, come sit here," Karen said, pointing to the seat next to hers.

They wandered to her, and Matías held the seat for Eli next to his mother, and he sat next to Eli with Sofía on his other side. He leaned over and kissed Sofía's cheek. "Thank you," he whispered.

Sofía smiled and winked.

Karen stayed standing and garnered everyone's attention. "I'm not one for speeches and lengthy monologues, so all I have to say is that I wish every one of you a wonderful, fulfilled life full of love, friendship and family."

"Here, here!"

"Dig in." Karen sat, picking up the bowl in front of her.

Matías watched as their families mingled, getting to know each other and finding new friends and acquaintances. His family had always been like this, but to know Eli's family was the same was amazing. He couldn't imagine what their birthday and anniversary and any other celebration parties were going to be like now. They'd end up hiring out a hall, eventually.

When they'd finished eating, Karen stood again. "Now, for the fun bit."

Eli groaned and dropped his head into his hands. "No, please, no."

"Pictionary."

Eli groaned even louder.

"When you are ready, if you could meet in the living room, we will pick teams."

Matías loved the game, though he wasn't very good at it. He elbowed Eli. "Do you not like the game?"

"I love the game, but I never win because Mum and Opal are so good at it."

"Never say never."

They wandered into the living room, guests sitting on sofas, the floor and chairs brought from the dining table. When everyone was present and accounted for, Karen clapped her hands.

"Okay, there are twelve of us, so I think three teams of four. Captains can be..." She looked around the room. "Alejo, Rafe and Lukas. Choose your team members. Alejo, go first."

"Mum."

"Jasmine," Rafe said.

"Justin," Lukas said with a grin.

Alejo rubbed his chin. "Karen."

"Eli." Rafe grinned at Matías's glare.

"Isabella." Lukas barely dodged Opal's backhand.

"Dad," Alejo said. "I get all the brains."

Rafe glanced around the room at who was left and sighed. "Matti, I suppose."

Matías rolled his eyes.

"Crap." Lukas sighed. "Opal."

"I love you, too, little brother."

"Okay. You go up one team at a time and, for those who don't know, try to guess the picture or phrase before the time runs out," Karen said. "If you guess it right, you get a point. If you don't guess it right, you don't get any points." She held up a pad. "I'll keep score. Alejo, your team first. Choose your first artist."

"Go on, Dad."

Diego chuckled and rose from the sofa with a groan. "After all the food, you better hope I don't fall asleep with the pen in my hand."

Everyone laughed. Matías's dad chose a card, and Karen started the timer. Diego drew a line across the whiteboard.

"A straight line!" Alejo shouted.

Diego drew a circle above it.

"Stickman!" Sofía called.

He drew wavy lines beneath the line.

"Sunset!" Karen said.

Diego pointed at her and drew an arrow pointing upwards.

"Sunrise!" Karen called.

"Yes!" Diego raised his arms in victory, and seconds later, the timer buzzed.

"One point to us," Alejo said with a grin. "I knew I picked the brainy bunch."

Karen said, "Rafe, choose your first victim."

"Matti." Rafe grinned.

"Asshole," Matías muttered.

Eli patted his back. "It doesn't matter. It's a game."

Matías knew it was, but he couldn't draw worth a damn. He picked a card and groaned. Karen started the timer, and he drew two vertical lines and several horizontal lines.

"A ladder!" Eli called.

He added some smaller vertical lines between each horizontal one.

"A piece of paper with writing on it?" Rafe said.

"A book," Jasmine said.

Matías pointed at her and waggled his hand back and forth. He drew a big square around the first picture and added a triangle on top.

"A door?"

"A shed?"

Matías groaned and drew a stickman inside the big square beside the first picture.

"A builder?"

Matías had no idea what else he could draw to get his point across. The timer buzzed, and his teammates groaned.

"What was it?" Eli asked.

"A library," Matías said, wiping the board clean.

"Ah, I see it now," Jasmine said.

They played several rounds, laughter and silly answers thrown around the room. He usually had fun with his family, but by throwing Eli's family into the mix, it was now a hilarious mashup of stand-up comedians and sarcastic barbs.

He'd never expected everyone to get on as well as they had, and Matías couldn't have been happier.

After a couple of hours, Matías's family bid their good-byes, leaving with promises of meeting up at another time. Rafe and Jasmine left, too. Together, if Matías wasn't mistaken. He'd have to remember to check in with Rafe the following day to make sure he behaved himself.

When Karen dropped back onto the sofa, she chuckled. "That was the most fun I've had in years. Your family is amazing, Matías. Thank you for sharing them with us."

It had never occurred to him that he got to share his family with Eli's family, and vice versa. Yes, he'd seen them in action together, but until the words had left Karen's mouth, it hadn't seemed like he was doing anything.

"I'm glad you had fun. There's no shortage of it around my family." He grinned. "And you've only met my immediate family, too."

"Do you want a drink?" Eli asked.

"A cup of tea would be lovely, sweetheart. Thank you," Karen said.

"Matti?"

"Same, thanks."

Eli disappeared, and Karen sat forward. "I can see you love my son, Matías, and I can see my son loves you. I want nothing more for him than to spend his life with someone who worships the ground he walks on. He's had a hard time of it, but you've brought him to life in ways I never thought anyone could. I can't thank you enough."

"I love him, Karen. Completely, unashamedly, forever. He's it."

"I know." Karen patted his arm. "Welcome to the family." She grimaced. "Give Robbie some time. He'll come around."

"He better," Eli said, entering with a tray of drinks. He handed one to his mum, then to Matías, and sat with his own.

Matías slid his arm around Eli and kissed his temple. It allowed him to inhale the scent of Eli's shampoo while keeping the connection with his lips.

"Are you okay?" Eli asked, pulling back a little.

Matías smiled. "Never better."

If this was his life from that moment forth, he would never need to wish for anything ever again.

Chapter 24

Eli

Eli's nervous energy bounced around his body, waking him at four o'clock. He tried to get back to sleep, but he couldn't. He didn't want to disturb Matías because he had to be up in an hour for his day shift, so he crawled out of bed and draped his dressing gown around him. He tiptoed down the stairs to the kitchen and flicked on the kettle. He may as well start his day early.

"What are you doing?" Matías's sleepy voice made Eli jump.

"Did I wake you? Sorry."

Matías stepped behind Eli and wrapped his arms around his waist, his morning wood pressing against the top of Eli's ass. "Don't be. What's wrong?"

Eli sighed. "Excitement, maybe. Nerves. Worry. Everything."

"You have nothing to be worried about." Matías kissed the curve of his neck. "She'll say yes."

"What if she doesn't like the terms?"

"Then you'll renegotiate."

Matías flicked off the kettle.

"Hey, I was going to make tea."

"No, you're coming back to bed. You need to sleep."

"But I can't."

Matías spun Eli around, dipped and lifted Eli into a fireman's hold and strode for the stairs. Eli laughed all the way, the air being punched out of his lungs with the movement.

"Put...me...down," he gasped.

Matías dropped him, and Eli bounced on the bed. Matías crawled over him, bracketing him with his arms and legs. "You'll sleep."

"My brain can't switch off just because you tell it to." Eli huffed, swiping his hair out of his face.

"I know. So I'm going to make it."

Eli should've guessed from the gleam in Matías's eye, but he didn't until Matías undid the belt on the dressing gown and bared him to his gaze.

"You don't have time..."

"I always have time for you."

Matías lowered his mouth and took Eli's breath. There were no soft kisses that morning, just deep, hard exploration that sent Eli's brain scrambling. Matías's hands skimmed over Eli's naked body, flicking over his nipples, scratching at his sides with blunt nails. The sensations were overwhelming, but Eli needed more. He always needed more.

Matías tore his mouth away, and Eli lifted his head to follow, but Matías grabbed his hips and spun him onto his stomach. He dragged the dressing gown down Eli's arms and off, the cool air replacing the warmth of the fabric and sending goosebumps travelling along his skin. Matías leaned over him, the heat of him warming where the cool air had touched. His mouth landed on Eli's nape, and Eli smiled, knowing what was coming.

A wet tongue followed the patterns and pictures inked into Eli's skin. He'd lost count of the times Matías had done this, and the result had always been worthwhile. Eli sank into the bed, closing his eyes and bringing the ink to life behind his eyelids. In his mind, he followed the same path Matías did, his skin reacting to the touch. Eli's breathing grew choppy the further Matías went down his back.

Eli knew when Matías reached the end because he paused and exhaled as if he was disappointed. Matías spread Eli's ass cheeks without warning and licked his pucker. Eli jerked and gasped.

"Holy shit!" It had been a long time since someone had done it to him. He gripped the covers beneath him and drew his knees under him, presenting his ass to Matías.

Matías chuckled but said nothing. He held Eli's cheeks and pushed his face into the space he'd made. A second later, Matías's tongue flicked against his hole repeatedly. The nerve endings set alight, and Eli squirmed. Matías wrapped an arm around his hips and held him still, firming his tongue against the entrance. More and more pressure until Matías worked his tongue inside.

Eli bit his lip, trying to contain the begging and cursing he wanted to say. The only sounds he made were groans and whimpers of need. His cock was rock hard and leaking like a champagne glass tower, and he needed more.

"Matti. Oh, god, please!"

Matías's free hand left his ass and encircled Eli's shaft. Eli nearly cried with relief, but Matías didn't move his hand. He used his thumb to rub against the nerves and his fingers to slide against the head while continuing his attack on his pucker. Eli slid a hand underneath him and rested a finger against his nipple, one of his most erogenous zones. He didn't actively move his finger, but with every twitch of his body, his nipple pressed against it, sending a zing of fire down his spine to his groin.

The unity of the different sensations sent Eli hurtling towards an orgasm. He opened his mouth to let Matías know, but all that came out was a keening cry as he unloaded onto the bed. His mind went offline, his body contracted and released, and lights flashed behind his eyelids until he slumped to the bed.

Matías removed his tongue and pressed a kiss to his ass, then swiped his hand over the head of his cock, making Eli hiss at the sensitivity. The sounds that came after would have been enough to make Eli stand to attention again, but he was too exhausted. He managed to blink his eyes and watch over his shoulder as Matías licked his hand clean.

"I wanted to taste you," Matías said.

Eli smiled sleepily and closed his eyes again.

"Get back into bed."

Eli mumbled something even he couldn't understand, but Matías picked him up and tucked him in.

"Wha' 'bou you?" Eli murmured.

Matías kissed his forehead. "You can make it up to me later. Love you."

"'uv you."

Eli's alarm woke him, and he fumbled to switch it off. When he found nothing on the bedside table, he reluctantly opened his eyes and searched for his phone. He found it on the chest of drawers and grumbled as he crawled out of bed to turn it off. Beside his phone was a note.

You talk in your sleep, you know. Thank you for the wake-up call. It gave me plenty of energy this morning. I moved your phone because I didn't think you'd want to wake up, and I know how important today is for you. I'll happily pay my penance later. Don't worry about Jasmine. She'll be over the moon with the agreement. Remember to eat break-fast. I'll see you at about six-thirty tonight. Love you. x

Eli smiled as he read about the penance. He was sure he could think of something suitable. He checked the time and headed for the shower. Time to make himself presentable.

An hour later, his stomach churned as he made a cup of green tea. Jasmine would be there any minute, and despite what Matías had said, he wasn't sure she would be happy with the contract he'd drawn up for her to become part of the business. There was nothing in there that wouldn't benefit her, but she might want more than being a partner. She might want her own business.

His heart stopped for a beat when the door opened, and Jasmine called out a greeting.

"You better have the kettle on. I need coffee!"

Eli smiled at the growl in her voice, and he turned to flick the kettle on again, pulling another mug from the cupboard.

"I wasn't sure if you'd want coffee or tea, so I hadn't made you one yet," he said.

"Coffee! Coffee! Coffff-ffeeee!"

Eli laughed. "Coffee it is."

Jasmine settled into the chair at the table and yawned. "It seems weird not having as much to do."

Eli's throat closed up. He poured the water into Jasmine's cup and made the coffee the way she liked, handing it to her.

"Come on. Let's go to the office. I have some things to go through with you."

He repeatedly swallowed as he led the way and settled behind his desk. He put the cup on the coaster and rested his hands on the folder containing the paperwork Jasmine needed to read through. Before she did that, he wanted to talk to her.

"You look serious," Jasmine said. "What's wrong?"

"Nothing." He licked his lips. "I have a proposition for you."

Jasmine's eyes brightened. "Is this what I think it is?"

Eli nodded. "But we need to go through some things first." He inhaled. "The first thing I want to say is sorry."

Jasmine's forehead creased. "Why?"

"Because I've held you back. I knew I struggled to let go of things, but I didn't see how much it affected those around me until you proved to me you were more than capable. Running Sarah's business for those few weeks was a feat, and you did it without complaint, without issue, and with more than enough ability."

"You don't need to be sorry, Eli. I love working with you."

Eli smiled. "Now, I don't know what plans you have, but you have two choices from my perspective. You can go off and create your own business, which I will happily support and help you with. I'll give you clients to get you going, reviews, anything you need."

"Or?" she said.

Eli inhaled. "Or you can become a partner in Devoted Weddings."

Jasmine's eyes widened. "A partner? I was expecting you to make me a wedding planner, not become a partner. I don't...What do I..." She covered her mouth and stared at him. "I don't have enough money to sink into a new business—or this one."

Eli smiled, body relaxing. "You don't need money." He held up his hand when she protested. "But if you insist, we can put a percentage of your wage into the business fund each month." He had no intention of letting her pay into the business, which was why when he'd spoken to his lawyer to draw the papers up, he'd included an extra ten per cent on her wage, knowing she wouldn't want to take the business on with no benefit to the company that she could see.

He could see her mind going through the idea, trying to see what it entailed. Lifting the folder, he handed it to her.

"Read through this. Note down any questions."

She glanced at the folder and smoothed a hand down it. "Is this really what you want, Eli?" She stared at him, tilting her head.

Eli didn't waver from her perusal. "Yes, Jasmine. I want this, but you need to do what's best for you. No matter what you choose, I will be there to help you."

Jasmine moved to the sofa and settled in with the folder on her lap and the cup of coffee in her hand. Eli watched her for a moment before turning to his laptop. He needed to get the details for the weddings this week. If Jasmine agreed to the contract and wanted to keep busy, she could take over some of his weddings—if the brides agreed—and he would have a bit of extra time to spend with Matías.

Comparing his schedule to Matías's had become second nature now, and after Eli went to bed that night, he knew he wouldn't see Matías for three days with Eli working during the day and Matías working at night. It couldn't be helped. If Jasmine came on board, though, he could potentially cut back the hours he worked on Matías's night shifts. He hadn't mentioned it to either of them yet, so it might not work out, but it was something to consider.

He made several phone calls, checking for stock levels and available dates and confirming details with the bride for the following day's wedding before Jasmine interrupted him.

"Are you kidding me, Eli?"

Eli snapped his gaze to Jasmine. "What?"

"This wage is ridiculous."

Eli smiled, his heart calming. "It is only slightly higher than what wedding planners get paid if they work for a larger company."

"Seriously?"

Eli nodded. "An assistant doesn't get paid as much, but a wedding planner does. Often not a fair balance with the amount of work an assistant sometimes has to do, but it is what it is."

"You have always been fair with the assistant wage."

Eli inclined his head. He paid his employees well. It was how he retained them, coupled with treating them right.

"This is too much."

"No, it's not, Jasmine. You're an amazing wedding planner. You deserve this."

Eli hadn't thought he would have to persuade her because she didn't think she deserved the price of her wage. He thought she'd want to go off on her own. Jasmine stared at the folder, biting her lip.

"You don't need to give me an answer now," Eli said. "Take it home. Think about it."

"I don't need to think about it." Jasmine strode over to the desk, slammed the folder down and grabbed the pen from his hand. She scribbled her name on the bottom without an ounce of hesitation.

"You should've got a lawyer to look over them." Eli frowned.

"You won't do me wrong, Eli. I know you. You'd prefer to cut off a limb before making a bad contract with someone."

Eli laughed. "I don't know about that."

"I do." She smiled. "When do I start?"

Eli stood and held out his hand. "Welcome on board, partner."

Jasmine rounded the table and threw her arms around him, jiggling them from side to side. Eli pulled back. "You can start whenever you want to."

"Now?"

Eli chuckled. "Sure. Let's go through the weddings we have booked and see which you might like to take over. I'll contact the brides and confirm they're happy for the transfer."

"But what about you?"

"What about me?"

"You love planning weddings. I don't want to take any away from you."

Eli sat in his chair and linked his fingers in his lap. "I'm looking forward to slowing down a little now. Matías's shifts conflict with mine sometimes, and it would be nice to work around him, so I can see him every day. You'll be doing me a favour. Going forward, though, we can split the weddings between us." He smiled. "Grab a chair."

Jasmine squealed and dragged a chair behind the desk.

"Hmm. We'll have to get another desk in here for you," Eli murmured, already thinking of the extra things he needed to buy to make sure Jasmine felt at home.

They went through the calendar, and Eli noted the ones that clashed with Matías's shift patterns, and Jasmine pointed out the ones she liked the sound of. It was an arduous job because Eli was booked solid for eighteen months. He averaged five weddings a week, which was over three hundred bookings.

He'd even paused and had to talk himself through going further than a few months because his head had told him he and Matías might not last that long. He'd given himself a pep talk, made another cup of tea and resumed the job in between answering calls.

After they'd put together a list, Jasmine went to grab their lunch from the bakery, and Eli made phone calls to the brides to see if they were happy for Jasmine to take over from Eli. He had one hundred calls to make, which wouldn't all be done that day. After all, they had a wedding to finalise for the following day, and Eli wouldn't drop the ball on this one because it was so close.

They had agreed while Eli worked the following day, Jasmine would begin calling their contacts and letting them know Jasmine would be taking bookings from now on as well. It never hurt to involve the other people in the business because then they wouldn't be thrown for a loop if Jasmine called them instead of Eli.

By the time their day ended, they were worn out.

"I knew you were busy, Eli, but I didn't expect it to be like this." Jasmine laughed.

Eli walked her to the door. "It's only while we figure out the logistics. It will become like it was with Sarah's business once we're settled."

"But you did a lot of the paperwork side of things for Sarah's business."

"And I will do the same for this business, too. I'm not going to throw you in the deep end, Jasmine. I'm here to support you and make sure you succeed. It's in my best interests, together with yours."

"You need to teach me the paperwork, too, though."

"I will, but not all at once. Slow and steady wins the race. That's what Mum always told me."

Jasmine laughed and hugged him. "You're amazing, Eli Jackson."

She opened the door and waved, and he watched her drive off. As he was about to close the door, Matías's car pulled up. He leaned against the door frame as he watched his boyfriend stalk up the path and drag Eli into a melting kiss. Eli slid his arms around Matías's neck and returned the kiss, the slightly smoky scent not at all off-putting.

When they pulled back, he said, "Good or bad day?"

Matías grinned. "Fantastic day."

Eli and Matías had discussed Matías's job, and Matías had explained some days were more difficult than others depending on what calls they'd attended. Eli had held him as Matías spoke about some of the deaths he'd experienced, and his heart had shattered alongside Matías's. From that moment on, Eli had promised himself to check in with Matías each time he returned to see what his mood was so Eli could gauge what he might need from him.

Matías had told him not to worry, but Eli wanted to support Matías as best he could, and it was the only way he knew at the moment.

"I'm glad to hear it. I haven't started dinner, I'm afraid." Matías's phone rang, and Eli quickly said, "Jasmine and I were celebrating, but I can get something started now."

Matías smiled, slid an arm around Eli's waist and answered the phone. "Hey, Mum." He made some agreeable noises. "Perfect. Bye." He put the phone away and slid his other arm around Eli. "Mum is making us dinner. All we have to do is turn up."

"She didn't have to do that."

"She isn't doing it for any other reason than that she wants to see us. It doesn't matter who feeds us—ourselves or our families or a takeaway service—provided we eat and are happy with our decision. Do you not want to go?"

Eli sighed and deflated. "Actually, I don't want to cook." He chuckled. "I didn't want you to think I was lazy and not willing to make you some dinner."

Matías kissed him. "You are the least lazy person I know. I don't care if you never cook. I'm happy to do it on my days off. I'm happy to eat takeaway every night. I'm happy if we flit from house to house where others cook for us each night. I don't care as long as I'm with you."

Eli grinned and grabbed Matías's head, pulling him down for another kiss. "Let's get you cleaned up before we go."

"Am I dirty?"

Eli pivoted and wandered towards the stairs, glancing over his shoulder. "Not yet."

Matías's mouth gaped, and Eli ran up the stairs, laughing when he heard Matías stomping behind him.

Chapter 25

Matías

Matías rubbed his forehead as he slammed the door of the fire engine. They'd had an awful shift, ending with the death of a man because the building had blown before the firefighters had even arrived. Each one of them took it hard when they lost someone, even if it wasn't their fault. No one wanted to hear bad news.

Nash stalked off out of the station, and Matías watched him go. He took every bad result as a personal weight on his shoulders, and nothing anyone said ever made him change his mind. Matías wished he could help him, but Nash would close up further if anyone tried—they'd learnt that the hard way when they'd first begun working together. Matías sighed, watching until Nash turned the corner and disappeared.

A hand clapped him on the shoulder. "He'll be fine. He's dealing with it the best way he knows how to," Pearce said.

"I know. I wish it was easier for him." Matías collected his equipment and carried it through to the locker room, ready to take home. "I'll be glad for these four days off."

Pearce exhaled. "You're not the only one."

"Yeah, don't rub it in, you guys," Layton grumbled.

Matías cracked a smile. "You love it. Stop complaining." He glanced at Bryan. "Although if you have to deal with these *green* guys, I don't blame you." He chuckled when Bryan threw something in his direction at his pun on their watch name.

"At least we don't have to put up with you," Bryan said.

Matías put his equipment on the floor in front of his locker, picked up what Bryan had thrown and threw it back, smacking the man straight in the face.

"Fucker!" Bryan glared at him and laughed. "Good aim."

"I wasn't aiming," Matías said.

Layton chuckled. "I dread to see you when you *do* aim."

"Maybe in college. I could've thrown it from one side of a field to the other, but now..." He shook his head.

"Rugby?" Layton asked.

Matías shook his head. "Baseball."

"I didn't realise they did that at schools here," Bryan said.

"Our year requested it, and when there was enough interest, they decided to set up a team." Matías shrugged. "As I said, it didn't last long. Once college finished, I was done."

"See you later," Pearce said before exiting the room.

"Where is everyone?" Bryan asked, looking around the room.

Matías sighed. "We lost someone. The rest of the crew have gone to their usual places to chill." He finished in his locker and closed the door, picking up his equipment. He paused. "It's something that never gets easier, does it?"

Both men shook their heads.

"Anyway, I'm heading out. I'll see you next set of shifts."

"See ya," Bryan said. "Take it easy, yeah?"

Matías curled his mouth in a semblance of a smile and headed to his car. Stowing his stuff in the boot, he climbed in and pulled out his phone, staring at it. He didn't want to go back to Eli's house feeling the way he did. Eli didn't deserve to be on the receiving end of his grief, so he aimed the car at his parents' house, hoping someone was home.

When he parked in the driveway, he didn't get out immediately. As usual, his mind ran through all the different scenarios that could make him be the one who died in a fire or his parents or his siblings or Eli. He scraped his fingers through his hair, gripping at the strands to try to stop the images. It was the one thing he could never truly ignore with his job. The reality of what he saw easily twisted and morphed into the what-if scenes. No matter how he tried to ignore them, they wouldn't leave him. Every time he closed his eyes, he saw a new person unable to escape from a fire.

His breath caught in his chest, and he curled forward, resting his head against the steering wheel. Inhaling and exhaling through his nose, he brought his pulse down, knowing he couldn't go to his parents like he was. They were worried enough about his job. He was glad the station offered counselling sessions to those who needed it. Sometimes, it was mandatory. Sometimes, not, but the option was there. Matías had used it several times, and the therapist had given him some coping mechanisms to get his brain back on track. Deep breathing and counting were some of the best ways for him, as was visiting his parents.

When he felt more centred, he climbed out of the car and let himself into the house with the key his parents had made sure each of their children had kept, even when they moved out. He kicked off his shoes.

"Matías! What a surprise," his father said. "Everything okay?"

Matías nodded. "Just a tough night."

Diego squeezed his shoulder and turned for the kitchen. "Tea?"

Matías followed. "Yes, please."

He folded himself into a chair, crossing his arms and resting his head on them. Closing his eyes, he listened to the sounds of the kitchen, breathing deeply. He wouldn't fall asleep, but the sounds were soothing. Sounds he'd grown up hearing and associated with calm and tranquillity.

Fingers threaded through his hair, and he opened his eyes, seeing his mum. "Hey, sweetheart. Would you like some breakfast?"

"No, thanks." He curled his hands around the cup his dad placed in front of him and removed them again when his phone rang. Eli. He stared at it. He knew he needed to speak to him, but it was difficult. He wasn't sure he had the words to explain how he felt at that moment. This was something he should've thought about talking to Eli about before it happened, but it had never crossed his mind.

The phone went to voicemail, but he didn't leave a message.

"You should talk to him," Sofía said. "He'd understand you need to take time to decompress."

"I know, but I hate I can't do it with him yet."

Sofía sank into the seat next to him. "He'll understand. You can't be expected to change your habits straight away. You've only been together..." She narrowed her eyes at him and continued, "You've only been together for a month. You're still finding your feet, hijo. I know Eli, and he'll understand."

Matías knew he would as well, which was why he couldn't understand not being able to pick up the phone and tell him. Sofía patted his hand.

"Rest, hijo. You can deal with it later."

Matías rose, kissed his mother on the cheek and bid goodnight, taking his tea with him. He climbed the stairs to his old bedroom, shutting out the world, and sank into the bed. He desperately needed a shower, but he needed to sleep more. Swallowing the rest of his drink, he laid down and closed his eyes, making a promise to talk things through with Eli when he woke.

He surfaced from sleep when he was jostled with someone climbing onto the bed.

"Hmm?" was all he could manage.

"Go to sleep, Matti."

Matías smiled and slept.

Matías woke and stretched, yawning. Rolling to his back, he slid his hands behind his head and remembered he was at his parents' house. He frowned. He swore Eli had been there with him, but there was no sign of him. Matías had probably dreamt it.

He flung the covers back, grabbed some spare clothes from his drawers and wandered to the bathroom. The shower didn't take too long to warm up, so he switched it on and stripped. By the time he climbed in, the water was warm. Standing under the spray, he thought about what he'd done. He should've called Eli and explained. He realised that now, but he had some grovelling to do when he next saw him. Which would be once he'd finished in the shower.

A plan made, he washed and dried, throwing on his joggers and a T-shirt with a hoodie, and went looking for his parents.

"There he is," Sofía said, opening her arms for a hug when he walked into the kitchen. "How are you?"

"Better, thanks." He pulled back. "I would stay, but I need to see..." He trailed off when he saw Eli sitting at the dining table with a cup of tea. "I didn't imagine it, did I?"

Eli smiled, though it was strained. "No."

Matías strode to him and dropped to his knees by his chair. "I'm so sorry, Eli. This was one aspect of firefighting I hadn't thought about in relation to us because it hadn't come up before now. I should've called you."

"Yes, you should have." Eli cleared his throat and cupped Matías's cheek. "When you didn't turn up as you'd said, I got worried. When you didn't answer the phone, even more so. I thought..." Eli shifted on the seat and clasped his hands together. "I know you're not my father, but it's hard to let it go sometimes."

Matías wrapped his arms around Eli's waist and rested his head on his lap. Eli's fingers stroked through his hair, and Matías closed his eyes. "I can understand what you thought, and I can only apologise again. I will explain everything, I promise. We can sort out a new routine."

"You don't need a new routine, Matti. I need to know if your plans change, that's all. I don't want to stop you from doing what you need to do. I was only concerned because you'd told me you were going to visit me before going home to sleep."

"I'm sorry."

"It's okay. We're good."

Matías lifted his head. "Weren't you supposed to be working today? You had a wedding this morning."

Eli smiled. "It's a good job I have an amazing partner who happened to be free today."

Matías grabbed Eli's hands and dropped his head to them. "I've messed up. I'm sorry."

Eli moved his hands to lift Matías's head and cup his cheeks. "You've not messed up. Yes, we should've talked about this, but until these things come up, we're not going to know what we need to talk about. I didn't think my father's leaving would crop up in moments like this, either. We're good. We learn from this and make plans for next time."

Eli dropped his head and kissed him. Matías opened beneath him, hoping to let him know how much he loved him. It wasn't enough. He pulled back.

"I love you."

Eli smiled. "And I love you. Now, get off the floor."

Matías chuckled. "Yeah, my knees aren't thanking me."

He stood and turned to his parents, but they weren't there.

"They left when we were talking. I think they wanted to give us some privacy," Eli said.

"Do you have the rest of the day off, or do you need to help Jasmine?"

"The rest of the day is ours."

"Good." Matías held Eli's hands and pulled him to standing.

"Why? What do you have planned?"

Matías slid his arms around Eli's waist and nuzzled his neck. "It's our one-month anniversary. I thought we could go back to Romano's for dinner."

"Or our three-month anniversary, depending who you ask."

Matías laughed. "I get the glare from Mum every time something comes up that reminds her of our ruse. Maybe we should celebrate from when we started our pretence because it didn't last for long."

"I don't think it can count because we didn't see each other often."

Matías shrugged. "Let us decide."

Eli stared at him, a smile curving his lips. "I think we should stick with one month. That way, I will have plenty of events to tell people of how we met and what you put me through."

Eli yelled and squirmed out of his arms when Matías tickled his sides. "You're mean." He pulled out his phone, navigated to his contacts and dialled Romano's.

"Romano's. How can I help?"

"Hi, do you have a table for two available tonight?" he asked, staring at Eli.

"Is there a specific time you're looking for?"

"Not really."

"In that case, we can fit you in at eight-thirty. Is that any good?"

Matías smiled. "Perfect, thanks."

"Could I take your name, please?"

"Matías Lopez."

"Okay, Mr Lopez. I've added it to our diary. We look forward to seeing you later tonight."

"Thank you." He ended the call. "Eight-thirty."

Eli dropped his head to Matías's shoulder. "It can be our new beginning."

Matías kissed his head. "I like our beginning. We don't need a new one."

"Well, if I need to be ready for our dinner, I should get home. I have work to do."

"You don't need to do anything to get ready. You're perfect."

Eli scoffed and strode out of the room. Matías chuckled. He could spend every breath he had for the rest of his life telling Eli he was perfect, but the man would never believe him. It was true, though, and Matías would never stop telling him.

"Are you heading out?" Diego asked.

Matías nodded. "We're going out for a meal tonight."

"Sounds lovely."

Eli shuffled to Sofía and hugged her. "Thank you for calling me."

"You're welcome, sweetheart. I knew he needed you, even if he didn't."

Their words were quiet and probably not meant for Matías's ears, but he couldn't help it. He wished he could backtrack over the past few hours and head straight for Eli instead of needing his parents' house, but he couldn't. Now all he could do was make better choices going forward. He would do anything to make it up to Eli because the idea he'd made Eli second-guess them, even for a second, was a painful reminder of what Eli had been through.

They said their goodbyes and walked out to their cars. When they stopped, Matías pulled Eli to him.

"I couldn't live without you, you know. Not now I know you."

Eli's cheeks darkened. "Same."

Matías lowered his head and kissed him. "See you in a few minutes. I have to nip home to grab some clothes first, but I'll be there. I promise."

"You don't need to promise, Matti. Just let me know if things change, that's all."

"I will."

He held the car door for Eli, then closed it and waved him off. Aiming his car for his apartment, he shook his head, knowing he'd had a close call. Now that he was more clear-headed and alert, he knew he should've called Eli, even if it was to say he couldn't talk, but he would explain later. Eli was so forgiving of him, especially when he did not need to be. After everything that had happened with his father, Eli had every right to be suspicious of people. Matías needed to sit down and discuss things with him, and he would make sure it was sooner rather than later.

Alejo was in the kitchen when he returned, the scent of tomatoes and spices heavy in the air.

"What are you making?"

Alejo glanced over his shoulder. "Lasagne with a kick."

Matías raised his eyebrows. "Spicy lasagne?" Alejo nodded. "Sounds different."

"I have no idea if it's going to work, but I like spicy food, and I like lasagne, so I thought I'd try it."

"Good luck."

"You want some?"

Matías held out his hand. "No, thanks. I'm going out with Eli. I have to make up for being a dick."

"What did you do?" Alejo put the spoon down and faced him.

"I had a crappy shift, so I went to Mum and Dad's. I didn't tell Eli."

Alejo grimaced. "Not good."

"I know. Eli has been very forgiving, but I want to make it up to him."

"You'll sort it out. You usually do."

Matías clapped his hands. "Anyway, talking about making it up to him, I need to get some clothes and get over to his place."

"Have a good night. I'm going to need a new roommate soon," he muttered.

Matías had thought about that, but Eli didn't seem to be the type of person to move too fast, so he put aside his thoughts of waking up and falling asleep next to him every day and night aside and gathered the items he needed. He had four days, or rather nights, of which he could spend with Eli, and he was looking forward to it. He knew Eli had to work the next day, but he sometimes helped in the background. Rarely, just occasionally. He didn't want to suffocate Eli, so he spent time with his friends and family when Eli was busy.

When his schedule was clear, they certainly made up for it.

By the time he reached Eli's house, he was already missing him, but when he found the man in the shower, he found a way he could begin his penance…on his knees.

Chapter 26

Eli

When Matías had "disappeared" all those months ago, Eli had panicked. Matías hadn't been answering his phone, and Eli hadn't been sure what to do. His first thought—as much as he wished it hadn't been—had been that he'd done what Eli's father had done. Within seconds, he'd known he was wrong, but he felt awful for having thought it in the first place. Sofía had called him within an hour of Matías arriving at her house and had assured him it was nothing to do with Eli and everything to do with what he usually did when he'd had a tough shift. The minute she'd said it, Eli couldn't help his need to be with him and help ease him. So, he'd called in a favour to Jasmine and raced over there. Sofía had reassured him again and invited him to stay for as long as he wanted.

He'd spent a couple of hours lying beside Matías and staring at him, which, when Matías had found out, had sounded creepy. But he'd felt more relaxed and content that nothing had happened to him. After their evening out to celebrate their first month anniversary—something they had now made a monthly date night—Matías had shown Eli exactly how sorry he was.

Even now, five months later, Matías was sorry for how he'd behaved, but Eli had put it all behind him. They had never been stronger than they were now, especially when Matías had laid everything out for him.

As a celebration of their six-month anniversary, Eli had told Matías they could visit Rafe at the club instead of going for the meal as they usually would. It was couple's night again, and although they couldn't always make it to the events, they tried to support Rafe when they could.

"So, Mr Jackson, how are we looking for this week?" Jasmine asked from her seat at her desk on the opposite side of the room from him.

Eli had bought a desk for her, and they'd rearranged the furniture a little, giving them both some semblance of privacy when meeting with clients. They sometimes brought out a screen to divide their areas if there were two meetings scheduled at the same time, although they tried their best to avoid the situation. Their shared calendar helped because they could see what the other person had booked.

Jasmine had found her feet with her side of the business and was offering services slightly different from Eli. It had built their reputation higher than ever, which they were both happy about.

"Well, we both have weddings on Wednesday, Friday and Saturday. You have one on Thursday, and I have two on Sunday. You also have a hen night booked for Friday night and a rehearsal dinner on Sunday. Why are you asking me when you can see the calendar as well as I can?" he asked with a smile.

Jasmine chuckled and rested her arms on her desk, twiddling her pen. "I want to make sure you realise how well you're doing."

"*We're* doing," he amended without looking up.

She rolled her eyes. "How well we're doing. I'm glad you've slowed down, Eli. I was worried for a bit that you were going to burn out."

Eli leaned back in his chair, staring at his paperwork but not seeing it. "Looking back now, I can see it. Although I hate to admit it, the fund my father gave us has taken the stress off me." He held up his hand. "Yes, I know it was stress I put on myself. No one asked me to do it. I know. It doesn't change the fact, though."

"Despite hating the man for what he did to you, I'm glad he's helped. You're so much happier now, and most of it has nothing to do with the money."

Eli laughed. "The money isn't mine. I haven't touched a penny, and I won't. But yes, I am happier. If you had told me a year ago, hell, even eight months ago, I'd be in a serious relationship with someone, I would've said you were nuts." He rested his chin on his hand. "Life changes in so many ways without you realising."

"That it does."

"Which reminds me, how are things with you and Rafe? Are you joining us for couple's night tonight?"

Jasmine's cheeks reddened, and she rubbed at them. "Things are good. Slow, but good."

Eli frowned. "What do you mean, slow? You've been together for almost as long as Matías and me."

Jasmine waggled her head back and forth. "Kind of."

"Spill."

She sighed. "Rafe keeps telling me he's not interested in anything long-term, which is fine, but I want more, Eli. But I also don't want to lose him."

"Have you told him?"

She shook her head. "I don't want to scare him off."

"Look, as someone who had a similar thing happen to him, let me tell you this. Talk to him, but understand he's given you his terms. He says he doesn't want long-term, so don't try to change his mind. Tell him where things stand for *you* and let him come to his own decisions."

"I know, and I'm trying. It's difficult, though, when he's everything I ever wanted in a guy." She shrugged. "I will be there tonight, anyway."

"Good. It's going to be fun."

"I'm surprised you and Matías are coming. I would've expected you to go to your usual dinner out instead."

Eli smiled. "Matías wanted to support Rafe, but our anniversary seems to coincide with the couple's nights each month, so we agreed to alternate. It's only fair."

"Let's get everything wrapped up today, and we can get our dancing shoes on."

They spent the next three hours finishing up their task lists, then Jasmine left, and Eli locked his office and climbed the stairs. Matías wasn't due for another hour, so Eli had time to relax in the bath before getting ready.

He'd finished filling the bath when the doorbell rang, and he cursed and slipped a dressing gown on. Matías stood on his doorstep looking like a wet rag, and Eli quickly pulled him inside.

"What happened?"

Matías dropped his bag on the floor and kicked off his shoes. "My car broke down a few streets over. I walked the rest of the way but didn't expect the deluge of rain to hit so suddenly." He stripped off his coat. "It was lucky I had a coat because I hadn't planned to bring one."

"What are you doing about your car?"

"Dad said he would get the car sorted. He has a spare key. Are you okay to drive tonight? Sorry."

Eli waved him away. "It's not a problem." He chuckled. "I know exactly what you need." He grabbed his hands and pulled him up the stairs and into the bathroom. "I'm sure with some manoeuvring, we can both get in there."

Matías shucked his clothes while Eli hung up his dressing gown. Matías held out his hand to Eli and helped him in before slipping in behind him. Eli was more on Matías's lap than in the bath, but it felt good all the same.

"Mmm, this is nice and warm."

"Considering your cold shower, I'm not surprised."

They lay in companionable silence, which Eli had always appreciated with Matías. The longer they had been together, the more they had realised the silence between them was as comfortable and meaningful as the words.

Matías reached for the shampoo and washed Eli's hair, and Eli twisted to face Matías and returned the favour. Even though their cocks were hardening because of the position they were in, neither pressed to do anything about them. The quiet, relaxing moment was what they needed before a frantic night out.

When the water cooled, Matías climbed out and held a towel for Eli, drying him off and securing it around his waist before sorting himself out. It was these little thoughtful things Matías did automatically that had Eli falling deeper in love with him every day. Things like dropping by with lunch from his favourite bakery or sending a text when he knew Eli was busy so he'd have something to smile about when he had the chance to read it or bringing him a cup of tea without being asked. Normal everyday things others might not care about.

Eli wandered to his wardrobe and chose his outfit. It was easy enough: dark, skinny jeans, a dark green shirt and a black waistcoat. He sat in front of his mirror, brushed his hair to remove the knots and tucked it behind his ears. He splashed on some aftershave, and he was done. Easy, simple, and he was ready to go. He stood.

Matías slid his arms around Eli's waist, rubbing his newly shaved chin on Eli's neck. Eli lifted his hand to Matías's hair and closed his eyes.

"Mmm. You smell delicious," Matías said, raking his teeth gently across Eli's shoulder.

"So do you."

"What I would do to you if we weren't going out."

Eli chuckled. "Save it for when we get home." He twisted in Matías's arms. "Do you want a tea before we go?"

Matías checked the clock and shook his head. "Better not. We're running behind schedule."

"Is there a schedule when it comes to nights like these?" Eli said, cocking an eyebrow and letting Matías step back.

Matías crossed to his bag and crouched, rifling through and pulling out some clothes. "I suppose not, but I want to make sure we're there when we said we would. You know I hate being late."

Eli grinned. "I know."

Early on in their relationship, Eli found out how much Matías hated being late. So much so he was always early. For the four days off Matías had that week, Eli timed how long he spent waiting about because he was earlier than his appointment time. It was three hours. Three hours, where he could do something other than waiting, but if it made Matías happy, then Eli didn't care. Eli didn't like being late, but he would never be purposefully too early. At first, it had annoyed Eli, but it had grown on him, and now, he thought it was cute.

By the time Matías was ready, he was itching to leave. Eli dragged him towards the door.

"Come on. Let's go. We're going to be too early, but never mind."

"We can wait in the car," Matías said.

Eli smiled. "We can." Eli had recently installed a puzzle app on his phone, so he had something to do when they were waiting.

They were twenty minutes early by the time they arrived, but Matías climbed out, and Eli followed.

"Rafe messaged to say he was here," Matías explained when Eli asked. His cheeks darkened. "I know you don't enjoy waiting around."

Eli kissed his cheek, the warmth heating his lips. "I don't mind when I'm with you."

They entered the club, heading for the booth Rafe kept for them when he knew they were coming. It held ten people, so it was a good table to have when they were meeting others, which they were tonight.

"Matti, my man! How are you?" Rafe said, grasping Matías's hand and pulling him in for a back slap.

"I'm good, as always. How's business?"

"Booming. These couple's nights have gone down well. I'm thinking of doing them twice a month."

"Sounds good." Matías glanced around. "Anyone else here yet?"

Rafe nodded. "Jason and Harry."

"Where's Jasmine?" Eli asked.

Rafe smiled. "She'll be here in half an hour. She said she had something to finish up."

Did she? Or did she want more people here to keep her occupied because Rafe was being an ass? He pulled his phone from his pocket and messaged her.

They joined Jason and Harry at their table and ordered their drinks.

"So, how's business?" Rafe asked.

Eli and Harry looked at each other for a second, then laughed. "You're going to have to be more specific. Who are you asking?"

Rafe glanced around the table and chuckled. "Both of you."

Eli waved at Harry to go first.

"Well, the firefighter calendar has given me more exposure, and the company I freelance for is sending more and more work my way. Hopefully, I'll be able to expand into landscape photos completely soon."

"Awesome. Eli?"

"Booming. You know Jasmine has been a boon to the business, and I've stepped back a bit. It's a balancing act, but it's working." Eli tilted his head. "Why?"

Rafe linked his fingers, resting them on the table. "I've been wondering about a collaboration."

Eli frowned. "In what way?"

"I would like to offer this place as a location for events, and my first thought was to ask you two. Harry, you could use it for different backgrounds if you wanted to, and Eli, you could use it for weddings. It seems a shame to leave it empty during the day when it could be useful."

"And you could make more money," Matías said with a grin.

Rafe opened his hands. "That, too. Win-win."

Eli glanced around the room, seeing it in a new light. "It's something to look into. Let's make a time to talk it over."

Rafe nodded. "Will do."

"Come on. No more work talk," Jason protested. "We're here to dance!"

Eli laughed and watched as Jason pushed Harry from the booth, grabbed his hand and dragged him towards the almost empty dance floor.

"I would say he calmed down, but I've not seen it yet," Matías said, palming his forehead.

"Nothing wrong with it. He wants to be with Harry." Eli threaded his arm through Matías's. "I know how he feels, but I could do without the dancing."

"Maybe later?" Matías looked hopeful.

"Maybe later."

Matías kissed him.

"Stop with the PDAs! Eww." Eli grinned and faced Paul and Quinn. "Sorry, couldn't resist. We get it from Eddie and Toby all the time."

"They're too old to care now, surely," Matías said.

"Nope. They still complain," Quinn said, sliding into the booth with Paul following. "Although I know for a fact they don't mind. They like our reaction."

"Your reaction to what?" Dean asked, appearing with Oliver.

"Eddie and Toby complaining about our PDAs," Paul explained.

"They're probably embarrassed because they do it themselves now," Oliver said, backtracking when Paul glared at him. "Or not because they're innocent angels who wouldn't dream of such a thing."

They all laughed. An hour later, when everyone had arrived, including Jasmine, Matías persuaded Eli to join him on the dance floor. Luckily, it was a slower song. Eli had no coordination when it came to fast songs. He slid his arms around Matías's neck, and Matías hugged him close. The heat pouring off the man was intoxicating, and Eli found his eyes fluttering closed. He rested his head on Matías's shoulder, letting himself relax in his arms.

"Are you happy?" Matías whispered when the song changed to another slow one.

Eli lifted his head and smiled. "Very."

Matías dropped his mouth to Eli's, and Eli felt the kiss deep inside. He gripped at the base of Matías's head, wanting more, but Matías pulled back and pulled him close again. Eli closed his eyes and held Matías as tight as he could.

The song faded out, and Rafe's voice took over. "Thank you to everyone for coming tonight. I really appreciate you supporting this club. I have a few quick announcements. First, I'm planning on putting on another couple's night, so I'll let you know what dates they will be once I've figured it out. Second, I would like to thank Jasmine for all her help with the club. I don't say it enough, sweetheart, but you're bloody amazing."

"Aww," sounded all around, and Eli grinned, trying to find her amongst the crowds but couldn't. Maybe she didn't have to worry as much as she thought.

"Finally, I have someone who would like to say something. Can we put the house lights up, please?"

The lights of the club brightened but not to full capacity. Matías pulled away and turned to face Eli, the tension visible in his face.

"What...?"

"Eli, I'm going to preface this with a note that I know we've only been together six months, but I want you to know how much I love you."

Eli's heart raced, and his mouth went dry. This couldn't be going where he thought it was, could it?

"Ever since I messed up and nearly lost you, I've known my life would never be the same without you. I know you have...insecurities about our relationship, and I want you to know I will be here for however long you want me to be. With that in mind..." He pulled something from his pocket and dropped to one knee.

Eli inhaled, feeling lightheaded.

"I know you always said you didn't want to get married, and it's absolutely fine. But I would like to give you this as a promise that if you are ever ready to get married, I'm all in. Say the word. And if you're never ready, that's okay, too. I want you to be able to look down at your hand and realise you have someone who is yours, truly and deeply. Will you accept this offer?"

Eli stared at him, smiled and pulled Matías to his feet. "Yes, I'll marry you."

A cheer sounded and feet stomped on the dance floor. Matías's mouth dropped open. "What?"

"I want to marry you, Matti. If it had been anyone else, I probably wouldn't have felt comfortable, but you're every-thing to me. I know my life would be empty without you, and I don't want that. Ever. Yes, I'll marry you."

Tears gathered in Matías's eyes as the music resumed, and Eli chuckled and held him still for a kiss. After Matías relaxed, Eli pulled back and looked down at the ring. It was a single band with a small diamond nestled into it. Matías took it out and slid it onto Eli's finger, then leaned down and kissed it.

"Thank you, Eli. I never imagined you'd agree to marry me. I thought you'd need more time."

"You're everything I want, Matti. I don't need to think about it because you've shown me repeatedly over the last few months that you are perfect for me."

"Woohoo! I knew it!" Jasmine bounded up and threw her arms around them both. "I'm so excited! Please tell me I can plan your wedding? Please? Please? Please? Pl—"

Eli covered her mouth with his hand and laughed. "Yes! Okay!"

"It's going to be epic. What date would you like? I have the calendar here." Jasmine pulled out her phone.

Eli stopped her. "Let this sink in first, Jasmine. Give me a minute."

Jasmine bit her lip. "Sorry. I'm so excited."

They made their way back to the booth and everyone greeted them with hugs and backslaps. When they settled down, Eli flopped onto the seat and rested against Matías. Despite his original misgivings about their relationship and what happened with Eli's father, he had been working his way through his issues. Now, instead of the fear he would've experienced months ago, all he felt was pure happiness. He couldn't wait to become Mr Eli Lopez. He wouldn't object if Matías wanted to be Matías Jackson, but he would never double barrel a name. It would be too much work.

"Are you happy?" Matías asked, repeating his earlier question.

Eli smiled. "Over the moon."

Chapter 27

Matías

Two Years Later

"It's time."

Matías faced his brother and exhaled, smoothing down the front of his suit.

"Are you nervous?" Alejo asked.

Matías smiled. "Not even a little. I've never been more excited in my life."

"I didn't think you would be. Mum said you would, but I knew different."

"Let's go get me married!"

They wandered from the tent, greeting the guests as they went, and settled into the front row to wait. He studied the decoration, knowing Jasmine went all out for Eli. The yellow and white theme looked amazing, especially with all the lights. She probably called in every favour she had to give the man the best wedding she could. He deserved every bit of it.

Matías closed his eyes and smiled, bringing forth memories of their almost three-year relationship. Birthdays, anniversaries, Christmases, and every other celebration he could think of had been filled with love. He was extremely happy with his life, but being able to say Eli was his husband was something he would struggle to top.

Alejo nudged him, so lost in his thoughts as he was, he hadn't realised the priest had called for him to stand.

Matías stepped forward, buttoning his grey jacket, and glanced down the aisle to where Eli would soon appear. He had no idea what outfit Eli had chosen. They had made all those decisions out of his eyesight and earshot, but he knew Eli would've considered his options carefully.

When they'd first started planning the wedding, Matías had thought Eli would want to decide it all and had left him to it. After their first huge fight, he'd realised Eli wanted a partner, not someone who let it happen and put up with whatever was chosen for him. As soon as he'd figured it out, they had sat and listed down all their likes and dislikes. Once it was done, they had their options to choose from. Matías had been involved in every step of the wedding, except for Eli's outfit.

As for his own outfit, he'd finally caved to the grey debate. Certain shades of grey did look good on him, although he would never truly admit it to Eli.

He caught his mother's gaze and smiled as she dabbed her eyes with her handkerchief. He held his hands in front of him and let his gaze wander as he waited. They had chosen an outdoor venue because they both loved nature, despite neither of them having much time to enjoy it. Between two large trees, the priest stood in front of an arch of white flowers and greenery with lights zigzagging across the space in between, giving a glow to the area. There were white flower petals scattered where Matías stood, making the grass seem softer somehow. The guests sat in wooden chairs with a white chiffon bow with yellow flowers secured inside. The combination of brown, green, white and yellow was fantastic.

Soft piano music started, and Matías stared down the aisle, impatiently waiting to see Eli. When he appeared, Matías's breath caught. The man was a vision in a black tailcoat and trousers with a white shirt and a soft yellow waistcoat and tie. The tie matched Matías's, but he'd never seen a yellow waistcoat before, but it matched Eli's personality perfectly. In Eli's hand, he held a candle encased in glass with white roses surrounding the base. Although Eli had wanted many candles in deference to Matías's job as a firefighter, Matías had only agreed when they had been put inside tall glasses to reduce the chance of fire.

Matías watched Eli walk down the aisle alone—a choice he'd made because he didn't want to upset any member of his family by choosing another. Matías licked his lips, unable to stop the smile from spreading across his face.

Catching Eli's gaze, he winked, and his smile grew when Eli flushed. Five steps later, the man was before him. Eli placed the candle on the small table between them and the priest and faced Matías.

"Family and friends, we are here today to celebrate the union of Matías Lopez and Eli Jackson. Marriage is not something to be taken lightly. It is a promise between people to be loyal and honest, but also to be there for them during dark times and discontent. Marriage is not a bandage to fix problems. It is a pledge to support the other. Matías and Eli have written their own vows for this wonderful celebration. Matías, would you like to go first?"

Matías's heart raced, and he swallowed hard. He gripped Eli's hand and stared into his eyes. "I love you. I cannot fully explain how those three words encompass how I feel about you. They seem so small in comparison to the size of my heart when I think about you. Our beginning may not have been ordinary, but everything about you, about us, feels right. The journey to this point has been wonderful, but the idea of spending my life with you is nothing short of incredible. You, Eli, have a heart of gold, enough compassion to care for the world, and shoulders big enough to support everyone you love. I can only hope my love is enough to carry you on those days when your well is running empty. I can only hope my compassion is enough to be a surrogate when your energy is ebbing. I can only hope my shoulders are wide enough to support those we love when your back is bruised. If you let me, I'll support you throughout our lives and love you until there is no more to give."

He exhaled, trying to keep his tears at bay now he'd managed to get his speech out. He squeezed Eli's hands and smiled at the tear tracks on his face. He mouthed, "Sorry," to which Eli chuckled and sniffed.

"Eli?" the priest said.

"How can I top that?" He sniffed again and wiped his cheeks as a chuckle wound around the guests. "Our lives will not be perfect. Our journey will not be without its mountains and valleys. But our love will be the thing to hold us together when those bumps try to pull us apart. As unique as our relationship began, I wouldn't change it for anything." He winced and glanced at Matías's mother. "It made us who we are today, and I believe we are stronger for it. I love you, Matías. I love how you care about those around you and help anyone who needs it. I love how you make me feel when I'm with you and how you make me smile in the hardest of times. I love that I can be your partner in everything. Our lives will not be perfect, but our journey will be ours, and no one can take that away from us. We belong together like salt and pepper pots, like a fire engine and its firefighters, like a wedding and a wedding planner." The guests laughed. "This life is short, but it's ours, and I'm so glad I get to share it with you."

Matías's tears had given up staying in his eyes, but he let them fall as the priest continued with his address. He stared at Eli, wanting nothing more than to pull him in for a scorching kiss and never let him go, but he had to be patient.

"Do you have the rings?"

Jasmine stepped forward with a small, specially made, yellow satin cushion that had two small indents in it to hold their rings securely.

"Eli, repeat after me. I, Eli Jackson, will take Matías Lopez to be my husband."

"I, Eli Jackson, will take Matías Lopez to be my husband." He slid the ring on Matías's finger.

"Matías, repeat after me. I, Matías Lopez, will take Eli Jackson to be my husband."

"I, Matías Lopez, will take Eli Jackson to be my husband." He pushed the ring onto Eli's finger.

"Before your family and friends, may I present Matías and Eli Lopez. Congratulations. You may kiss."

Matías pulled on Eli's hand and fused their lips, trying to keep it clean as there were kids present. He drew back and rested their foreheads together. "Thank you."

"For what?"

"For being my everything."

Matías wrapped his arms around Eli and held on as the cheers and conversation seeped into his consciousness. He stepped back, pulled Eli's arm through his and led him back down the aisle. They followed Jasmine to the location for the photographs, where two fire engines waited on either side of another arch of lights and flowers. Harry, who had agreed to be their photographer, placed them in between the engines. Matías slid his arm around Eli's waist and gripped his other hand, bringing it to his chest.

"I love you."

Eli smiled. "And I love you."

Matías kissed him and felt a brush against his cheek. He pulled back and looked up, seeing two firefighters on the top of two ladders, dropping rose petals over them. Matías and Eli laughed. This had been a perfect day.

After several rounds of photos, they wandered through the small cluster of trees to a clearing where there were several long tables with chairs beneath a canopy of fairy lights. Although Matías had known this was what it would be, the effect was far more astonishing in person. He and

Eli settled in at the head table with their parents on either side of them, and Matías took a sip of water.

"This is everything I could have wished for," Eli said, leaning his head on Matías's shoulder.

Matías kissed his head. "You took the words right out of my mouth."

Sign up to my newsletter to get a free stories, exclusive content and early access: https://elouiseeast.com/news letter

Would you like more from this world? Check out the Crush series, starting with *Instant Desire*, and join a group of friends who find love throughout the series.

About Elouise East

I am Elouise East but feel free to call me Elli. I write sweet and steamy connections in gay romance. I also touch on taboo stories under the name Elouise R East.

Books that tell the stories where friendship and family are the focal point - be it blood family or chosen - is very important to me. That's why I include a variety of personalities, talents, ages, situations and abilities as I believe a story or a character needs. I want my characters to be real, to be relatable, to be free to have whatever views they tell me they have. And trust me, most of the time, I do not have *any* say in the matter!

My characters come to life on the page for me as well as my readers. Their stories unfold in front of me, and I have very little input into how they want to be shown. Just like real life, the lives of my characters change with every choice, every interaction and every conversation. And I wouldn't have it any other way.

I write books that are emotionally realistic, even if liberties are taken with other aspects of my stories. I don't know any other way to write. It comes from deep inside.

Who am I? A single parent to two children who make life worth living. An avid reader who still devours every book she can get her hands on. A student of learning about any subject that takes her fancy. An author of books she would read herself. And a romantic at heart who loves anything cheesy.

Who's in?

Stalk me here... ;-)
Website: https://elouiseeast.com
Newsletter: https://elouiseeast.com/newsletter
All links: https://elouiseeast.com/links

Books by Elouise East

Love in Flames
Fight Fire with Fire
Up in Smoke
Smoke Signals
Smoke & Mirrors

Club Royal
Rogue Royal
Secretive Royal
Grieving Royal
Disowned Royal
Trained Royal
Awakened Royal
Commanding Royal

Crush
Love Conquers
Instant Desire
Primary Seduction

Deep Down
A Crush for Christmas
Life Support
Covert Strength
Love Scene
Lawful Attraction

Just A Little Crush
First Kiss
He's Behind You
A Special Love

Daddy
Love Me, Daddy
Soothe Me, Daddy
Spoil Me, Daddy
The Complete Daddy Series

Standalone
Treehouse Whispers
Star-Crossed
Protecting the Thief
Sizzling Chauffeur
A Home for Barney
Mattie

Elouise R East (taboo)
Dark & Divergent
Forbidden Temptation
Too Many Secrets: A Life of Secrets

Too Many Secrets: The Lake House
Secrets in his Eyes

Collide

When Fantasies Collide
When Dreams Collide
When Pleasures Collide
When Cravings Collide
When Hungers Collide